GRAY TIDINGS

HAILEY EDWARDS

Copyright © 2022 Black Dog Books, LLC

All rights reserved.

No part of this book may be reproduced in any form or by any electronic or mechanical means, including information storage and retrieval systems, without written permission from the author, except for the use of brief quotations in a book review.

This is a work of fiction. Names, characters, businesses, places, events and incidents are either the products of the author's imagination or used in a fictitious manner. Any resemblance to actual persons, living or dead, or actual events is purely coincidental.

Edited by Sasha Knight
Copy Edited by Kimberly Cannon
Proofread by Lillie's Literary Services
Cover by Damonza
Illustration by NextJenCo

GRAY TIDINGS

Black Hat Bureau, Book 6

Corpses are vanishing from New Orleans morgues, there's talk of a sea monster in Lake Pontchartrain, and Hiram Nádasdy is turning the French Quarter upside down in search of a witch with the power to bring the dead back to life.

When the director assigns Rue the case, she suspects he's sending her hunting all right. For her father, not the creature. Too bad she's got her hands full with dueling covens, drunk revelers, and a whole lot of pool noodles. Oh. And it's Mardi Gras. Of course it is. But as the locals say, *laissez les bons temps rouler*.

1

Cage diving with sharks had nothing on spending the day in my office. Sharp-toothed predators circled, a carousel of menace, bumping against my newfound authority, testing for weak spots, hoping for an easy meal. The bars protected as much as they confined me, but I had entered this cage, agreed to swim with these carnivores, of my own free will. Though it didn't help that the director had tied a juicy steak around my neck when he announced my relationship to him along with my promotion. That steak? Raw and bloody.

Just like I would be if I didn't figure out my next move soon.

"More coffee?" Inga placed a fresh mug on my leather blotter before I could answer. "Another donut?"

"I'm good." I signed off on the sixth warrant of the day with a hand already cramping. "Send in Clay."

Please kept trying to wiggle in there, but I couldn't afford politeness. It would only be seen as weakness.

"Yes, ma'am."

On dainty hooves, the cervitaur exited with a swish of the fluffy white tail that might get her killed one of these days.

Light glinted off the enchanted *Deputy Director* plaque affixed to the door, a warning of what lay in wait if you dared enter. The ash wood door with its ornate silver vine inlay and cold iron knob were beautiful.

The symbology, however, was grotesque.

Ash wood? Silver? Cold iron?

They were banes, each element lethal to a faction of my allies.

Witches. Wargs. Dae.

The placement made it clear the director wanted them kept out of my office.

And my life.

"You're growling," Asa noted from behind me. "You're also clutching the letter opener again."

Swiveling in my chair, I found him right where I left him four hours ago. One ankle crossed over his knee, knitting needles clacking in his clever fingers, and a tablet with the pattern for a shawl resting on his thigh.

The official line was I had demanded a security detail. The truth was, I didn't want to be alone.

On my own, I was vulnerable to the memories of this place. The *tap-tap-tap* of the director's cane across the marble floors. The phantom pain as he cracked that cane across my knuckles. The ache of broken bones mending. The well of hatred filling me until it threatened to drown my fledgling conscience.

I could become who I once was here. I could become that black witch again. I could become his heir in truth as well as in title.

Some days, Asa was the only barrier between the dark memories pounding in my head and the identity I had spent so long crafting from the qualities I wanted to embody. Rue Hollis was more than a checklist. I had breathed life into her, and Asa's presence reminded me to keep filling my lungs and not suffocate on the past.

Today his earrings and septum piercing were orange coral, and so was his neat pocket square. The bright color popped against his immaculate suit and brought out the vibrant green of his eyes. For no particular reason, I had braided his hair in a single queue that hung down his back, but now I missed his usual style.

The sleek black pantsuit with matching stilettos I wore had me missing my usual style too. And the white blouse? Worst idea *ever*. Had these people never seen me eat? I would have to get my tops spell treated to repel stains or wear my lunch down my chest every time I overpoured hot sauce on Taco Tuesdays.

"Inga clips, and she clops, and she swishes her tail." I flicked a finger back and forth. "At *you*."

I drove the blade an inch into my desktop with an angry stab I pretended fell between two doe eyes.

"I haven't noticed." He got distracted by a tangle in his burgundy yarn. "Except for the growling."

"*If* I killed her, and I'm not saying I would, but *if* I did, no one would blame me."

"You're the deputy director." He lifted his gaze to mine. "No one would dare blame you. For anything."

Ugh.

The reminder of the power in my hands unclamped my fingers from the comfort of the handle I was too lazy to dig out of the wood. He was right. I knew he was right. But I still wanted to mount Inga's head on my wall.

"A *cervitaur*." I spat the word. "He chose a *cervitaur* for my assistant."

A rare breed of centaur, Inga was half impossibly beautiful woman and half sleek deer.

Deer.

Had the Silver Stag survived, I bet the director would have drafted him to fetch and file for me too.

The unsubtle reminder of the case that cleaved me from Black Hat's bosom kept my molars grinding.

"Inga had no say in her assignment." He zoomed in on his pattern, searching for where he left off. "This is just another job for her."

"How is she in Black Hat anyway? Was she pulling the sleigh when Grandma got run over by a reindeer?"

"Rue." A tender smile spreading across his face, he set aside his project. "You're doing it again."

"Fascination is exhausting." I slumped in my chair. "I'm tired of being jealous all the time."

"You want to talk about jealousy?" He cocked an eyebrow. "Really?"

"Not this again." I dismissed what I knew was coming with an annoyed huff. "He wasn't serious."

"He threw a vial of his blood at you and chanted an invocation to bind your souls for eternity."

The *he* in question was a black witch whose name escaped me.

"And I kicked him in the balls so hard he sprouted a second uvula." I rubbed underneath my chin. "That's the dangly thing in the back of your throat, right?" I hummed. "Or would it be second *and* third uvula?"

As the first woman deputy director in the history of the Black Hat Bureau, I was experiencing a mutualist phenomenon akin to ballsy pilot fish ridding a lethal shark of parasites in exchange for not getting eaten.

And no, I had no idea why I kept circling back to sharks.

But it fit, what with the director chumming the water the second I dipped a toe into the family business.

I still couldn't believe he had outed me as his granddaughter to the entire Bureau.

On the heels of that bombshell, I expected the outrage from those who cried nepotism. I anticipated the pushback from good ol' boys like Marty who didn't want to take orders from *a girl*. Unexpected? The opportunists who viewed me as the next gleaming rung within reach on the corporate ladder rather than the long fall to the bottom awaiting them.

After I kicked them in the teeth for thinking they had some claim on me.

"Keep a kill list." Clay slipped in and shut the door behind him. "Write down the name of every person you want to kill and why. After you fill up a notebook, leak it. It's better than a fart for clearing a room."

As the second half of my security detail, Clay wore a comms charm spelled into a chunky vintage Rolex wristwatch that allowed us to communicate. For emergencies. But, as he proved by jumping right into our conversation, he often used it to eavesdrop on Asa and me out of boredom from his post in the hall.

Does the existence of the comms charm imply I could have summoned him myself?

Yes.

But then I wouldn't have had an excuse to get rid of the director's handpicked spy for a few minutes.

"You had me up until the end." I angled my chair to see them both. "Well?"

"The line wasn't too bad today." He flopped into the chair across from me, one I'd had reinforced to support him. "Seven guys with diamonds in their pockets. One woman with fresh hearts, with provenance, on ice in a cooler. And four assassins I fed to Earl." He pulled one of the light-brown curls in his wig straight then let it spring back into a coil. "You remember Earl, right?"

"That literal void in the floor?" He did have his own office, though. "I didn't realize it—*he*—had a name."

"Maybe not an official one, but he's got that Earl look to him. Real down-to-earth guy, that Earl."

"Of course, he's down-to-earth." I snorted a laugh. "He's a *hole*."

"I'm not familiar with Earl." Asa stood and stretched, a show which I did not mind watching one bit. "What, exactly, is he?"

"There's some speculation *Earl* is a portal to Faerie," I told Asa, who had not been allowed much access to the manor or the compound prior to meeting me. "One time a high fae staggered out and peed on a rug in the hall." I lifted a shoulder. "He was drunk and claimed he thought it was his bathroom."

"The director keeps a portal in the compound?" Asa raised his eyebrows. "A *two*-way portal?"

"The benefits outweigh the risks." Clay pulled a candy bar from his pocket. "Earl has been a valued member of the Bureau for two centuries. He makes body disposal *so* much easier, and there's only been that one security breach. If the director awarded employee of the decade, Earl would win every time. I'm telling you. He's good people."

"The director isn't concerned he *might* be dumping dead bodies at an undisclosed location in Faerie?"

"The void, aka Earl, is naturally occurring." Clay crammed the whole thing in his mouth. "His office?" I don't think he even chewed before swallowing. "It was built around him."

That was news to me, but I saw the appeal of having unlimited access to a magical landfill.

A buzz in my pocket informed me it was time for our team strategy session, and I couldn't stop my smile.

With a tap of my finger on the desk, I activated a soundproof ward that coated the inside of the room. A variation on the spell I used to soundproof our hotel rooms, I had anchored this one semi-permanently to make activating it quick and deactivating it even faster. Just in case Inga got curious about the silence.

"Agent Smarty Fuzz Butt," I greeted Colby as I put my phone on speaker. "What do you have to report?"

"Saint received your message," she answered with a distracted air. "He's in New Orleans."

"Makes sense." Clay drummed his fingers on his armrests. "New Orleans is a mecca of the paranormal."

"Black witches flock there in droves," Asa agreed. "You can source almost anything in the Quarter."

Like a miracle.

One big enough to bring Mom back to life.

Proving he had the same thought, Clay asked, "Do you think his quest is Luca approved?"

"I doubt it." I began working the letter opener back and forth, splintering the desk as I pried it free. "I bet he dropped her like a hot potato."

I had yet to identify Luca, but she must be Black Hat to have gained access to Dad once, let alone several times while she built trust with him. However, their earth-shattering bargain had been struck *prior* to his reunion with Mom. Now he had no time for another woman in his life.

Ask me how I know.

"The Toussaint coven owns the French Quarter." Clay twisted his lips into a corkscrew. "Rue and I have had dealings with them. They're not fans of ours. We had to put down their matriarch a couple decades back."

"She was eating teenagers," I explained to Asa. "She lured them into a Mardi Gras float garage with a charm that wafted magical cannabis smoke."

"To be fair," Clay countered, "she was so high from inhaling her own potion in such close quarters, she thought I was a giant talking pizza."

"She kept asking me why they left off the bell peppers."

"No," Clay chided me. "Red pepper flakes."

"Ah." I snapped my fingers. "That makes more sense."

Clay, whose mind was a vault and his stomach an abyss, sketched a small bow from his seat.

Asa, used to us getting sidetracked by food, asked, "Do you think Saint is searching for Howl's bones?"

Jai Parish, the former deputy director, had strewn Mom's remains across the world. Maybe across multiple worlds. He was fae, after all. I doubted she would be put back together again anytime soon. There were simply too many missing pieces.

"Bones or a cure." I sobered in the face of that reality. "Or both."

There was no cure for death, but that was beside the point as far as Dad was concerned.

"On the upside," Colby said, her keyboard clicking, "the tracking chip is working."

After Dad and Mom ditched me—and no, I wasn't still bitter, why do you ask?—I sent him a short note via the bottle he magicked to travel my creek like our personal mail route. Colby had hidden a sliver of metal in the cork that reported its location to her. I couldn't begin to guess how long it would last before he found it, his magic nullified it, or the water fried it, but I wanted to keep tabs on him for as long as possible.

"Hey." Clay chucked me on the chin. "He might lead us straight to Luca."

To the heart of a rebellion that I hadn't decided whether to join or to crush.

"She might come hunting him." Asa reclaimed his chair. "She'll expect a return on her investment."

While I appreciated Luca discovering my dad was alive and then springing him from his prison cell below the compound, I had my doubts as to the nobility of her quest to bring down Black Hat and the director.

Parish's death had drummed one simple truth into my brain: As bad as things are, they can always get worse.

With Luca stirring the pot, encouraging rogue behavior, and generally making my life miserable, I had reason to doubt she had altruistic motives for, well, anything. A nice chat would go a long way toward convincing me where I ought to fall on the line she was quickly drawing down the center of the Bureau.

"We'll find her before that happens." Clay folded his hands behind his head. "She can't hide forever."

"If Saint breaks faith with Luca, she may come to us." Asa slanted his eyes toward me. "To you."

"Come *to* me or come *after* me?"

"Saint is a nuclear option. He'll mushroom cloud if she harms Rue." Clay spread his fingers. "Ka-*boom*."

I wish I had their confidence, but I doubted Dad would notice me if I was writhing and screaming on a lit pyre in the French Quarter, burning while the director toasted marshmallows in the flames and tourists sipped café au laits, crammed sugary beignets in their maws, and marveled at the New Orleans performance art scene. Claps would ring out as I was rendered to ash and blown across the hot pavement into nothingness.

Yeah.

That was grim.

Even by my standards.

"What you need—" Clay's eyes glittered, "—is to escape this claustrophobic office for a few hours."

That sounded better than doodling in the margin of my notepad to avoid more paperwork. "Oh?"

"What she needs," Colby cut in, "is to come home." Her voice went soft. "I miss you, Rue."

"I miss you too." I rubbed the aching spot over my breastbone. "I'll be home tomorrow, okay?"

Since my big promotion, I wasn't there as much. The commute was a nightmare, but worse, it was dangerous to let people believe I had an important reason for returning so often to Samford. The more curious among them might decide they ought to pay a visit and discover its hold over me for themselves.

Until I conjured a more permanent solution, Aedan was sleeping in Clay's room.

Colby wasn't alone, but it wasn't the same.

For any of us.

"We'll have the whole weekend together," Clay added. "Forty-eight hours to kill the kraken. I bet you and Blay do it in twenty-four."

The kraken.

From the Mystic Realms pirate expansion pack.

That I bought in a fit of soul-crushing guilt when I realized this job meant leaving Colby in Samford.

There must be another way to keep our family together, and safe, but I hadn't found it yet.

Until I did, I would continue to support the Mystic Realms franchise as very expensive penance.

A knock on the door had me tapping my desk to break the ward, and I muted the call before Inga pranced in.

"The director asked me to hand-deliver this." Bright eyes on Asa, she leaned across the desk, giving us both an eyeful of perky boobs and me a thick red file. I recognized it as a new case, and Clay was quick to snatch it and begin skimming. "He said the content is relevant to your interests."

"We're having a cookout this weekend, Inga." Clay played the innocent. "Would you like to come?"

"Oh." Jerking her gaze to me, she registered my murderous scowl and her proximity to the letter opener that kept creeping into my palm. "I..."

"Rue makes a mean venison burger." Clay tilted his head, eyes on her tawny flanks. "Steak too."

"T-t-thank you." The color drained from her face as she shot upright, quivering on her hooves. "But no."

A quick pivot on her hind legs and she trotted out with impressive speed across the slick tiles.

Pretending I was above such pettiness, I chided Clay for spooking her. "That was uncalled for."

"From where I was sitting, it was very called for. She needs to realize that being in heat doesn't grant her exemption to flirt with a dae in fascination." Clay philosophized at the closed door. "I saved her life, really."

As much as I wanted to disagree, I couldn't, not when the letter opener spoke for itself. "In heat?"

"Those cutesy tail flicks?" Clay's brows slanted down. "She's flinging pheromones. *Everywhere.* Your office is basically a personal ad for her need to get it on that she's hoping Ace will circle in red pen."

That, I could forgive. Biology was biology. But if Clay noticed, then no doubt Asa had too.

"Inga has been courting you *in my office*." Claws sprouted from my fingertips. "Why didn't you tell me?"

"It didn't bother you—"

"—only because I didn't know it was happening!"

"I'm taken." Asa spun my chair to face him and slid his hands behind my knees to keep me right where he wanted me. "What do I care about other women?"

"Or their secretions," Clay added helpfully.

Mouth set in a hard line, I refused to soften for Asa when he pressed his lips to mine. But when his long fingers traced the inside seam on my pants, rising higher, I decided maybe I ought to let him apologize.

Really, it was the least I could do.

"New Orleans."

Pulse racing as Asa's thumb reached the apex of my thighs, I mumbled a vague *mmm-hmm* noise at Clay.

"New Orleans," he said again, and whacked me over the head with the file. "That's where the case—" He jumped back when his new vantage, standing behind my chair, gave him a bird's-eye view of my lap. "What is it with you people?" He hit Asa between the eyes with a paperclip. "Are the pheromones finally hitting you?"

The idea of another woman turning Asa on, however unintentional for him, shriveled my enthusiasm.

Breaking from Asa with a murmured apology, I resumed my position, angled between the two of them.

"You two haven't...?" Clay began to sit then paused with his butt hovering above the seat. "In my chair?"

"No." *Hello, pettiness, my old friend.* "I mean, we tried, but the armrests got in the way."

Straightening to his full height, he wiped his hands on his pants. "You two are the absolute worst."

"As long as you stay off the desk, my chair, his chair, a few of the shelves, and the floor, you'll be fine."

"I quit." Clay dusted his palms together then waved to me. "See you in ten years."

"You're never going to let that go, are you?"

"Not a chance, Dollface."

"I suppose I deserve that."

"We have a case." He shook the file. "Put your…" he gestured vaguely at Asa, "…back in your pants and pay attention."

"Okay." I hooked a finger through Asa's belt, urging him closer, onto his feet. "You heard the man."

"That's not what I meant." Clay dropped his face into his hands. "Rue, do not put Ace in your pants."

And that was how the director found me, after letting himself in, which meant Inga was still hiding.

With Clay wishing for lightning to strike him dead where he stood.

And Asa standing between my thighs as I made zipping noises with his fly to further horrify Clay.

The director was an unimposing man by design. Late forties, maybe early fifties. Old enough to pass for a dad, but not a grandfather. I don't know how long ago he decided to stop showing his age, but he hadn't sprouted a single extra gray hair at his temples since I came to live with him.

He wore the template for the company uniform. Black suit, white shirt, glossy shoes. Thick black frames completed the look. Goddess only knows what those lenses showed him. His vision was already perfect.

Tap. Tap. Tap.

The black lacquer cane with mother-of-pearl inlays glinted under the lights, and my fingers curled into my palms, ready for the strike I never stopped anticipating.

"I do hope I'm not interrupting." He ignored Asa, and my fists. "The door was ajar."

Cold sweat glazed my spine, and my heart gave serious consideration to bursting through my ribs.

"Not at all," I rasped, my throat going tight as he leaned on his cane with the casual ease of a habit.

Asa performed his disappearing trick, fading into the background of the room until he might as well have been wallpaper. I hated when he lessened himself, but it was on my orders. It was too dangerous for the director to view him as more than a pretty bauble that decorated my office and kept my bed warm.

"Have you read the file?" *Tap. Tap. Tap.* "It's an interesting case, yes?"

Sliding my gaze to Clay, the only one who had skimmed it, I waited for his nod to go ahead and lie.

Turning my back on Asa in a clear dismissal made my heart ache, but it kept the director focused on me.

"Interesting is a good word."

I wasn't lying. I was misdirecting. It gave me room for plausible deniability later.

"I expect you to spearhead the investigation." He flexed his hand. "You will report to me directly."

"I'm the deputy director." I gestured to a pile of unfinished paperwork in a tray. "Not a field agent."

"You are what I say you are, *Granddaughter*, and you do what I tell you to do."

"How high?"

For a heartbeat, I savored his confusion before he demanded, "What?"

"You told me to jump, so I'm asking how high."

"At times, your lips move, but it's your mother's lowbrow humor that falls out of your mouth."

"Thank you."

"It wasn't a compliment." His knuckles whitened on the head of his cane. "Quite the opposite, in fact."

With only one pertinent card in my deck, I played it to the hilt. "I'll leave for New Orleans immediately."

"See that you do." He rested a hand on Clay's shoulder. "Stay close to her."

A gray film dulled Clay's eyes as the order sank in, but then he gritted out, "Yes, sir."

Orders given, the director exited the room and left the way open behind him.

When I said *immediately*, I hadn't meant I would follow him out, but clearly that was his interpretation.

"You can put it down now," Asa said gently. "He's gone."

How it got there, I don't know, but I clutched the letter opener in my hand, where it rested on my thigh.

One day, I would kill the director for what he had done to my family, and that most definitely included Clay.

Until then, I would have to settle for a brief respite as the door on my self-made cage slid open.

As I wiggled out and kicked to the surface to fill my lungs, I let myself pretend I was free. Truly free. That I didn't have to dive back in when this case was over. It was a lie, but a necessary one, and I relished it.

Too bad I had no clue what this breath of fresh air was costing me.

2

Guilt led me by the nose to Hollis Apothecary that afternoon, where I stood on the cracked sidewalk, gazing through the pristine front window into a snapshot of an idyllic life that had never been truly mine, no matter how I wished for it.

A metallic tinkling noise caught my attention, and I grunted as impact drove me into the glass. *"Oomph."*

"Rue." Camber held on while she bounced on the balls of her feet. "We weren't expecting you."

"Rue?" Arden stuck her head out the door. "I hardly recognized you."

Hard to blame her for ribbing me when the Black Hat uniform was antithesis to my usual wardrobe.

Another hit knocked me against the brick as she smacked into my side. "*Oomph* again."

The door opened a third time, but I couldn't see past the happy tears blinding me.

"Excuse you." Aedan bumped Camber out of his way then nudged Arden aside. "Pardon you."

"Hey." I accepted his hug with a sniffle. "I missed you."

"Him?" Camber peeled him off me. "What about us?"

"Yeah." Arden bulled him out of her way. "What about us?"

"I meant to say *I missed you all.*" I gestured to the three of them. "All of you. Missed equally. By me."

"Hmph." Camber turned up her nose. "I'll allow it."

"Fine." Arden melted under the heat in Aedan's smile. "I accept your apology."

"Don't believe them," Aedan cautioned me. "They're only saying that because they need a favor."

"That doesn't sound like us." Camber punched his arm. "I'm sure I don't know what you mean."

"You're worse than siblings." I separated Aedan from them. "Always poking and tattling on each other."

"We're not siblings," Aedan and Arden chorused as Camber said, "There's been no poking. *Yet.*"

Snorting at their sorely missed antics, I plunged right in. "What's the favor?"

"Uncle Nolan emailed last night. He invited us to New Orleans for Mardi Gras." Camber raised her hands over her head and did a little dance. "He rented a townhouse on Toulouse Street."

A cold stone dropped into my stomach and didn't quit sinking until it smashed my toes flat.

What were the odds of Nolan being in New Orleans ahead of us? Or including the girls in his trip?

Thin.

Paper thin.

Tissue paper thin.

And we all knew how easily that tore.

"We're closed on Sundays," Arden rushed to fill in the blanks. "That only leaves Saturday." Her gaze slid to my third employee. "Aedan offered to cover the shop so we can go."

Mardi Gras. I groaned. *Why did it have to be Mardi Gras?*

This case would already be total chaos between the parades, the alcohol, and the bead-hungry tourists.

The only thing worse I could think of was having Camber and Arden smack in the middle of it.

"Mardi Gras is dangerous." I blurted the first protest that came to mind. "I don't think it's a good idea."

Especially with Nolan Laurens, wildlife photographer and absentee uncle extraordinaire, as chaperone.

The last time I saw Nolan, he was camping on my property, without my permission, with a massive zoom lens, stalking Colby. To send him on his way, I held his precious equipment hostage but offered to ship it back to him at no cost, so long as he provided an address that was out of the state. Minimum. Out of the country would have been preferable, but he only made it as far as Colorado.

Ready with her argument, Arden began, "Uncle Nolan—"

"What if I pay for a St. Patrick's Day weekend in Savannah? You've more than earned it. They even dye the water in their fountains. There's plenty to do and see and eat. It's safer. And greener. You'll love it."

And it kept them far away from New Orleans.

"It's two more weeks," Aedan said to their chorus of groans. "I hear River Street is amazing."

No surprise, he zeroed in on the cobbled row of shops and restaurants overlooking the Savannah River.

"We've been to Savannah." Camber yanked on my arm. "We've never been to New Orleans."

"Come on, Rue." Arden rested her head on my shoulder. "It'll be fun."

There was no good way to ask why Nolan had invited them out of the blue without them getting defensive. I didn't want to pick a fight during one of our rare visits, but I didn't trust this sudden offer to spend a weekend where I had been dispatched to solve a problem that might dispatch me first if I lost my focus.

"Gran can work my shift Saturday, and Aedan can cover for Arden." Camber dusted her hands. "Problem solved."

Miss Dotha had quit the shop after the girls' abduction. I wasn't as sure as Camber that she would reprise her role anytime soon, even as a favor for her granddaughter.

"It's not about the schedule." I still sounded like a party pooper. "I'm worried about your safety."

"Then come with us." Arden gathered my hands in hers. "You could use a vacation."

Little did they know, this was my vacation, an escape from my new official duties.

"We never see you anymore." Camber piled the guilt higher. "A girls' trip sounds perfect to me."

From their smiles alone, I knew I had lost the battle. "I can't stop you from going, can I?"

"Nope."

"Nah-ah."

"Take Aedan," I bargained, hands on my hips, "and I'll close the shop for a three-day weekend."

"You're not going?" Camber's expression fell. "Aedan is nice, but he's not you."

Arden rested her hand on Aedan's forearm to apologize for Camber's bluntness.

"Those are my terms." I hardened my expression. "Take 'em or leave 'em."

"We'll take him." Arden flushed hot enough to cook an egg on her face. "I mean 'em. The terms."

As if only realizing she still held on to him, she jerked back and shuffled closer to Camber as if her hands had minds of their own and she couldn't always control them.

Oh, how well I knew that feeling.

"I came home to pack a fresh bag." I examined the sidewalk to avoid watching their faces fall, but my peripheral vision was kind enough to fill in the blanks. "I'm heading out again in a few hours."

"We're just a speed bump on your way somewhere else, huh?" Camber tucked her chin. "See you, Rue."

"Cam..." Arden shot me a sympathetic glance then chased her friend. "Slow down."

Alone on the sidewalk with Aedan, I rested my forehead against the cool glass and shut my eyes.

"They can't visit New Orleans right now." I exhaled slowly. "That's where I'm heading."

"For work?" A curious edge crept into his voice. "What's going on there?"

"A sea monster."

Aedan huffed out a laugh.

"No, really." I thought back to that damnable file Inga probably infused with her *secretions* before dumping it on my desk per the director's orders. "Though I suppose it's technically a lake monster."

"Lake Pontchartrain?"

"Yep." I might as well tell him the rest. "A ready source of food appeared, and so did it."

"I'm afraid to ask." He made an educated guess. "Swimmers?"

"The next best thing." I opened my eyes and straightened. "Dead bodies."

"Bodies?" His gaze was drawn to where Arden stood behind the register. "Serial killer?"

"That would be too normal." By Black Hat standards, anyway. "These were stolen from area morgues."

"That's...odd."

"The culprits might be taking organs or bones for spellwork then dumping what's left. Hard to tell, given the monster and all."

The on-site team hadn't seen enough of the creature to identify its species.

"I see why you didn't want the girls near this." He rubbed his jaw. "Maybe I can talk them out of it."

"You can try." I squeezed his shoulder. "I wish you luck."

Once Camber dug in her heels, it was a done deal. This was

happening. I couldn't stop it. Not without a better reason than *because I said so*. All we could do now was damage control.

"I'll run interference as best I can," he promised. "Stay in touch so I know where not to let them go."

"I will." I hugged him again. "Thanks for taking such good care of them."

"It's no problem." His tone softened as he stared through the glass again. "I'm glad I can help."

Withdrawing from him, I smoothed a hand down my blouse. "I should go."

"Are Asa and Clay at the farm?"

"Yeah." I tucked a stray hair behind my ear. "Asa had a meeting scheduled with Moran, and Clay had an errand to run there too." I rocked back on my heels. "Look, I don't know what Nolan is up to, but you can bet it's nothing good. I really don't like that he's in New Orleans right now."

"He's a wildlife photographer, right?"

"Yes." I couldn't think of a worse person to be nosing around us. "He saw a photo with Colby in the background and decided to hunt her down."

"Do you think it gave him a taste for documenting paranormals?"

"He was leaning toward Colby being a new or invasive species, but he was camped out for *days*. I can't be sure how much he saw before I caught him or what evidence he left with in his photo storage cloud." Modern technology was the bane of my, and every other paranormal creature's, existence. "My gut says if he had any useable footage of her, he would have sold it to the highest bidder already."

If he had viable proof of her existence, naturalists would have been swarming our yard like cockroaches.

"Then this sea monster might be his new holy grail."

"A discovery like that would earn him a spot in the history books, which would appeal to his ego, but how could he have heard about it?"

"You'd think if he was going monster hunting, even with a telephoto lens, he wouldn't want the girls anywhere near it."

For that to be true, he would have to think about someone other than himself. Not really his style. Which made it believable he would invite the girls, even if we didn't know why.

"Text me the address once you're settled in." I chewed my bottom lip. "I'll sneak over and ward it."

A magical barrier wouldn't protect the girls' hearts if Nolan ditched them again, but I would sleep better if they were as safe as I could make them.

"I'll do that." The muscles in his cheek twitched. "I'll also try to find out why Nolan extended the invite."

"Make sure that townhouse has three bedrooms." I pointed a warning finger at him. "Minimum of two."

Worst-case scenario, he could pack an inflatable mattress and crash in the living room.

"And the two in that one better be Camber and Arden." He saluted me. "I have my marching orders."

"I better get a move on too." I checked the time on my phone. "Talk soon."

He waved, I waved, Camber and Arden pretended not to see me leave...

All in all, it could have gone worse.

I don't know how, but I preferred not to tempt fate by wondering.

Fairhope Farm, which Asa purchased for the centuria after my promotion, sprawled over twenty acres on the outskirts of Samford. There was a small farmhouse, but it leaned to one side as if tired of its years overseeing the tilling of fields and tending of cattle. However, the barn was in much better shape.

While the former owner's kid had had no interest in the extensive renovations necessary to make his childhood home livable, the barn was useful as storage. That had earned it a patched roof and electricity, which would do for the daemons until we tapped into the house's existing septic tank and plumbing to give them indoor bathrooms and running water.

"What do you think?" Wrench in hand, Clay wiped sweat from his brow. "This is the last one."

"Nice." I scanned the open area that had been swept down to the bare concrete floor. "Very nice."

Portable AC units plugged the windows, humming and blowing cool air. Bunk beds lined the rear wall in a tidy row, and Clay leaned against the set he'd just finished assembling to toss back a bottle of cold water. I could see condensation on its exterior. Curious where he got it, I meandered toward the former tack room and found it had been outfitted with six fridges, four freezers, and two microwaves.

"I bought two more grills." Clay appeared at my elbow. "That brings them up to four."

"I saw the washers and dryers under tarps." I angled toward him. "Who's paying for all this?"

"That would be me." He polished off his bottle and helped himself to a second. "No strings attached."

"I can't let you renovate this place into a chic barndominium and not pitch in."

"If you want to get technical, these are Asa's people." He winked. "How about I bill him?"

"I want to help." I cracked open a freezer to find it full of frozen slabs of beef. "I don't have the funds you guys do, but I would like to contribute."

If I had been eligible to inherit my parents' estate, Dad would probably be sticking his hand out right about now.

"Okay." He measured me. "You can cover the couches for the living room." He held up his fingers. "Six."

A wave of breathlessness swept through me as the cost of my generosity registered with painful clarity.

"You forget—" I wiped the smug look off his face, "—I have a little moth with a nose for sniffing out sales."

Most of our furniture, clothes, and appliances were secondhand or discontinued items.

"I would say that's cheating, but Shorty wants to help too."

Heart swelling for the thoughtful little girl she was, I had to remind myself the reason she was so good at bargain shopping was her mercenary streak. It was wider than she was tall.

A metallic glint on his wrist caught my eye, and I suppressed a groan. "What's that?"

"You mean this old thing?" He stuck out his arm. "It's a smartwatch to make calling and texting easier."

As much trouble as he had operating his jumbo phone, I had doubts a tiny watch was the solution, but it was shiny new tech. That alone justified the purchase in his mind.

Though, if he had told me in advance he wanted a smartwatch, I could have saved myself the hassle of charming his Rolex. Then again, maybe that was what had given him the idea to splurge.

"Where is everyone?" I peered around but turned up none of the daemons. "Patrol?"

"Asa and Moran are sparring." He twiddled his thumbs in clear view. "Shirtless. Sweaty. On the hill."

"I thought they were in a meeting."

"Yeah." He tilted his head. "They are."

"A shirtless meeting?" I gave serious consideration to crushing the water bottle against his forehead. "It didn't occur to you to tell me this sooner?"

"Oh, it did." He tossed the plastic in a recycling bin I hadn't noticed. "But you were on a self-guided tour, and I hated to interrupt a potential investor while she valuated the work we've already done."

"One day," I told him, "I'm going to set your wig on fire." I flicked the end of his nose. "While you're still wearing it."

"Warn me in advance? I have a couple I wouldn't mind sacrificing for the greater good."

"Uh, no." I wasn't enabling his purchasing guilt-free replacements. "Then it wouldn't be a punishment."

Exiting the barn, I stood in the driveway until I heard a faint commotion that sounded promising.

The former cotton fields were barren, which made for easy walking, but it was a sad sight. I crouched and scooped up a handful of dirt. The top layer was dry as dust, but rich soil greeted me an inch or so deeper.

"This place has potential." I stood and wiped my palms on my pants. "How do daemons feel about gardening?"

"Depends on the daemon, I imagine." Clay caught up to me. "What are you thinking?"

"I could use a local supplier for the herbs and flowers in the shop's most popular blends." I let the idea percolate. "I might rent an acre on the edge of the property, hire some daemons to tend it. It could give the centuria some disposable income." I wasn't sure they would stick around after their duties had been fulfilled, but it would be a better use of their time than returning to the monotony of their prior existence. "It's an idea."

"I seriously doubt Ace would accept rent from you." He let his focus drift across the neglected field. "It's good thinking, though. Gardening is therapeutic. Plus, they could grow some of their own food, which would help, given the volume the males put away daily."

Asa would never complain about the grocery bill, not when the centuria was under his protection, but pitching in would give the daemons a sense of pride and accomplishment as well.

"They used to raise cattle here too, but livestock are a lot of work."

And a whole lot of money was required in start-up costs for fencing, feed, and hay, as there was no grass. Not to mention the animals themselves. Plus shelter. Plus vet care. Plus sweat equity.

"Cowboy daemons." Clay slapped his knee. "Yee-haw."

"Hold on, partner." I reined him in before he got too carried away. "Don't start buying Stetsons yet."

"I would be willing to sponsor your idea with two teeny-tiny little caveats."

"You can't have a pony, so if that's what you're wanting, the answer is no."

Horses can carry up to twenty percent of their body weight. For a four-hundred-pound golem, we would need to locate a two-thousand-pound animal. Bare minimum. Think Belgian draft horse.

"I own a horse farm in Kentucky." He flicked my nose as payback. "I already have *all* the ponies."

Mouth falling open, I struggled to find my voice. "How did I not know this?"

"You vanished for ten years." His brows slanted downward. "You don't get to tell me how to cope."

"You bought it off eBay, didn't you?"

"Online shopping counts as therapy." He crossed his arms over his chest. "Ask anyone."

"Okay, okay." I lifted my hands, palms out. "What are your conditions?"

"You attend barbecue school with me." He held up one finger. "Myron Mixon has a school in Unadilla, Georgia. He's that guy on *BBQ Pitmasters*. Catch the reruns, pleb, so you don't embarrass me when we get there." He lifted another. "*And* we establish an annual cook-off judged by Samfordians."

"The mayor would love that." I caught on to his annoyance. "No, really." I laughed. "I mean it."

"You hate Mayor Tate."

"No," I corrected him. "Mayor Tate hates me."

From the moment I stumbled into town, she had made it plain she wanted me to keep right on going.

A ruckus ahead urged me into a brisk walk, and I crested a small hill to find Asa shirtless, as promised, on his back. Moran, in a leather sports bra, stood over him with a blade aimed at his heart.

The cheering faded to a dull whine that muted the world as I broke into a sprint.

The phantom taste of copper filled my mouth, and my jaw clenched until my teeth ached.

I flung myself at Moran, knocking her off him, and landed astride her. Fingernails sharp and deadly, I swiped at her face, her fierce grip on my wrist the only thing that saved her left eye. Her grin was wide as she grappled with me, and she laughed as she punched me in the gut.

Air whooshed from my lungs, but I could still taste blood in my mouth, and I couldn't stop.

Swinging my free arm, I clocked her in the jaw then clamped a hand around her throat.

"Rue."

Crimson rivulets spilled down the sides of her neck, and my tongue dried to sandpaper. The urge to bend down, lick her skin clean, then finish what I started beat in my chest as loud as her heart.

Bah-bump. Bah-bump. Bah-bump.

Exhilaration tasted much the same as fear, adrenaline sweetening the flavor.

"*Rue.*" A gentle hand landed on my shoulder as Asa's voice drifted to me. "You have to let her up now."

Had he spoken in Mandarin, he would have made more sense to the fraying edges of my control.

"She would have tapped out by now," Clay drawled, "if you weren't trying so hard to kill her."

Kill her?

Kill her?

"Goddess." I hung my head. "I'm sorry, Moran." Breathed in. Breathed out. "I was totally out of line."

Once I got my head screwed on straight, Asa backed away slowly to avoid provoking me again.

"You have nothing to apologize for." She grinned up at me through pink teeth. "Your bond is strong."

"That doesn't mean you should let me off the hook easy." I offered her a hand up she accepted without hesitation. "I had no right to turn your match into a melee." I kept my grip. "I mean it, Moran. I'm sorry."

"You have impressive reflexes." She ignored my second attempt to make amends. "Who taught you?"

"That would be me." Clay preened as Moran sized him up with a frown. "Rue was my best pupil."

"Then I shudder to think what condition your other pupils might be in."

"You just praised her reflexes," he spluttered. "Rue is talented."

"A talented witch? Yes. A talented fighter? No." Her neutral tone reminded me of one of my former tutors, and I cringed from her assessment. "Her tactical thinking is poor, and her form is barely recognizable."

"Gee." Warmth spread through my cheeks as I shook the talons from my fingertips. "Thanks?"

"You're a creature of instinct." Moran glowed with approval. "I respect that."

As much as I wanted to blame fascination for my hair trigger, I was raised to never make excuses.

To show I valued her opinion, I pressed for her to continue. "But?"

"You could be so much more lethal with proper instruction."

"I do enjoy being lethal." I was only half kidding. "Okay. Yeah. I'll let you kick my butt into shape."

"This is what I mean." She cocked her head to one side. "Kicking a butt serves no purpose."

Biting the inside of my cheek to avoid laughing, I offered a solemn nod instead. "I have much to learn."

"Maybe I'll join you for those classes." Clay cracked his neck. "I could use a remedial workout."

"As you wish, golem." Challenge rang through her words. "Name the time and place."

"Anytime, anyplace." He hesitated. "Except not right here or right now. I'm on my way out of town."

"Good comeback." I patted him on the shoulder. "You really brought your A game."

"It's okay to be impressed with me." Clay smoothed his hair back. "Most people are."

"Clearly," Moran drawled, "you're impressed with yourself enough for us all."

"Burn." I laughed at his puckered expression. "She got you there."

Whatever was said next, I missed as I watched Asa shrugging on his shirt, his fingers deftly fastening the buttons. He caught me ogling him and held my stare while tucking in his shirt with exaggerated motions.

I wished it was my hand shoved down his pants.

"Rue." Clay clamped his hands on Moran's ears. "Keep your dirty thoughts to yourself."

A flash of her palm shot his head back, and he stumbled a few steps before regaining his balance.

"Looks like she wants you to keep your hands to yourself." I smothered a laugh. "Nice move, Moran."

Laughter bright in her eyes, she acknowledged the compliment with a straight face.

Smart enough to know when he was beaten, Clay switched topics to give his bruised ego time to heal.

"I finished the bunks." He tested his tender nose. "The mattresses and sheets will be delivered soon."

Differences set aside, for the moment, she clasped her hands in front of her. "Thank you."

"You have my number." He bobbed a shoulder. "Call if you need anything else."

"I thought that was Aedan's job." I arched an eyebrow at them.

"He's the liaison, right?"

"Yes." Moran dropped her gaze, her lips curling. "Of course."

Clay, who also found the ground interesting, scrubbed the back of his neck with his palm.

Me?

I found the two of them, and their shy glances, far more interesting than dirt.

"We'll work on a training schedule when I get back." I twisted my lips. "Again, really sorry about earlier."

"Now that we've all kissed and made up," Clay said, checking the time, "we should go."

"Will you be joining her?" Moran cocked an eyebrow. At Clay. "Or are you all talk?"

"I don't know." He pretended to consider her. "If my form is that bad, I might be beyond hope."

"There's always hope," she said softly. "Failing that, I have a large stick and excellent aim."

"Tempting," he rumbled. "Very tempting."

Hooking my arm through his, I dragged him away from Moran and steered him out of earshot.

"You got a wee bit excited back there when she mentioned the size of her stick."

A blush crept up his throat into his cheeks. "I hate you."

"What do you get when you cross a golem with a daemon? A daelem? A golmon?"

"Not funny." He pried my fingers off him. "The last thing I need right now is a relationship."

"*Oooh.*" I clutched my hands to my chest. "*Relationship* sounds serious."

"I assembled bunk beds for the woman," he protested. Loudly. "I didn't braid her a hair bracelet."

With that, he stomped off toward the SUV, leaving me to savor a taste of sweet, sweet payback.

"Are they interested in one another?" Asa watched him storm away. "Or are you torturing him for fun?"

"There was blushing, some innuendo." I pinched two fingers together. "So, mostly torture for fun." A soft chuckle that warmed me to my bones was his response. "I ought to apologize to you too, for how I behaved earlier, but I'm sure you're tired of hearing how sorry I am by now."

"I'm daemon enough that I will never grow tired of your swift and vicious jealousy."

"Thanks?" I slid my arm around his waist and leaned my head against his shoulder. "I swear I'm not always so murderous." I heard myself and backtracked fast. "Okay, well, I am pretty murderous even under the best circumstances, but—"

"I don't mind." He slowed, turning so he faced me. "No one has ever coveted me." He cupped my cheek. "I enjoy it." His lips hitched to one side. "You're beautiful in your fury."

"Pretty sure I look unhinged, but to each his own." I kissed his palm. "How was the meeting?"

"Productive." He raked his fingers through my hair, the ends curling around his hand as he used his grip to drag my mouth to his. "The centuria are settling in. They're happier than I can remember them being in a long time."

"They have a purpose." I shivered as his lips moved down my throat. "They're also somewhere new. A change in scenery can do wonders for morale."

"Mmm-hmm."

"We need to go." I didn't budge an inch. I might have even tilted my chin, exposing more of my skin. "We can make out when we get home."

"Or we could make out here."

"I like the way you think." I jolted when I noticed a lone figure over his shoulder. "Aedan?"

When he reached us, he spoke four little words everyone dreaded hearing. "We need to talk."

3

The grim set of Aedan's features warned me bad news was incoming.

Had Nolan come for the girls? Had they ditched Aedan? Had he uncovered a dark motive for the trip?

"Camber wants to bring a friend."

Certain it must be dire to warrant him delivering the update in person, I braced for impact. "Okay."

"A guy."

Confused when he didn't elaborate further, I rallied my wits. "Okay?"

"The guy wants to bring a friend too." Aedan paced in front of me. "Another guy." His hands flexed down by his sides. "For Arden."

Missing corpses, a hungry sea monster, and Dad visiting the Big Easy. How it all fit together, I wasn't sure yet, but it must. Otherwise, the director wouldn't have dispatched me to oversee the case personally. As much as those elements mixing worried me, I had to tune out those fears and listen to my cousin.

Even if heartache was the only way forward, I could spare a few minutes while he vented his frustration.

"A guy for Arden isn't the worst idea." I gripped his forearm to hold him still. "If both girls are distracted, they'll be easier for you to manage." I hung on while temper flushed his cheeks. "You care about Arden, I get that, but you have to be ready for what a relationship with her means if that's what you want."

"I would have to tell her…everything." His anger deflated like a popped balloon. "That I'm a daemon."

The domino effect would take care of the rest. I would have to confess, and it would get uglier from there. We might all lose her if he chose that road, but he couldn't have her otherwise. Not fully.

"Eventually, yeah." I loosened my grip. "She's a smart girl, and one slip would expose you."

"What do I do?" His shoulders drooped as reality dogpiled on him. "After what she's been through…"

"She might recall some of what happened to her if you decide to cross that line." I hated to say it, but I had to for him to make the most informed decision. "Right now, it's all hazy. Fading more by the day. But human minds are tricky. Sometimes a drop of truth can burst the dam."

"She could remember how that black witch caged her and left her in the water to die."

Closing my eyes, I tried to shut out the memory of how I found them, but it breached my defenses.

Camber and Arden huddled together, their fingers laced, and their heads bowed until their hair tangled.

For a month after their rescue from the murky depths of Tadpole Swim, they used baby wipes and dry shampoo to avoid showers. I had to increase the dosage on the tea I brewed for them and smudge their memories a bit more before they could bear water on their skin without trembling in half-forgotten fear.

"I'm Aquatae." He studied the faint webbing present between his fingers even through his glamour. "She'll never love water the way I do."

I heard *she'll never love me the way I love her*, and I felt his anguish like a dull knife sliding between my ribs.

This must be empathy.

As if the turmoil of my own feelings wasn't bad enough, I could now imagine their impact on others.

This was one attribute I should have struck through on my *Ten Steps to a Better Rue* list.

"You decided to wait, to let her heal." I pulled him in for a hug. "You did all the right things."

As much as he wanted more, he had accepted her friendship as enough. For now.

"Time won't fix this," he murmured with heartbreaking certainty.

"I don't know how she would take the truth." I released him. "I've been too much of a coward to try."

My being a witch hadn't mattered when I first met the girls. I hadn't used more than a sprinkle of magic to enrich the teas, salves, and tinctures we sold at Hollis Apothecary. Barely any at all. Just enough to give me a competitive edge.

It hadn't felt like lying, then. Not really. I was so used to pasting on new identities, adopting affectations, that I didn't blink. There was no moral question. No doubt. There was only me, doing what I had been trained to do. To blend.

Had I been smart, I would have run the second it occurred to me that I loved my home, my town, my neighbors. I should have sacrificed my own happiness for their protection back then, before my roots grew too tangled with Samford and its residents to ever fully tear free.

Now? The past sat in my stomach, heavy as lead. A lie that would end everything. How could it not?

Part of me wished Aedan would damn the consequences, tell her the truth, and force me to suffer the fallout right alongside him. But that was selfish of me, to wish him to take the arrow meant for my heart.

"I'll go on the trip." He squared his shoulders. "But I won't come back."

Heart lodged in my throat, I asked the hard question, "Back to the shop or back to Samford?"

For minutes that spanned years, he didn't answer. I wasn't sure he had made up his mind yet.

"I'll bunk with the centuria," he decided, "after I see this through to the end."

An end I could no longer picture, with so many factions in play. "And then?"

"I'll move on." He turned. "I'll have to, or one day I won't be strong enough to keep silent."

Aedan left without looking back, each step heavy with determination.

"He won't stay away forever."

Warmth encased my spine as Asa pressed against me. "How can you tell?"

"He's in fascination with her," he breathed over my nape. "He has been, for weeks now."

"I didn't think—" No, that was a lie. "I *hoped* it hadn't gone that far for him."

"You've done all you can to heal Arden, and I could say the same for Aedan."

"Will it be enough?"

"I'm not sure." He pressed his warm lips to my skin. "I hope they both find the love they deserve."

"Me too." I tipped my head back to rest on his shoulder. "This trip will be miserable for him."

If I punched through his ribs, fisted his beating heart in my palm, and squeezed, it would hurt less.

"Maybe standing at a crossroads will help him decide which path to take."

As much as I wanted to believe this was for the best, I worried his next path would lead him out of Samford, and my life, for good.

On the floor in my bedroom, legs crossed, I restocked my kit for the trip from the dwindling supply in my closet. I had already checked the safe, and its contents, but the dark artifacts I had collected over my career were tucked safely behind their wards. Including the stash I pilfered from the Boo Brothers.

Black magic wasn't the kind of stink that went unnoticed, so I felt confident there had been no leakage. It was more difficult for me to parse the scent in trace amounts, since it had been a part of me for so long, but Asa always checked behind me to ensure I wasn't leaving Colby in a miasma of dark energies.

Inviting himself in, Clay rested his hip against my dresser. "How bad is it?"

"Oh, you know." I relaxed in my battered jeans and soft tee, grateful to be comfy again. "Boy loves girl. Girl has no idea boy is a daemon. Girl finds out the truth, the whole truth, and either she loses her mind, or she gains an HEA."

"Poor Aedan."

"Poor Arden too." I avoided the safe to keep from drawing Clay's attention to its glamour. "She's got it just as bad for him."

"Feelings are dumb." His gaze slid over the chest full of dried herbs, never touching on my forbidden collection. "Hearts are stupid."

"That's what I've been telling you." I slapped his thigh. "Why does no one ever listen to me?"

"Hmm?" He scrunched up his face. "Did you say something?"

The glare I shot him was sharp enough to draw blood, if he had any.

"I did come in here for a reason." He inclined his head. "Other than to pester you."

And Asa wondered where I learned to relish tormenting those I loved most.

"Aedan got Colby the address of Nolan's rental, and she verified his name is on the lease." He checked the calendar on his watch. "Starting two days ago."

And here I expected it to be a VacayNStay, the preferred vacation rental app of anyone up to no good.

"A lease implies he came to New Orleans with a purpose, not on a whim." I toyed with the lowest hinge, opening and shutting the door to annoy Clay into ignoring the closet's contents. "I don't suppose under *reason for moving* he was thoughtful enough to spell out his dastardly plans?"

"Sadly, no, but Colby did a quick background check to see what he's been up to since Colorado."

"Nothing good, I take it?"

"Nothing period." A grimness settled over him. "Nolan Laurens has fallen off the face of the planet."

He emailed me the file to skim, but the bare-bones outline troubled rather than thrilled me.

No forwarding address. No work contracts on record. No deposits or withdrawals from his bank.

Not for food, not for travel, and not for the rental.

"Maybe I scared him straight."

"Maybe something he caught on film spooked him."

"Straight to the worst-case scenario." I shook a jar of black pyramid salt. "That's what I like about you."

"What can I say?" He played it off with a smile. "I'm a likeable guy."

"Arden told me he disappears for months at a time when he's on assignment." I checked my stores for a sprig of holly but came up empty. "Do you think he could have been hired to document the creature?"

Had he discovered footage that sent him into hiding? Living off grid? Or worse, had it sent him digging deeper?

Contacts made in the paranormal sector during research could have netted him intel on the sea monster and a gig capturing it on film.

"I could buy that." Clay ran his palm over the wood, frowning at the dust. "Validation after you stomped on his ego would be sweet. He might be foolish enough to believe entrée into paranormal society would protect him from you if he went after Colby again."

"What if he expects me to show, and he wants to use the girls as his shield?"

"You know, Dollface." Clay wiped his hand on his pants. "It's not too late to stop them from going."

"They're adults." I would have called their moms otherwise. "I can't tell them what to do."

"It never stopped you before."

"With me being gone all the time, we're not in a good place. If I put my foot down without giving them a solid reason, they'll rebel to spite me." I hurt them, and they would want to hurt me back. "I trust Aedan to keep them out of trouble, and we'll be local if things go sideways with Nolan."

How I would explain us riding to the rescue, if they needed it, I had no idea, but I could improvise.

"Let's break in, hack the owner's surveillance, and ward the place before they get there."

"Lawlessness does make me feel better." I squinted at him. "How do you know there's surveillance?"

"Do you hear that?" He cupped his ear. "Colby's calling me." He shot to his feet. "I gotta go."

Now that I thought about it, the hacking was probably her idea. And the breaking, and the entering.

Lawlessness and I weren't in what you would call a mutually exclusive relationship.

Asa, almost bowled over by Clay's exit, lingered on the threshold, waiting for an invitation he never took for granted. One of these days, I would break him of that habit. But not, apparently, today.

"Welcome to my humble abode," I teased, waving him in. "Can you shut that behind you?"

Once we were locked inside, I raised the wards to soundproof my room with the ease of long practice.

"Are the artifacts behaving?" He sat on the edge of the bed. "Any jailbreaks?"

Hand going to the pendant at my throat, where the grimoire remained tightly contained, I exhaled with relief. "Yes and no."

The choker's golden threads wove through the pendant's original chain, bright against its ancient patina. An odd light had come into the ruby in recent days, another reason why I kept all five carats of it tucked into my shirt. The other being its baroque-style frame was slightly hideous, in my humble opinion.

"I almost forgot." I snapped my fingers. "Can you check around the safe?"

Sliding to his knees, he breathed in deep, holding the air in his lungs before exhaling slowly.

"I smell herbs and fabric softener, a hint of hydrangea, but no black magic."

The rich floral scent of hydrangeas called to mind Mom's white magic, and my heart wrenched to realize I would never smell it again. The dead had no spellcasting abilities. That part of her life, that part of her identity, was gone. All that remained was a faded echo within my own powers.

"Excellent." I nudged the bifold doors closed with a foot that had fallen asleep. "I was counting on the purifying quality of Colby's magic to cleanse it."

With pins and needles stabbing one leg, I climbed onto the bed and patted the mattress beside me.

"Have you determined what the new objects do?" He sat and tugged me flush against his side. "Are any of them worth bringing to test in the field?"

"One of them tempts me," I admitted, leaning into him. "A quartz lapel pin that stores magic."

"Similar to how a familiar acts as a battery?"

"Except, as best I can tell, it produces no magic of its own. It collects power like iron filings drawn to a magnet."

"Any idea of its capacity?"

"No clue." I had never seen craftsmanship like it. "I worry if I wear it for long periods outside the range of other magic users, it will decide the only way to fill its tank is to suck Colby dry."

"Less than ideal." A furrow cut across his brow. "Any luck tracing their origins?"

"None so far." I was slacking in that department. "I can't risk taking them to work with me, they would be too vulnerable to discovery, and I'm never home to fiddle with them."

Like a kid using a cellphone in class instead of listening to their teacher, I would be begging the director to confiscate any artifacts I brought to work. Inga, a clip-clopping spy if ever I heard one, would sell me out in a heartbeat. And leaving an object of power at our current hotel was a good way to have it stolen.

Little Miss Tail Swish booked our rooms. Not Colby. Meaning the hotel was likely in Black Hat's pocket.

"You're growling." Asa leaned over, catching my ear between his teeth. "What are you thinking about?"

"Inga." I wrinkled my nose. "She's an intrusive thought I can't get rid of."

And yet, there was a super simple solution to the problem.

If we mated officially, the boiling rage in my gut would evaporate.

All it would cost me was Colby's life, if Blay ever lost a match against any of his daemon challengers.

Lucky for me, Asa seemed content to bask in my jealousy while it lasted. He had little enough experience with being loved. He was enjoying every rage-inducing moment of my territorial fury. Even if it cost friends, allies, and family the occasional pint of blood.

Hey, I was evol*ving*. The *ing* being the critical part. I wasn't done yet.

"I don't think about her." He pressed a kiss to the underside of my jaw. "Neither should you."

"You're distracting me," I huffed, aware he could feel my pulse racing for him. "How very sneaky."

I felt his smile against my skin and couldn't help but grin in response.

"I've been practicing." He chuckled. "Have you considered banishing anything else to the djinn's lair?"

"I did briefly fantasize about dumping the contents of my safe in there so it would be all in one place."

"Then you realized if anyone discovered your trove, they would behead you and steal it."

"Yeah." I amazed myself by laughing at the idea. "That seemed kind of lame, so I passed."

"I'll pretend I didn't hear that." His lips twitched. "Blay's feelings would be hurt."

"He does enjoy a good head-ripping-off."

The finishing move was his favorite way to end any battle or mild disagreement.

"I need to speak to Aedan." He got to his feet. "You need to finish packing."

"Aedan?" I hadn't seen him since he left the farm. "He's back?"

"We're establishing a communication protocol for the centuria until he returns from New Orleans."

"Okay." I let him go without even a quick fondle. "Meet you guys outside in a few."

Alone with my worry for Aedan, I attempted to frame how a life without him might look. I hadn't known him long, but he was family. More than that. He was a good person. I didn't want his heart broken. But I didn't want to shatter Arden's worldview either.

No matter what I did, I knew in my bones I would lose one of them.

And that truly sucked.

4

As soon as I stepped out onto the porch after locking up the house, I could tell something was wrong. On one side of the SUV, Clay stood with his thick arms crossed over his wide chest. Across from him, Asa, on the verge of giving in to his transformation, rumbled a low warning to whatever they saw that I didn't.

Colby had gone ahead, tucked in Clay's pocket, and the desire to sprint to her almost overwhelmed me. I kept my strides tight, my pace steady, as if I hadn't noticed their unease as I circled around to Asa.

"What's the holdup?" I kept my tone soft, in case sensitive ears were listening in. "I thought we…"

Up the driveway strutted Orion Pollux Stavros, High King of Hael, Master of Agonae, blah blah blah.

Had I been able to see our *y'nai*, I would have strangled the life out of them. With Asa's braids.

But those murderous thoughts took a backseat to the utter shock at Stavros's latest bribe.

The horse, if you could call it that, stood a head taller than him at its withers. Its short coat was the color of sun-bleached bones. There was a prismatic quality to its fine hairs that cast rainbows down its sides. Its mane and tail were decadent, the long strands glistening like poured silver. Two glittering nubs peeked above its forelock, the beginnings of horns. Rather than hooves, it walked on the thick paw pads of a lion, its sickle claws flexing as its pink nostrils flared in indignation.

"That's a nightmare," Clay breathed, his fingers twitching to pet it. "An albino."

As if it understood him, the creature slanted its bright-pink eyes toward Clay.

"Beloved—" Stavros began his pitch, stroking the mare's velvet muzzle, "—I bring you a token of my esteem."

"Come closer." I crooked a finger, a vicious smile on my lips. "I would love to scratch behind its ears."

As soon as I touched his present, I could flip his *return to sender* spell on him.

"I admire your cunning in turning my magic against me."

"Yes, well, I couldn't resist giving you a literal *go to hell*."

"Actually, it was Mobile, Alabama."

Huh.

I didn't see that one coming.

The *return to sender* spell teleported unwanted gifts Stavros sent me back to him. I hadn't stopped to think before dismissing him—and the cupcakes he bought from the bakery Asa used to send me treats—from my sight. Apparently, if Stavros was in possession of the item, it latched on to the origin of the next best thing: the gift.

Good to know.

Especially since this beast looked like it belonged running wild on the steppes of Hael.

"Her name is Armistice," he continued silkily, "in honor of the truce I hope you grant me."

"I don't care what you call her, I don't want her—or anything else—from you." I yanked Asa to me. "*This* is my mate." I gestured up and down him like he was a prize on display. "This guy, right here. Not you. *Never* you." I edged in front of him as Stavros thinned his lips. "Allow me to make my point."

Over the years I spent living in Samford, I had sunk a lot of time into maintaining the wards surrounding my home. They were anchored along my property line with my blood, my love, my hope. They were strong. Colby coming into her familiar powers had only strengthened them.

Drawing the athame from my kit, I cut a line across my palm, allowing crimson to spill through my fingers onto the thirsty soil. I kicked off my shoes, shucked my socks, and wiggled my toes into the earth. Grounded like this, power tickled my toes, and I drew on that to fuel a massive banishment spell.

Hot sun beating down. Dead bodies piling up at my feet. Fried not-crickets served in pinkish sauce.

I broke a sweat opening the portal to the tournament realm behind Stavros, but I got the job done.

Eyes locking on the trespasser, I beseeched the land to reject his presence. It answered me in a rippling wave of roiling earth that flung him off his feet, right through the portal. His grip on the mare's reins let him hold on as the vortex whirled around him, sucking him deeper as the spell barred him return entry.

The mare, stamping and whipping its head to dislodge Stavros, was dragged through the gateway with a snarled lip that exposed dainty teeth as clear as cut crystal.

With an effort that sent me crashing to my knees, I slammed the portal shut behind them.

"Your dad must be more of a lover than a fighter." Clay snorted. "He hasn't raised a hand against Rue."

Out of breath, I settled for glaring at Clay, who grimaced when he replayed his words in his head.

"It's coming," Asa said quietly. "As soon as he realizes she's serious, that this isn't all a game, he'll resort to less flowery methods to get what he wants. He enjoys the chase until he works up a sweat."

"I can handle him."

"The women he targets can't say no." He stared at the drag marks leading nowhere. "You can't get too comfortable with him ceding victories to you. A novelty is only a novelty until it becomes an imposition."

Allowing him to help me up, I kept hold of his hand and gave it a reassuring squeeze.

"Pity about Armistice." Clay walked to the furrows and crouched. "I've never seen an albino nightmare. I saw an entire herd once. I didn't realize they came in a color other than black." He shrugged. "Since albinism is a congenital absence of melanin, I guess they technically don't."

"I'm not home enough these days to keep a pet."

"I didn't mean for you." He lifted a few glittering hairs Armistice left behind. "I meant for *me*."

"Can you imagine how much it costs to feed one of those things? Beef ain't cheap."

"But did you see its little horns? One day they'll be long enough to impale a man."

"You have enough ponies without adding a murder pony to your stable."

"I never should have told you that."

"We need to get moving." I puffed out my cheeks. "Before Stavros gets back."

The portal was mine, so he couldn't activate it. That meant he would have to use his within the pocket world to return to his realm and then journey back to ours. Time worked for him and against me while he was in there, so I couldn't gauge how long it might take him to come back with even cheesier pick-up lines. And an even more dangerous gift.

This was the one place Stavros knew I would always return to, and that made it a vulnerability.

I hated him for ruining home for me.

I hated myself for the same reason.

But I was glad to switch things up and dump the fault in his lap for a few hours, until the guilt crept back in to remind me of the cost of trying to live a normal life. There was no such thing as normal for people like me. Even among other paranormals, we were different.

More ruthless. More powerful. More craven.

With a gentle hand on my lower back, Asa led me to the SUV and opened the door.

"I won't let him hurt you," he promised, his thoughts lingering on Stavros. "I'll kill him first."

"We'll figure it out," I promised right back. "Even if *I* have to kill him first."

"How do you make plotting patricide sound so ooey-gooey?" Clay climbed in the backseat. "It shouldn't be possible, and yet, I can't shake the image of you and Ace doing the *no, you hang up first* thing like teens on a phone call. Except face-to-face, and with murder."

A rustle of motion announced Colby exiting his pocket, dragging her phone and earbuds out behind her.

Oblivious to our conversation, she started her own, holding her screen up to him. "3D printed nail decals. With food on them. They look *so* real. There's a whole line of desserts too."

Forcing her eyes round, she turned her pitiful gaze on Clay, begging without saying a word.

"I'll buy them." He fell for the act hook, line, and sinker. "But you're applying them."

"Oh, I will." A shudder rocked her. "I learned my lesson the last time I let you paint your nails alone."

"You're the one who told me waiting to dry between coats was for losers."

"Time out." I made a T shape with my hands. "Do you have our hotel booked?"

To compensate for our late start, and to avoid Stavros, we would spend the day in Slidell, catching up on our sleep, then drive to New Orleans tomorrow afternoon.

"Yep." She grinned at me. "It's probably even safe."

"That's the kind of ringing endorsement I like to hear." I switched to a thumbs-up sign. "As you were."

Their quiet bickering lulled me to sleep, where I dreamed rainbow nightmares.

5

We rolled into New Orleans about an hour before sundown, having slept the day away. It was refreshing to stay in an establishment for longer than ten minutes without someone trying to murder us even once.

However, the night was young, and I was sure someone would give it the old college try before bedtime.

"I don't know what I'm smelling—" Clay rubbed his stomach, "—but I want it in my belly, stat."

"What?" I yelled over a conga line weaving through the tight crowd on the sidewalk. "I can't hear you."

"Food." He mimed bringing a fork to his mouth. "Must eat."

"You've already swallowed three po' boys." I swatted his hand. "You're fine."

Bars on every corner sold the iconic sandwiches to revelers hand over fist.

A chewy baguette piled high with shrimp, crawfish, catfish, duck, alligator, chicken, oysters, rabbit, and anything else you could batter and fry, po' boys were quintessential New Orleans fare. Fully dressed, they came loaded with shredded lettuce, sliced tomatoes, pickles, and spicy remoulade sauce.

They were quick to make, cheap to buy, and insanely good. Not that Clay had offered to share.

"Turn right." Asa applied gentle pressure on my arm. "The rental is on the left."

Standing three stories tall, its lush galleries draped in creeping fig vines, the townhouse was a true gem.

Faking interest in the overflowing planter boxes mounted under bright-blue hurricane shutters, I homed in on the space within, listening for a heartbeat. The guys perked their ears too, but I had evolved to pick that specific noise out as easy as breathing.

Even with a samba blaring the next street over as jazz musicians poured their souls into their music.

"Time to play with our new toy," Clay announced to Colby as he pulled a black box from thin air like a magician and flipped a bright red switch. "A Wi-Fi jammer."

"The jammer blocks Wi-Fi," she explained for my benefit from the depths of his pocket, "and their home security system is a network of hubs bought at a big box store. Knock out the Wi-Fi, and they won't see us coming."

"Clever," Asa praised her. "I wouldn't have thought of that."

"I hit the purchase button," Clay grumbled. "I'm clever too."

"Of course you are." I patted him on the head. "Good golem."

I smiled.

He didn't.

But Colby laughed with childish abandon, which was music to both our ears.

"No one's home." I took the front steps like I had every right to be there then fed magic into the lock until the old latch gave and the front door swung open under my hand. "You guys start at the top and work your way to the bottom." I waited for Colby to wriggle free of Clay's pocket. "Do what you do best, smarty fuzz butt." She fluttered toward what looked to be a home office. "I'll begin setting the wards."

While the guys thumped and bumped upstairs, I layered protections, moving from the ground floor up to avoid us being under each other's feet. As satisfying as it would have been to bar Nolan entrance, I didn't want him experiencing another brush with the supernatural on my watch. Best to keep it simple and straightforward in the shared spaces.

Speaking of shared spaces...

A seven-inch digital display sat in plain sight in every room. Some pretended to be clocks. Others flashed slideshows of photos taken in New Orleans. A dot blinked in the center of each one, and speakers were visible at the bottom.

Cameras.

Every single one of them with built-in microphones.

There was no privacy in this house.

Had Nolan or his landlord done this? Either way, it disturbed me that the girls would be staying here.

Hypocritical of me? Yes. But there you go.

On the second floor, I located the guest suites. Each held an assortment of Mardi Gras paraphernalia. Mini king cakes. Beads in gold, green, and purple. Top hats made of striped felt that would look at home on The Cat in the Hat.

Matching plush animals sat on their pillows, as if the girls were much younger, and I almost regretted the suspicion that surged through me whenever Nolan's name was mentioned. This was thoughtful of him, not a word I typically associated with their uncle.

"Three and two are clear," Clay told me on his way down. "On your way to three?"

"Yep." I winked at Asa when I passed him on the stairs. "Three and then I'm done."

The top floor was a master suite with huge bedroom, en suite, bar, and sitting area. The clothing and mishmash of camera equipment told me Nolan had claimed the space for himself. That plastic-y, ozone smell I associated with new electronics left me questioning if he had replaced his gear. Maybe he didn't trust me not to have hexed the originals. In this mess, I doubted he would notice if I rooted through his things to find out, but if the guys hadn't scented anything worrisome, then it wasn't worth the risk.

One person's chaos is another person's organized chaos.

Quick as I could, I added protections on the windows and doors to keep out evil.

"My work here is done." Colby returned to me and lit on my shoulder. "Eyes and ears go live in five."

"You little miracle worker, you." I checked behind me. "Let's get out of here."

Colby holding on tight, I took the stairs at a jog and bumped into Asa halfway.

"Aedan is looking for parking." He grasped my hand and tugged me after him. "We need to go."

"Come on, Shorty." Clay held open his pocket. "Do your thing."

The four of us slipped out the door, locked up, and hit the street, allowing the crowd to swallow us.

"One last thing." Clay flipped the red switch on his black box with maniacal glee. "Let there be Wi-Fi!"

Adrenaline kept my heart pumping loudly, but the dozens upon dozens of competing beats drowned out my own rhythm. The crush of bodies pressed in on me, the salt of their skin more potent than the spices in the air. Humans held no appeal, but there were witches, fae, wargs, and vampires. *So* many vampires.

The dancing, singing, and feasting made for absolute chaos. And the parades hadn't even started yet.

"We need to get out of here." I wet my lips, my mouth dry. "I can't hear myself think."

"Thinking is overrated." Clay swung into a dance with an old man, his dark skin sheened with sweat, who handed him off to a young woman with metallic streamers tucked into her braids. Laughing, he made his way back to us. "Now this is what I call a party."

As much as I hated to be the party pooper, we were here to work. Not play. And I was getting...

...hungry.

Back at the SUV, two girls in cropped LSU tees draped themselves over Clay. Giggling maniacally, they begged him to buy them hurricanes. Prying their fingers off him, I shoved him into the backseat before they dragged him to the nearest bar.

Shielding me from their slurred profanities and excessive pouting, Asa opened my door for me, and I climbed in, relieved to have a barrier between me and the whirl of colors and blaring sounds.

A clinking noise filled my ears, and I whirled to find it was Clay, laden with several pounds of beads.

The throbbing in my temples had eased enough for me to notice what I missed earlier.

Lipstick prints covered his cheeks, nose, forehead, and lips. He smelled of perfume, shrimp, and whiskey.

"I can't take you anywhere." I waited for Asa to get behind the wheel. "Colby, you're up."

Before we set out all willy-nilly, we needed to establish our base and alert the other team of our arrival.

"I already programmed it in," Colby confirmed, and when I checked on her, she wore a single strand of purple beads looped four or five times around her neck. "It's about six miles from here. Maybe fifteen minutes?"

"Not in this traffic." I sank back into my seat. "Tell me about our rental."

As much as I wanted to light VacayNStay on fire, I had to admit it made travel easier. Plus, it meant we could rent off the grid, depending on the assignment, and minimize casualties. Of the innocent variety, anyway.

"It's a houseboat," she trilled. "Two bedrooms, one bath, and a rooftop deck with couches."

"We're hunting for a sea monster—" Asa met her eyes in the rearview mirror, "—on a houseboat?"

Cranking my head around, I locked gazes with Clay. "Do you want to say it, or should I?"

"We're not going to need a bigger boat." He backed up his partner in crime. "We need to be as stealthy as possible."

"A houseboat says stealth to you?" A smile curled my lips. "At least tell me there's a harpoon cannon mounted on the deck."

"The lake monster is likely a sea serpent." Colby vibrated with excitement. "Maybe a bakunawa."

"How can it be a sea serpent," Asa asked, "if it's in a lake?"

Sailing onto his shoulder, she said, in a very *I'm glad you asked* voice, "Lake Pontchartrain is an estuary."

"Estuary." He laughed softly at her wings tickling his ear. "Those have direct access to the sea, right?"

"They're also fed by rivers, so they're brackish. They can support freshwater *and* saltwater life."

"The bridge we crossed was the Lake Pontchartrain Causeway," Clay mused. "What's its deal?"

"It's the longest continuous bridge over a body of water in the *world*." She beamed. "Cool, huh?"

"Very." He looped another strand of beads around her neck, this one gold, and she tipped off balance under its weight. "There's a power line too, right?"

The gleam in his eyes warned me what giant leap of logic came next, and I cut him off quick.

"We're not going to reenact that scene from *Jaws 2* where the shark bites through the cable and gets fried," I warned him. "We really would need a bigger boat for that."

"Or a helicopter." Colby clutched Asa's silver hoop earring to keep from falling backward. "The towers are on caissons, so, no. The sea monster won't conveniently bite through the cable and solve our problems."

"Word is the Loch Ness monster was a plesiosaur." Clay rubbed his throat. "Neck like that, he might make it."

"No one's neck is that long." Colby flitted onto his head and patted his wig, a sedate black undercut. "And plesiosaurs are extinct."

"You believe in bakunawa but not in dinosaurs?"

"I believe they existed, but I don't think any are left."

"How do you know? Something like eighty percent of the world's oceans are unexplored."

"The deepest point in the lake is Seabrook Hole, and that's only ninety feet. The rest is like sixty-five."

"Maybe it's a baby."

The two of them dissolved into a debate on the likelihood oceanic dinosaurs were still alive, freeing me up to dig some white willow bark from my kit to chew in lieu of aspirin. Sometimes the old remedies were the best ones.

"Hearts." Asa cut his eyes toward me. "That's why you're jittery."

"Withdrawal?" I caught his look of concern. "Oh." I shook my head to clear it. "Hearing so many."

"I didn't consider how difficult it must have been after you opened your senses at the townhouse."

The nearest comparison was placing a bloody steak in front of a lion then snatching it back.

"I'll be fine in a bit." I drummed my fingers on the door. "All that dancing, singing, playing instruments. It jogs the pulse. Gets their hearts pumping. It's hard for me to ignore it the way I can when a crowd is all human."

"Do you see that?" Clay pointed his arm at the windshield. "Smoke on the water."

The GPS prompted Asa to turn in to a marina, right as people ran screaming past us on the main road.

"What in the world?" I leaned forward, peering out at the water. "Oh crap."

"That's us, isn't it?" Asa craned his neck, but the smoke was thick and so was the crowd. "Our boat?"

At the end of a pier sat a cute little baby-pink houseboat that had been waiting for us to board it for our adventure when someone blew it to bits. Debris scattered the picnic area, setting small fires on the dry tables, and people limped past with shrapnel wounds staining their shirts and pants crimson.

"That's us," Colby confirmed. "Or it *was* us."

"Fireworks displays are nicer at night." Clay tried to bluff away his concern. "Twilight just doesn't hit the same."

Asa parked on the shoulder of the road, and we waded against the flow of panicked tourists to reach our berth, where our rental belched smoke and spat flames.

On my phone, I snapped several photos then texted them to the director, per his orders.

The entire purpose of him outing me was to throw as many obstacles in my face as humanly possible then watch to see if I sank or swam. Had I been on the boat when it exploded, and survived it, I would have done both. Sank then swam. I would point that out to him, but he didn't appreciate my sense of humor.

"The other team is probably up to their necks already, but we need to find out what caused this."

"I'll call the cleaners," Asa offered, and I pretended not to notice he had them on speed dial now.

"Don't you mean *who*?" Clay sidled up to me as Asa walked toward a line of RVs to get away from the noise. "Who knew we were coming? How did they find our rental? Why did they have to go and explode the pralines fixings I had dropped off at the back door?"

"I booked the reservation as usual," Colby said slowly. "Maybe they hacked the VacayNStay app?"

For added layers of safety, she booked us under aliases of our aliases these days. Anyone looking for Rue Hollis, Asa Montenegro, or Clayton Kerr wouldn't find them, but paper identities weren't bulletproof.

"That still required them to expect *us*." Clay pursed his lips. "Our company credit cards are untraceable."

Follow the money led to a dead end with those purchases. But, again, a rectangular piece of plastic was a poor shield when someone had you in their sights.

"Unless you're a member of the company," I grumbled. "The Kellies could do it."

Which meant any hacker with above average skills and the right access could too.

"We're not the only people tracking Saint," Colby ventured. "One of them could have done this."

The director.

Luca.

Me.

Lots of folks had a vested interest in keeping tabs on him.

"Well, this case started out with a bang," Clay said cheerfully. "Or maybe it was more of a boom?"

"At least it wasn't a gulp." I turned my back on the fire, my skin hot and tight. "Who in their right mind would pick Mardi Gras to lure a maneater into a lake twenty minutes away from the French Quarter?"

"No one good." He shielded his eyes against the glare. "Otherwise, the director wouldn't have sent you."

He knows your dad is here, a little voice whispered in my head. *He wants to test your loyalties.*

Shut up, I told it with a slap of thought. *People will think I'm crazy if I start talking to myself.*

Too late, it hit back. *RIP your reputation.*

If this was having a conscience, I wanted a refund. I had enough self-doubt without myself doubting me.

"I hate it when you're right." I tuned out those pesky doubts. "Thank the goddess it doesn't happen often."

"Rude." He glowered at me. "I thought we were friends."

"We are friends." I smiled toothily. "Before, I was giving you the bestie discount on my sarcasm rate."

"You're a cruel woman, Rue." He patted his pocket, where his new BFF resided. "We need new digs."

"Perhaps I can help with that."

A boy no more than five or six stood with his chubby hands shoved into the pockets of his filthy overalls. He wore no shirt or shoes, and his gray-blond hair was a wild tangle around his head. He grinned at me, his teeth black and broken, his tongue a vibrant blue through the gaps.

"Oh?" I touched my wand for comfort through the fabric of my pants. "And you are?"

"Frederick Allan Murphy."

The name rang a distant bell, but I didn't have to dig for the connection. Not with Clay and his steel-trap of a mind beside me. His encyclopedic knowledge made me think I ought to invest in a notebook or app or something to train me to match faces to names. I had a knack for spells, but I never applied the talent to people. My antisocial tendencies hadn't hurt me before, but as the deputy director, ignorance might get me killed one of these days.

"You're still kicking around?" Clay clapped the child on the back. "What are you doing here?"

"Fishing." He fingered a necklace of carved bone hooks. "What else?"

"What else indeed," Clay murmured, his unease palpable as he studied Frederick's jewelry.

I elected not to ask if they were human, but I wasn't fooling myself that they weren't.

"I'm also the AIC." He squinted at the horizon. "I was on my way to greet you but that happened first."

This was a first for me, meeting an agent in charge who could pass for a kindergartener, but appearance didn't equate age in this line of work.

"How did you know we arrived?" I wasn't shy with my suspicion. "I hadn't notified anyone."

"I'm two berths down." He indicated another houseboat, this one rotting and hanging low in the water. I worried his slight weight might be enough to sink it. "I was fishing, as I said, when I saw the SUV turn in." His blueish lips curved at me. "Once I spotted Clay, I knew you for Bureau."

"Where are my manners?" Clay slung an arm around my shoulders. "Freddie, this is Rue Hollis."

"Our new deputy director." He picked his teeth with a dirty fingernail then spat out a fish scale. "Your grandfather must be so proud, you following in his footsteps and the like."

"He's so happy, he could die."

"And should he die," Freddie said, eyes sparkling, "you would be so happy."

Asa, who had done his disappearing trick, spoke in a fluid language to the boy, who broke into laughter.

"You're one of us, eh?" He awarded Asa his full attention. "But not quite."

"Your team beat mine here." I killed that line of inquiry. "What have you learned so far?"

"The beast is kept to a feeding schedule." He spat a red globule on the dirt. "That much I know."

"The report claims no one has seen it." Asa took the question out of my mouth. "Has that changed?"

"I spend nights and most days on the water." He sucked on his teeth. "I've a glimpse here or there."

"You're a good man," Clay said dryly. "Patrolling the lake at all hours with your bucket of worms."

"I'm no man at all, thank you very much." He canted his head as a low siren warbled through the air. "The police are on the way. Best not linger. Come on then."

"Forgive me for being rude..." I planted my feet, not liking my options. "Where did you have in mind?"

"My home. Where else?" Freddie gestured to the dilapidated boat. "You can stay with me until you find a place of your own. I have all the best wards and concealment charms. Only those I want to can see me coming." He swept his arm out to usher us onboard. "Any friend of Kerr's is a friend of mine."

"Turn your back on him," Clay warned us, "and he'll drown you."

"You're still holding that against me?" Freddie pouted. "It was only the one time, and I was curious."

"I could have told you golems don't float."

"You should have spoken up sooner."

"You didn't ask."

More sirens wailed in a creeping procession, and I nudged Clay in his side. "You still hungry?"

"Only always."

"Let's eat." I wanted to avoid the human police. "We can decide where to stay over dinner."

"I approve of this plan." He stared down at Frederick. "You're welcome to join us."

"A meal as compensation for your generous offer," Asa said, dipping his chin, "which we must decline."

"I prefer to hunt for my food." He fiddled with his necklace. "A charred carcass dumped on a plate isn't half as tempting as raw meat between my teeth."

Toddling off to his boat, he climbed aboard, plunked down in a peeling metal lawn chair, and began baiting a hook.

"One more thing," I called. "Where's the rest of your team?"

"At the In and Out, last I heard."

"That's a burger joint, right?"

"That would be In-N-Out." Clay turned me on my heel and led me away. "In and Out is a nickname for a local brothel catering to para kinks."

"Madame Lalaine's Peculiarities," Asa told me. "That's its formal name."

Whipping my head toward him, I demanded, "How do you know that?"

His gaze bored a hole through the back of Clay's head, but he kept mum on the topic.

"I keep forgetting you two were bachelors on the town together."

"Ace was a wet blanket, if it makes you feel any better. Downright musty. Moldy even." Clay shook his head. "He wouldn't look at the girls, let alone touch them. I was tempted to have him add a clerical collar to his wardrobe to explain my chaste friend to Madame, but there's nothing more appealing in a room full of ladies of a certain profession than the opportunity to corrupt an innocent."

"Which was why Clay wore one the next time he visited, and I opted to stay at the hotel."

The urge to locate the brothel and set it ablaze somewhat abated. "That sounds about right."

Goddess bless, I had to get over this. Arson was not the answer.

Except when it is, my inner voice encouraged. *Fire sends a strong message.*

Yeah, I agreed. *That I'm an insecure, rage-fueled pyromaniac.*

Better a rage-fueled pyromaniac than a doormat.

For the sake of my mental health, I chose not to believe myself, which, yeah. Probably more mental than healthy.

People talked about letting their conscience be their guide, but I hadn't known they meant it literally. Or why mine doled out some of the absolute worst advice I had ever heard—thought?—without fail.

"That sea monster is bad news if Freddie is here," Clay said, once we were back in the SUV. "He's Jenny Greenteeth's son. Rumor has it his father was a grindylow. I say *was*, because rumor also has it that Jenny fed him to baby Freddie. Chopped him up, ground him down, mushed him into baby mash."

"I can see how he ended up in Black Hat." I checked my phone and found a short update on Camber and Arden. "Aedan says the girls are settling in. They're going to eat and then catch a parade."

"Has he seen Nolan?" Asa waited until the firetruck, police car, and ambulance sped past us into the lot before pulling back onto the main road. "His scent wasn't in the house."

"You didn't mention that." I twisted in my seat. "Do you think it's because he's been out hunting?"

"Most likely." Asa kept his eyes on the road and all the worried boaters standing in the middle of it. "He camped out on your property for days without any creature comforts. The gear was scuffed. Faded. He'd used it often. He built his career on rare footage taken from remote locations. Lake Pontchartrain is tame in comparison. It's also forty miles long and twenty-four miles wide. He could be anywhere."

"Good point." I glanced back at Colby. "Any luck with the surveillance footage from the morgues?"

"Each location suffered a security blackout for exactly one hour on the night they were hit."

"That means they were hacked," Clay explained to me slowly. "Hacked is when—"

"I know what hacked means." I turned around and slid down in my seat. "I'm not that out of the loop."

Neither he nor Colby said anything for a beat, and again, I lamented encouraging their unholy alliance.

"I found a rental," Colby announced, escaping from Clay's pocket, "but you're not going to like it."

"Pickings are slim." Quick to defend her, he patted her head. "I'm shocked you found anything."

"What's the problem?" I toyed with my seatbelt. "Does it cost a billion dollars a night?"

"It's a townhouse." Her wings twitched. "Across the street from where Camber and Arden are staying."

"You're right." A sense of foreboding clanged through me like witch bells. "I don't like it."

We just got into town, and already the threads of my lives were tangling. Those kinds of knots required a deft hand, and I didn't believe for a hot second it was a coincidence.

What, exactly, had the director gotten me into here?

"That's the only listing. On the whole app." She climbed onto the seat and opened her laptop to the page she had been viewing on her phone. "I can't refresh the VacayNStay homepage, either." Her antennae bristled with annoyance. "Every time I try, I get shunted back to the same page."

Clueless, I broke down and asked, "What does that mean?"

To me, a failed refresh equaled a poor internet connection. To her, it obviously portended much more.

"I've been hacked." A gleam sparkled in her eyes that I dared label as eagerness. "Hello, there." She kept pounding the keys. "I see you." Her wings tucked in close. "You won't get away from me so easily." Indignation spiked through her, and she gawked at me, clearly in shock. "The Kellies found my back door."

The secret entrance she carved into the Black Hat database to conceal her more dangerous searches.

"Why would the Kellies target the VacayNStay app?"

Even if they knew the girls were here, what purpose would it serve to book us across from them?

"I doubt they did," she muttered, her focus narrowing on her screen. "They infected my computer."

"It spread from your computer to the VacayNStay app?"

"No." She popped up her head. "No, you're right." Her frantic typing resumed. "So, how...?"

Further conversation got me shooshed, but I was willing to let it slide, given the gravity of the situation.

Plus, I had no idea what she was talking about, so it was for the best that I let her work in peace.

"How serious is this?" I turned to Clay, who knew better than to bug her. "Can she handle it alone?"

"The worst that will happen is an inquiry as to who owns the laptop. As far as they need to know, that would be you. And you being you, you might get spanked for using an unregistered device to break in when you're cleared to use the front door." He wavered a hand in the air. "You're the deputy director now, so maybe not even that."

"If they reach out to her, let me know, and I'll handle it."

"Hey." Clay poked Colby in the shoulder until she broke her trance. "Do you have backups?"

"Backups of my backups." She curled protectively over her laptop. "What are you thinking?"

Rather than answer, he craned his neck, vying for Asa's attention. "Can you find a spot and pull over?"

"All right." Asa drove until he found a turnoff that allowed for privacy. "Will this work?"

"Yeah." Clay slammed her laptop shut. "Sorry, Shorty." He passed it to me. "I need you to check this."

A snort escaped Colby at the idea of me unhacking her computer, or whatever you called it, but there was only one reason why Clay would have handed it to me.

"Watch it, smarty fuzz butt." I took it outside and set it on the ground then dug in my pack for a pinch of salt, an ounce of dried lemongrass, and a few sage leaves. I mixed them in my palm then laid a circle around the computer. "Here goes nothing."

Tapping my wand to the edge of the circle, I ignited a spell to cleanse it of any curses or hexes.

Sure enough, faint orange smoke wafted from the laptop, curling into the shape of a ferret that bared its teeth in a silent hiss before evaporating into nothing.

"What was that?" Colby shot from Clay's window and swooped over my head. "It was *in* my computer?"

"A hex," I confirmed. "I've never known the Kellies to use magitech. It's a point of pride for them."

They definitely didn't sign their work, which was what the ferret symbolized—a signature.

"Well, Shorty?" Clay stuck out his hand. "Any guesses how long ago your laptop was compromised?"

"I run complete systems scans twice a day. More than that if I'm working a case." She sailed onto his outstretched palm. "That thing couldn't have been with me long. Maybe two hours?"

A groan tore out of me as I did the math. "About the time you hacked the townhouse security system?"

"Yeah," she said slowly, her cheeks pinkening. "That sounds about right."

With our rental going kaboom, we hadn't had time to notice the mess we had stepped in.

Asa, twisting to see out Clay's door, puzzled over it. "We didn't detect any magic in the house."

"Magi-tech is a new field with few practitioners. I don't understand mundane technology well enough to guess at its magically augmented counterpart." I would have to change that soon or be left behind in the Stone Age. "The magi-virus—yes, I just coined that term—could have lain dormant until Colby poked the security system. Then it could have woken up, assessed the danger, and took action to fulfill its purpose."

"Its purpose being to destroy any information after the hacker collected it by corrupting the system."

Fumbling with the lingo, I asked, "And if Colby had cured the virus?"

"Depends," Clay said, "on how badly the owners want what goes on in that house to stay in that house."

"You think there's a secondary strain?" Colby scrunched up her face. "A tracker?"

"Odds are good we don't have to worry about it." He eyed the laptop. "The hacker smoked you."

Most people don't associate moths with boiling, seething rage, but they hadn't seen Colby's tiny face after she got out hacked on her home turf.

"As far as I'm concerned—" Clay noticed too late he was holding a puffed-up ball of indignant moth girl with revenge on her mind, "—this proves Nolan is savvy to the supernatural."

The facts did lend themselves to that conclusion, but the dearth of evidence in his suite bothered me.

"We need more information." We also needed to make progress on our actual case and figure out if the demise of our houseboat was related to that...or this. "The home security system is a no-go. We can't risk infection again. We need another plan."

"I have to patch up the hole the Kellies made in my defenses," Colby said. "They didn't have time to dig into my files, they're all encrypted anyway, but I can't use the laptop until I've cleaned it top to bottom."

An acrid scent filled my nose as the circle dissipated, and I got a bad feeling about the laptop's longevity.

"I'm no technomancer," I murmured, "but laptops aren't supposed to smoke like that, right?"

"Oh no." Colby darted for the computer. "You just bought that for me." I plucked her out of the air. "Maybe I can—"

Orange flames erupted around the laptop, engulfing it, rendering it to char that scattered on the wind.

Wings drooping down my arms, antennae trembling, Colby buried her face against my shirt.

"Don't cry, Shorty." Clay got out his phone and started scrolling. "We'll get you a new one."

"Hey, being deputy director ought to have some perks." I patted her back. "I'm willing to expense your laptop, since it died as a result of a direct order."

Anyone who knew me would assume I had flambéed it in a fit of technophobic temper, which worked fine for me. Her legit legwork, signed in under my name, did its job of making me look active online during investigations. That would more than cover my butt when I filed the paperwork for whatever new laptop she chose.

"Really?" She wiped her face. "You're not mad?"

"Sweetie, you only did what I asked you to do." I kissed her soggy cheek. "Now, go tell Uncle Clay what you want."

He understood the lingo, and he already had the nearest big box store pulled up on his phone.

"What's my price limit?"

Leaning down, I whispered in her ear. "You don't have one."

A piercing squeal left her as she blasted out of my arms, shot back into the SUV, and lit on Clay's shoulder. She couldn't hold still. She was too excited. Her wings were fluttering a mile a minute.

Once I kicked the remains of the circle and the ash, mixing it with dirt and leaves, I got back in the SUV.

"Food," Clay reminded me. "I was promised food."

"Food it is." I pulled out my phone to scroll menus. "What is everyone in the mood for?"

"As long as they have bread pudding and bourbon sauce," Clay proclaimed, "I'm good."

"Asa?"

Now that we had left the taste-testing portion of fascination behind us, he had redeveloped his own palate, though I missed our weirdo food fetish.

"Crawfish étouffée or corn maque choux." The flavor of the words made me wonder if he spoke French, and the question must have been plain on my face. "Mon amoureuse."

"I speak French too." Clay popped the back of Asa's head. "Not in front of the kid."

Curious what Asa called me, I turned to my old pal Google Translate.

My lover.

"Aww." I leaned my head against Asa's shoulder. "Back at you."

"Mon rayon de soleil," he murmured, smiling against my hair. "Je t'aime chaque jour davantage."

"You're his sunshine," Clay deadpanned, "and he loves you more each day."

"That's one way to kill the mood." I heaved a sigh. "If only slaying your appetite was so easy."

"Never gonna happen." Clay's groan was almost a growl. "I'm starving."

Taking his hand off the wheel, Asa squeezed my knee. "Me too."

For a second, I thought he got away with it, but then Clay thumped us both soundly on the ear.

"Tout est juste dans l'amour et la guerre." Clay cackled with glee. "All is fair in love and war."

And in the spirit of that sentiment, I chose the one place I could find *without* bread pudding.

6

"We got lucky with the houseboat," Colby said from her spot on the bench beside Clay, tucked safely under the table. "There's nothing available for a couple hours outside the city."

I toyed with a shrimp in my bowl of cioppino, made with fresh Gulf seafood and tomato brodo.

Clay snubbed me for ordering an Italian dish at a Cajun restaurant, but you didn't have to look far to see the influence of Italians on New Orleans cuisine. Take the muffuletta, for instance. The iconic sandwich was first served in Central Grocery in the French Quarter by Sicilian immigrant, Salvatore Lupo, in 1906.

I pointed that out to him, but he was in a mood. Probably over the lack of bread pudding.

Oops.

The guys made up for my choice with their picks. Clay went for fried alligator with chili aioli, an oyster and bacon sandwich, and a crawfish pie. Asa got his crawfish étouffée fix and a side of corn maque choux.

Busy punishing Clay, I hadn't noticed that not only was there no bread pudding on the menu, there was no dessert. Period.

I had cut off my nose to spite my face, and my face wasn't happy. Specifically, my mouth.

"How does Black Hat not own any real estate down here?" I clinked my spoon against the chipped edge of the bowl. "This town is a hotbed of paranormal activity."

"There's a boarding house," Clay informed me, casual as you please. "Folks sign up a year in advance for a chance to Mardi Gras in style."

"What I'm hearing is, we might end up living out of the SUV until we solve this case."

"We could always take Freddie up on his offer of hospitality."

"I might have found us something." Colby texted me a link. "What do you think?"

"An RV?" I skimmed the listing. "Wait." I gawked at the attached photo. "That's a party bus."

"You can rent this model overnight," she told me. "There are six bunks in the back."

Party all night, sleep it off the next day was one of their catchy slogans.

They tacked on a hefty fee for your very own designated driver, but we didn't plan on moving the RV. Its home away from home for the next however many days would be the marina. If it had available space. Which it probably would, in light of the explosion of our prior accommodations.

"That could be fun." Clay's eyes brightened. "Does it have a stripper pole?"

Beside me, Asa choked on his next spoonful and had to spit into his napkin.

"What's a stripper pole?" Colby sounded intrigued by the idea. "Why do you want one?"

"It's a new workout everyone's trying," I fudged, thinking back on what Meg's descendant—Derry Mayhew—told us about his wife's aerobics class. "You hang off a metal pole to build muscle. Sometimes it's set to music, like a dance routine."

The clothing-optional rule that often went hand in hand where poles were concerned, I glossed over.

"Oh." She considered this before asking him, "Don't you have enough muscle?"

"You can never have enough wigs," he told her solemnly, "or muscles."

"Is there a bathroom?" I could tell this was a losing battle. "A kitchen?"

"There's a bathroom," she confirmed. "There's also a mini fridge and microwave."

"We're in *New Orleans*," Clay emphasized. "All the food we need is right here."

"Book it." I caved like they knew I would. "It's not like we have any other options."

"There are two slots left at the marina for RVs," Colby informed us. "One is waterfront, and one is presidential, whatever that means."

"Waterfront would be best." I drummed my fingers. "We'll need a boat."

"That ought to be easy enough." Clay's outlook brightened. "We can requisition one from the Bureau."

"Are you sure?" Asa pushed his bowl back, signaling he was finished. "How many do they have?"

"If it's a Bureau resource, I can get it." I cringed at the authority in my voice. "Who's in charge of the field office?"

"I can handle the paperwork," Colby volunteered. "As long as you let me borrow your laptop."

I had the thought, as I scraped my work onto her plate, that I ought to pay her a salary. Or get her a refillable gift card for Mystic Realms that allowed me to add money where all hers went anyway.

"Thanks." I pushed my bowl away too. "How long will it take the RV to get here?"

RV sounded much better than *party bus.*

"The site says they'll deliver it to the marina for a fee."

"Works for me." I waved my hand, then realized she couldn't see it from her position. "Do it."

"We're set," she announced a couple minutes later. "It will be delivered within the hour."

"That gives us time for dessert." Asa, who had been quiet during our meal, smiled. "Ice cream, anyone?"

"I knew I loved you for a reason." I smooched him, just because I could. "Where do you have in mind?"

◈

An hour later, we got a text that our RV had arrived, and the driver was waiting on us to sign for it.

Progress was slow, due to the fact Clay demanded we split something called a Tchoupitoulas from a creamery a few doors down.

Eight scoops of ice cream, eight you-pick toppings, wafers, whipped cream, and a cherry on top.

Pretty sure if I cried, sprinkles would rain down my cheeks.

Asa didn't look much better off. Most of the brownie bites had been on his half.

Clay, of course, was fine. His cast-iron stomach remained hale and hearty. He was even licking a to-go cone.

The marina was quiet in the wake of the earlier panic. I noticed Freddie and his boat were missing, but we had a more immediate concern. Namely, the eyesore idling in the driveway. The party bus had been an upscale RV at one point in its life. The center had been gutted of anything useful, that much I could see through the tall windows lining both sides. So much for privacy.

A young woman with a spring in her step caught me gawking and grinned. "You Ms. Hollis?"

Her skin was pale and smooth, her cheeks high and rosy. Strawberry-blonde hair teased her shoulders, which were bare above her strapless top. Cut-off shorts revealed the freckled legs of a runner. Her eyes, though. They snared and held my attention. They were gray-green and empty. They clashed with the girl-next-door vibe she was striving for. So did her bright-red lips, but I was in no position to judge another woman's makeup choices when I never remembered to wear any.

"Give me a minute." I took in the wrap covering the RV, a billboard of half-naked women. "I'm still deciding."

"You're not our usual for sure." She swept her gaze over me. "Why'd you need a party bus?"

"Last-minute trip," I explained. "This was the best option we could find."

"Yeah." A grimace twisted her face. "This time of year is nuts." Her smile bounced back. "Leave your name with a few hotels." Her gaze remained a flat contrast to her warm tone. "Maybe you'll get lucky and they'll have a cancellation."

The line of people who had already cast themselves upon the mercy of kind concierges ahead of us must stretch a mile long.

"Thank you." Asa drew on the manners I had forgotten as the hairs on my nape stood on end. "We'll try that."

"Where do you want me to park her?" She began backing away. "I'll show you guys how to hook up real quick, but then I have to go. I'm attending a midnight ball, and makeup takes hours."

Always willing to lend a hand to a pretty face, Clay stepped up with a grin, not bothered by her one bit.

"It's right over there." He pointed to a waterfront slot. "Can you give me a lift?"

"Sure thing, sugar." She winked at him. "You don't mind getting your hands dirty?"

"Not at all." He grinned back. "Feel free to dirty me up however you see fit."

Once she led him away, I filled my lungs but scented nothing out of the ordinary. "Good grief."

"He does have a type," Asa mused, leaning against the SUV beside me to watch the show.

"Yeah." I shook off my unease. "Female with a pulse."

Soft laughter shook his frame. "This is shaping up to be an interesting case."

"We've been here for hours, and we have nothing to show for it except a party bus, a pile of laptop ashes, and a smoking barge that used to be our cute little houseboat."

"There does seem to be a theme." Asa watched the woman park the RV without breaking a sweat. "Too bad the bus wasn't parked here rather than the boat when the pyromaniac struck."

"You mean you're not looking forward to resting in a coffinlike bunk down the hall from stripper poles?"

"You know a spell to sanitize the interior, I take it."

"Do you think I would have agreed to it otherwise?"

Given the big draw for buses of this type were bachelorette parties, I wasn't worried about semen as much as pee, vomit, and other fun bodily fluids that came standard with the drunken *last night as a free woman* set.

"We can keep looking," he offered. "Maybe we'll get lucky and something else will open up."

"I did consider tossing an unfortunate few out of the Bureau bunkhouse, but I wouldn't sleep a wink down the hall from so many agents. Colby aside, I can't shake the paranoia that everyone is out to get me."

"Everyone is out to get you." He smiled at me. "The job is, apparently, to die for."

"I see what you did there." I drilled a finger into his side. "I killed Jai Parish, as far as anyone knows, and Jai killed Mikkelsen before him. So forth and so on."

A shrill whistle drew our attention to where Clay waved us over. The lot was so jammed, there was no parking, except within your rented slot. Not even the explosion had warned people away. That might change overnight, but for now, it meant we needed to move the SUV before it got hit or towed.

As we stepped out, the woman passed Clay her card. "I do private parties, if you're interested."

"I..." He rubbed the card between his fingers. "I'll keep that in mind."

"Do we need to call you a ride?" I was eager to get her gone and start sanitizing. "It's crazy out there."

"No need." She pointed to the road leading to the marina. "That's my ride."

A woman with black hair peeking out from under her helmet sat astride a hulking motorcycle. She was so thin a stiff breeze ought to have blown her away, but that hunk of metal anchored her just fine.

"Nan worries." The woman waved to her friend then winked at Clay. "She's available as well."

A chuckle rumbled out of Clay. "Good to know."

Once she reached the bike and climbed on, I pivoted toward Clay with my eyebrows lifted.

"Look at you, turning down a hot girl's number." I tapped my chin. "Wonder why that is?"

Under my breath, I hummed *The Bridal Chorus*.

"I have her number—it's on the card you saw her give me—and I would have to pay for her company." He tucked it in his pocket. "I'm not that desperate." He worked his jaw. "Yet."

Tempted to remind him of his patronage at the In and Out, I bit my tongue to avoid hurting him.

There were reasons he sometimes chose strangers as sexual partners, and it was none of my business.

"Give me ten minutes." I patted him on the shoulder. "Then you guys can come in."

From the aisle, I could tell the bus was divided into quarters. The cockpit—yes, there was a sticker—then an open space with leather couches snugged against the sides, complete with *two* stripper poles. A small bathroom came next, with the kitchenette opposite. Aside from the microwave, the space was crammed with shelves of hard spirits and drink fixings in every color and flavor. Lots of glasses, umbrellas, and straws. The promised fridge was tiny, its freezer mostly dedicated to ice in various shapes and sizes.

New Orleans was a city for eating, Clay was right about that, so the lack of a kitchen wasn't a total bust.

Five minutes into my cleaning spell, which left behind a rather nice pine scent, I got a call. "Hey."

"We're here," Arden announced. "Safe and sound at the townhouse. Well, not anymore. We're eating."

"Just thought you'd want to know," Camber said in the background. "Also? It's super nice."

"I'm glad on both counts." I tensed when I heard masculine voices. "Is your uncle there?"

"He texted." Arden's disappointment rang clear. "He said he might not be home until breakfast."

First an email and then a text. Nolan was nothing if not reliable in his neglect.

As much as I wanted to comment on that, I let it pass. "Then who's with you?"

Scuffling noises broke out, and Arden groaned before the line whooshed and crackled in my ear.

"Wyatt and Carter." Camber took over the story. "We went to school with them. We've known them *forever*." She toned it down a notch. "Arden had the worst crush on Wyatt, but he was captain of the football team and basically a walking cliché factory."

For Arden to let that slide, she must no longer be in earshot. "And he's not that now?"

"Oh no." She laughed. "He is." She pitched her voice low. "I'm hoping seeing them together will force Aedan to pull his head out of his ass and ask her out already. That, or it'll convince him to back off. You don't know how depressing work has gotten. It's all longing sighs and lingering glances. It's driving me nuts. They need to get together or get over it."

If only it were so simple. "Let me know if you guys need anything."

"Will do." She sucked in a breath. "I, uh, have to go. My plan might be working too well."

"Why do you say—?"

The line went dead before I could find out what happened to send her running.

Telling myself it was fine, that everything was okay, I exited the bus and caught a whiff of rot I hadn't noticed before the cleaning spell scoured my nostrils clear.

"Clay." I sniffed around him. "Where did you put that card?"

"Not this again." He folded his arms across his chest. "Let it go."

"No." I stuck out my hand. "It's not that." I flexed my fingers. "Let me see it."

With a grumble, he passed it to me, and I brought it to my nose. "There's magic on this."

"Let me see." Asa reached for it and inhaled along the side. "You're right. I didn't notice before."

"It's not spelled, or it would be stronger." I took it back. "It's transference, I think."

The driver, whose name wasn't listed, only her number, hadn't tweaked any of our noses.

"She was a witch?" Clay stared down the road. "A black witch, since we're debating stink levels."

"When will Colby's laptop be here?" I crumpled the paper in my fist. "We need her to verify the woman's credentials."

"Do you think it's a trap?" Asa eyed the vehicle, as if glad for an excuse to avoid it. "Did you sense anything?"

"No." I tightened my fingers. "I didn't pick up on this until I stepped outside."

"A coven, or whatever faction the driver is affiliated with," Asa said, "might be using the RV for easy money."

Another reason paranormals flocked to cities that liked to party was for this very reason. They preyed on tourism, in every sense of the word.

"There was this one coven," Clay said thoughtfully. "They ran a taxi service." He scrunched up his face. "They spelled high-value paras, harvested their organs while they were unconscious, then dropped them off where they had originally paid to go."

"Why would you put that idea in my head?" I jabbed a finger at him. "Do *not* tell Colby."

"A mobile organ donor service," Asa mused, eyes crinkling when he noticed my pinched expression. "You have to admit, it's clever."

Another side effect of fascination was my newfound ability to get squeamish. I don't think my stomach minded, exactly. Pretty sure it was all mental. Some instinct ordering me to recoil from the unsavory. It wasn't my favorite thing. This job was easier when nothing bothered me, but maybe it was a good thing to be bothered, to *feel*.

Or maybe the feelings were plotting against me, convincing me that embracing them was a good idea.

Emotions were as untrustworthy as Clay left alone with a dozen cookies fresh from the oven, so it was hard to tell.

"Can you shutter the windows?" Asa gripped the door. "I'd like for Blay to take a look around."

A spark of warmth filled my chest at the mention of the daemon, and I followed Asa in to figure out the controls. Sure enough, we were able to lower shades to conceal the interior, and as soon as they latched in place, Blay burst from Asa's skin with boundless energy.

"*Rue.*"

The bus swayed as he sprinted to me, sweeping me up in a bone-crushing hug.

"Hey," I wheezed as my lungs cried for oxygen, "Blay."

"Blay search for magic now." He set me down, angling his wrist so his bracelet caught the light, and I made the appropriate noises. Like I did every time he flashed his bling. "Just wanted to say hi to Rue."

"Well, hello to you too." I sat in the driver's seat to give him room to work. "Hopefully, you can stretch your legs more on this trip."

With all the hours I had been spending at the office, Blay had been on lockdown. Asa had perfected the art of blending into his surroundings. Blay? Not so much. Crimson skin and horns didn't lend themselves to camouflage. Plus, he got bored sitting in the same spot all day.

Me too, Blay. Me too.

"Swim in lake?" He poked his head in each of the bunks. "Catch fish?"

"Sure." I quickly added a caveat, "We'll have to take you out far enough no one can see you."

"People see lake monster," he grumbled. "Why not see me?"

A pang ricocheted through my chest that, like Colby, much of his life was lived in the shadows. I hated it for both of them, but I wasn't sure how I could fix it for either of them.

"Rue sad." He circled back to me. "Don't be sad, Rue." He patted my head. "Blay swim in dark."

"I wish you didn't have to hide." I settled back in my seat. "It sucks."

"Blay get tired sometimes." He rolled a massive shoulder. "Asa know best."

With that wisdom imparted, he turned and resumed his inspection of the bus, leaving me to wonder.

Was his exhaustion new? Something that always happened? Could Asa tell? And did it determine when and for how long the daemon half surfaced?

Names have power, and we had given Blay one. I worried it might shift the balance within Asa too far in Blay's direction, but I hoped it hadn't done the opposite. I couldn't see how, but I wanted to be sure I hadn't harmed either of them.

"No bad smell," he announced, cutting into my worries. "Play with Colby?"

"Sure thing." I stood then groaned. "I forgot. Her laptop is broken. She can't play Mystic Seas right now."

While she could borrow my computer, it was for work only and monitored by the Kellies. She would have to sign into her account, and she was paranoid that Black Hat feelers might latch on to us that way. Given the umbilical stretching between Mystic Realms and my wallet, I agreed it was a valid concern. One that would cause her to double or triple down on her protections as soon as her new device arrived.

"Okay." He stuck out his bottom lip. "Swim later?"

"Absolutely." I shot him two thumbs-up. "Do you want your own swim trunks?"

"Yes." He flashed his bracelet. "Blay likes having Blay things."

"I'll get you a pair." I could add them in to our grocery delivery. "Anything else?"

"Oranges," he said solemnly. "Scurvy is an ever-present threat."

That sounded like a sound bite direct from the game. Or Colby. Which wasn't much different.

"Oranges it is." I was still smiling when he gave Asa back to me. "Blay wants to go swimming."

"I know." He tapped the side of his head. "He wants to pet the sea monster."

The two of them could open a pathway that allowed them to share thoughts and experiences, but I hadn't realized they could communicate so clearly.

"That's new," I ventured, my earlier fears redoubling. "Anything to worry about?"

"No." He sank to his knees before me. "You've given him a voice, and he's using it."

"I hope I didn't make things worse." I cupped his cheeks, stroking his temples with my thumbs. "The divide, I mean."

"You've made it clearer, I think." He turned his face into my touch and kissed my palm. "There's less friction between us. He lets go more easily, and so do I, to repay him."

Because Asa didn't have to worry when or if he would return.

A fear he hadn't shared with me until now.

One that caused an arctic level chill to sweep down my spine.

Worried I would hurt Blay by asking, I had to chance it. "I'm not going to lose you one day, am I?"

"Not even if you tried." He shut his eyes, enjoying pets as much as his daemon half. "He and I aren't at war." He cracked them open. "Anymore."

Fragile hope tingled through me, but I was too jittery to focus. "Okay."

Heavy banging on the door interrupted what few moments we might have stolen alone together.

"Everything okay?" Clay cupped his hands around his eyes like binoculars then pressed them to the door. "Computer's here, and Shorty's already swimming through her loot like Scrooge McDuck."

"All clear," Asa told him, then sank into the chair beside me.

Arms bristling with bags, Clay waded into the RV and dumped tech store debris everywhere.

"Did you buy her a computer, or did you buy her a DIY supervillain lair?"

"We got a few new toys while we were at it." He didn't elaborate. "We also secured a boat."

"Good." I got to my feet. "That's the first thing that's gone right since we got here."

Colby emerged from a bag and lit on the tower of boxes. "I'm queen of the mountain."

"And you're expected to stay locked inside the castle while we're gone." Clay booped the end of her proboscis. "You've got plenty of work to occupy you while we're out on the water."

Lost in the depths of her plastic fortress, she must not have heard over the ripping and tearing.

"You two ready to go?" Clay hooked his thumb over his shoulder. "Our ride's here."

"Yeah." I ignored the prickle of unease at the base of my skull. "Let's find us a sea monster."

7

The moment I stepped foot on the grass, a boy of about ten or twelve eased into view.

Familiarity niggled my memory, but recognition failed me until he flashed a black-toothed grin.

"Freddie," I greeted him with a horrible premonition about our ride. "You've grown."

"Seven a boy, seven a man, seven a codger."

As if that explained everything when it left me with even more questions about his appearance.

Asa and Clay joined us, and Clay produced a rusted nail he handed me.

"Keep it on you." He flashed me its twin on his palm. "It'll keep you safe."

"What about Asa?" I tucked the cold iron nail into my kit then cleaned my hands to prevent transferring any residue to him. "What will protect him?"

"From the vicious glint in your eye," Freddie cackled with sly amusement, "I'd say you, girlie."

Holding his gaze, allowing every ounce of menace in me to show, I agreed, "I'm good with that."

"Figured it'd suit you." He set off with a spring in his step. "You reek of fascination. Positively stink of it."

The look I shot Clay called his sanity into question, but he dangled his nail in my face then pocketed it.

"He's the AIC, and he owns a boat. He's the obvious fit." He pitched his voice lower. "Let him get away with sitting on his thumb during a case, and he'll think you're afraid of him." He leaned even closer. "That would be a *very* bad idea, given how much time we're about to spend on the water."

The brat would drown me. That was what he meant. Either ride in his floating shanty or appear weak.

There was no room for weakness in our world, except in the belly of the strong.

The houseboat made an ominous creaking noise when Clay stepped onto the deck. I'm not proud to admit I waited to see if it would sink before trying my luck. It protested my weight and grumbled about Asa, dipping lower in the water and moaning as if the cabin were about to split in two.

"Are you sure this is safe, Freddie?" I jerked my chin toward Clay. "We carry a lot of extra weight."

The extra weight in question glared daggers at me and sucked in his already flat stomach.

"Eh." Freddie patted the side of his house. "We can always use the golem as an anchor, if we must."

"Do you want me to fix that slant for you?" Clay lifted the corner on a polycarbonate panel corrugated to resemble tin roofing. "I have plenty of *iron* nails."

The threat sank in, and Freddie bared his crumbling teeth at Clay, his eyes going black around the edges.

"I welcomed you into my home." Freddie palmed a wicked-looking fishing spear. "You would disrespect me so?"

"I heard no formal acknowledgment of guest rights." Clay spread his hands. "Are you offering?"

The trap Clay set for him snapped closed, leaving Freddie a choice of hosting us or dishonoring himself.

"No harm will come to you by my hand," he grumbled, "so long as you offer none in return."

"We appreciate your hospitality," Asa said for all of us. "You do your mother proud."

From what I recalled of the lore of Jenny Greenteeth, she lured the elderly and children to their deaths. Drowned them and ate them. Left their bones to decorate the bottom of her lake. Not someone whose pride I would want to earn, but I couldn't throw stones, not with my gnarled and twisted family tree.

"It would warm the cockles of her heart to hear you say so, I'm sure." Freddie set aside his weapon. "If she had one." His eyes turned soft. "Cold as a fish, is my mom. No better woman alive. Or dead, for that matter." His blue tongue winked through his smile. "But then, some mothers are better off dead."

Faint warning bells rang in the back of my head, fear he knew Mom's condition, but that was impossible.

More than likely, he was searching for a scab to pick. Thanks to the director, I had plenty of open wounds for him to choose from. Everyone knew my mother was dead. Everyone thought Dad was too.

They didn't know he was alive, for now, and she was back among the living. Also for now.

"It's nice that you're close with your mom," I said blandly. "Hard to find that bond these days."

"Aye," he agreed, and his face sharpened before my eyes into early adolescence. "Pity that."

Whistling a jaunty tune, he disappeared belowdecks, and I was relieved to see him go.

The steady rumble of the engine beneath my feet fueled my hope we wouldn't end up marooned in sea monster-infested waters. The boat resembled a shipwreck dredged from the bottom of the lake, but the problem with fae was they sprinkled glamour over everything the way others seasoned with salt. Even the modest wake was concealed so that it appeared we slid across the water like it was glass.

An easy fix was adding hag stones to my kit. As finicky as magic was around water, I should have thought of that before we left. Peer through the hole worn away by nature in the stone's center, and you can see through basic illusions.

Right about now, I would love to know if this vessel was sea—or lake—worthy.

Preferably before the sea monster came to investigate, and we found out the hard way.

Freddie returned with a can full of dirt and wriggling worms in hand and sank into his lawn chair.

"How is the monster being fed?" I drifted closer. "Are the bodies being dumped at the shore or—?"

"The bridge." He selected a cane fishing pole. "They're thrown off at a minute past midnight."

"The same time every night?" Asa slanted me a glance. "They're establishing a feeding schedule."

"That makes it sound like a pet." I caught myself staring at every ripple on the water, reminding myself it was content dining on the dead. As if sensing my trepidation, Freddie chortled at me. "Anything else unusual happening we ought to be made aware of?"

Say, a powerful black witch rising from the dead? And bringing his wife's spirit along for the ride?

"This is New Orleans, during Mardi Gras." He belted out a wild laugh. "Usual has no place here."

"I walked into that one," I allowed. "Anything we should be concerned about?"

"Amaury Garnier has misplaced his eldest daughter. Covens are combing the streets for her, but there has been no news for days. He claims she's a Lazarus, a fool thing to do, announcing it like that while she is out of his hands. No one knows who her mother is, but all the same. That bloodline ran dry ages ago." He twirled a hook between his fingers, ready to bait another line. "Necromancers eradicated them."

"Lazarus." I swallowed a ball of dread. "As in the resurrection myth?"

"The very same."

"Four days dead," Asa murmured. "Then Lazarus rose."

Mom had been dead a lot longer than four days. Or four weeks. Or four months. Or four years.

But hope had fishhooks that pierced your skin and tore your flesh if you tried to rip it out.

"It's time." Clay checked his smartwatch. "Where will the body drop take place?"

"Just ahead," Freddie assured us. "We've a prime view for the show."

I marked it on my phone with a pin in a navigation app then took photos and filmed the dark underbelly of the causeway. I didn't expect to find anything, and I wasn't disappointed. There was nothing there.

"We need to search the bridge." I gripped the frayed rope railing. "Maybe there's a marker up there."

"Have you ever had catfish?" Freddie indicated a stand with more poles. "The bones give it a nice crunch."

I was beginning to see why we had so little information to go on, if the AIC was spending his days with a bait can. Not the worst idea, *if* he was fishing for the monster and not a snack. Which seemed doubtful.

How Black Hat got anything done was often a mystery to me. Then it occurred to me, as deputy director, it was my job to make them do theirs. But how, aside from threats and violence, could I motivate them?

Not my circus, I reminded myself. *Not my monkeys.*

"How do we get up there?" I ignored his wormy offer. "What's the fastest way?"

"It's the longest continuous bridge over a body of water." Asa repeated what Colby told us earlier. "We don't have time to walk it before the body drop, and we can't afford to miss that."

"I have an idea." A smile blossomed across my face. "Blay did say he wanted to go for a swim."

To find what we needed, we didn't have to search the entire causeway. Not tonight. Just this one spot.

"Now?" Asa checked with our resident expert. "Is it safe for us to go in the water?"

"As long as you don't smell like a ripe corpse," Freddie decided, "you two ought to be fine."

"That's good enough for me." I was antsy to make progress on any front, and I really hoped that wasn't misplaced pride in my new title propelling me onward, into the breach. "Asa, do you mind?"

Flame erupted around Asa as the daemon burst from his skin with a grin from ear to ear.

"Swim?" His sudden appearance gave Freddie a fright. "You and me?"

"Can you help me climb the pilings to reach the top of the bridge?"

"Yes." He broke into a huge smile. "Blay carry."

He picked me up, slung me onto his back, and jumped off the boat before I could protest.

As the water closed over my head, I heard Clay laughing at my expense.

"This fun." Blay swam with powerful strokes. "Swim tomorrow too?"

"Maybe," I coughed out. "We'll see how it goes."

When we reached the giant cement support, Blay didn't hesitate. He found his footing and climbed as if he were half mountain goat rather than half fae, while I clung to his neck and hoped I didn't go splat.

"Rue safe." He must have felt my tension. "Climb easy."

"I trust you, big guy." I loosened my death grip. "This bridge just looks a lot higher from under here."

Traffic ran steady, lights flashing as vehicles passed, meaning we couldn't count on darkness to hide us.

"I'm going to make us invisible, okay?" I shut my eyes to focus. "That way you can come with me."

The magic was slower to encase us, with us both drenched. Not to mention, the spell recognized the same divide between Asa and Blay as I did. Probably because I was the one doing the casting.

The images I used to conceal Asa didn't work for Blay. I had to picture him, his unique appearance, his individual voice, how he laughed when he played with Colby, his new borderline hypochondriacal fear of scurvy, and from there, I finally drew a veil of concealment over us.

"This fun." Laughter pumped through him as he hauled us over the railing. "Do again?"

Pretty sure I left my stomach back on the boat, so that would be a hard no from me. "Maybe?"

Thankfully, he hadn't yet learned from Colby that *maybe* generally meant *no*.

When he slid me down his back onto my feet, every vibration through the bridge ran up my wobbly legs, and I swayed against the railing for support.

"Rue okay?" Blay stroked my head, his sharp nails tangling in my soaked hair. "Sit down?"

"I'm good." I dredged up a smile for him. "I just need to get my land legs back."

"Smell death." He filled his lungs. "And fish. Dead fish."

"*Death* and dead fish?"

"And jambalaya." Head turning toward the city, he filled his lungs again. "With andouille."

"I'll bring some back to the RV for you tomorrow, okay?"

If travel had taught me one thing, it was cities that never sleep sure put their restaurants to bed early.

"Deal."

While he hunted down a new scent, I brought out my wand and began dousing for signs of magic that might have been used. I gave it a few minutes, but I turned up nothing. That didn't mean there was none involved, or that the persons responsible weren't magical, only that they hadn't used any while disposing of the bodies, which meant they hadn't been using the topside of the bridge for feedings.

Without glamour, which I should have been able to pick up traces of, how were they rolling up and dumping bodies nightly without getting caught? Mardi Gras might forgive a multitude of sins, but it wouldn't explain away a feeding frenzy.

"Find anything?" I asked Blay as he searched the opposite direction. "I'm coming up empty."

"No." He wandered past. "Check here too."

"Okay." I peered over the edge and saw Clay wave up at me from the boat. "Sounds like a plan."

A scuffling noise brought my attention swinging back to Blay as he climbed over the side of the bridge.

"Hey." I rushed over and clutched his hands. "What are you doing?"

"Be right back," he assured me. "Need look at bottom."

"Bottom of the causeway?" I tried for clarity. "Do you mean the spans, or the pilings?"

"Spans," he confirmed then ducked out of sight. "BRB, Rue."

Left without much choice, I stood there, waiting for his results.

He didn't leave me for long.

"Found trail," he called up. "Rue want to see?"

No, Rue did not want to see, but Rue had a job to do. "Show me."

"I come get." He swung over the railing like a kindergartner on a jungle gym. "*Blay* come get."

Unable to fight my smile, I couldn't hold his fondness for using the third person against him. He'd had nothing to call himself until now, and he was making up for lost time.

Grunting as he flung me across his shoulders, I clasped my arms around his neck. "I'm starting to feel like a superhero cape."

"Like superheroes." He climbed down, more gently this time. "Make good movies. Lots of explosions."

As we descended into deeper shadow, I developed a tingle across my skin that warned of old magic.

"Someone's been down here." I caught a whiff of moss, earthy decay, and mildew. "Often."

Between the grooves in the supports, a path had been worn, but I sensed nothing. That could be blamed on the water's erosive effect on magic, or on the nature of the person who made the nightly trek.

"The end." Blay paused in the middle of the arch, the highest point of the causeway. "No more trail."

"They're coming here to feed, where it's safest, then leaving." As I stared down at our ride, my stomach swooped with vertigo. "Back to the boat, please."

With absolutely no warning whatsoever, Blay released the support and plummeted toward the water.

Former black witch or not, I wasn't ashamed of the scream that ripped out of my throat, the shriek so startling to Blay that Asa wrestled away control seconds before impact. The breath whooshed out of me as I hit chest first, and I swallowed half the lake. Gripping my wrist, Asa swam us to the surface while I coughed up a lung.

"What happened?" Asa whipped his head, searching for danger. "Did you see the sea monster?"

The sudden urge to reach into Asa and rip out the daemon so I could smack him stung in my palms.

"He let go," I growled and spluttered, my nose and ears plugged with water. "I'm going to kill him."

"Gods," he breathed then had the gall to laugh. "I have butterflies in my stomach."

"I have a gallon of water in mine." I spit to clear my mouth. "What was he thinking?"

"He would have protected you, but I panicked." Asa paddled us toward the boat. "I couldn't tell what had happened. All I could smell was your fear. He wasn't reacting to it, so I stole the chance from him."

Grateful for the hand Clay offered, I almost thanked him before I noticed he was filming the whole thing.

"Did I just get played?" I grew my nails sharp enough to poke him. "If so, justice will be swift and brutal."

"You can't blame this on me." He shook me off him then tucked his phone down the front of his pants to protect it. Way down. Not in, say, a sanitary pocket. "I'm innocent."

So innocent, he had probably already texted it to Colby…and Aedan. "Mmm-hmm."

"Best get out of the water." Freddie reeled in his catch. "A drop from that height might summon the beast early."

Asa gripped the frayed railing and swung me onto the deck before climbing up himself. We sat, shoulder to shoulder, our legs folded under us, and waited to see if we might get lucky and spot the creature.

Once we settled in, Freddie put the boat in gear and backed a safe distance from the causeway.

From here, we fell into the eight-mile stretch on the twenty-four-mile causeway where land wasn't visible in any direction. There was only us, the boat, and the bridge.

An hour passed, and nothing of interest happened, leaving us on the cusp of feeding time.

"Should we be this close?" I fixed my eyes on the horizon. "How big is the creature?"

"We're safe enough," Freddie assured me. "The beast won't breach the water."

Taking him at his word, we stood watch, yanked to attention

when a white-wrapped bundle that reminded me of steak in butcher's paper appeared out of nowhere, striking the water with a slap.

Dinner had been served, and we hadn't seen a thing.

"They're keeping this low-key." I peered up at the spans, stumped over what just happened. "Surprising, when I can't imagine any use for a sea monster that doesn't involve terrifying humans or eating them."

"Maybe someone wants him for a pet."

"Home aquariums don't come in this size." I nipped that thought in the bud. "Don't get any ideas."

With the temptation of a fresh corpse, I hoped we didn't have to wait much longer to see action.

Sure enough, within ten minutes, a subtle bump underneath us launched my heart into my throat.

Clay, proving he lacked all sense of self-preservation, leaned over the railing, shining a flashlight on the subtle waves. Its glare burned my eyes after sitting for so long in the dark, and I blinked to clear my vision.

"Look." He knelt to get closer. "Can you see it?"

A massive presence glided past us, but I couldn't make out its shape. Skin a rich aubergine, its olive markings reminded me of a topographic map that went on for miles. Its dark eyes were ringed with an eerie luminescence, but it paid us no mind, too intent on its meal.

"I'm going to name him Pontchy." Clay grew pensive. "He looks like a Pontchy, doesn't he?"

The body bobbed, dunked, bobbed, dunked, and then went under and stayed that way.

"Name it whatever you want." I curled my toes away from the edge. "It's still not coming home with us."

"First Armistice, and now Pontchy. What's a guy gotta do to get a pet around here?"

"How about I buy you a pack of sea monkeys and a fishbowl when we get home?"

"Sea monkeys? That's so..." He opened his mouth, closed it, furrowed his brow. "Actually, they're pretty cool. Make it one of the tanks with a Ferris wheel and carnival rides for them, and you've got a deal."

Pretty sure he was thinking of flea circus attractions, but I wasn't about to tell him that.

"Fine." I could deal with brine shrimp for their six-month lifespan. "Deal."

Thirty minutes later, we were still sitting, still waiting, but apparently that was it. The show was over.

Pontchy, whatever he was, had returned to wherever he came from.

"Time to head back." Freddie reached in the bucket where he stored his catches, pulled out a fat catfish, and bit off its head. "I prefer not to be on the water come morning, and I have things to do."

As the AIC, the only thing he *had* to do was what he was doing now, but I didn't pull rank on him. I'd had enough adventure for one night. I wanted to get back to dry land and Colby and think.

Much like Pontchy, I needed time to digest.

8

Despite the late hour, bright lights and loud music assailed us as soon as we stepped foot on dry land.

"Someone's having fun." Asa took my elbow to steady me. "Are party buses soundproof?"

"You'd think so." That was a happy thought. "I'll have to ask Colby."

"You mentioned a spell?" He paused on level ground. "Are you casting now or later?"

The downtime on the water had given me the bright idea to cast a *don't look here* spell to blur the dock and shoreline. It was easier preventing mistakes with humans than correcting them later.

The effect might not last, it was hard to tell, but it was better than nothing.

"Now," I decided. "It won't take long."

With a nod, Asa stood watch while I got down to business. Maybe five minutes later, I was done.

"Easy as falling off a log." I dusted my hands together. "Ready to go?"

"Ready to breathe air that doesn't smell like decaying fish and decomposing algae."

However bad it was for me, and it had been foul on the boat, it must be ten times worse for him.

Halfway to our slot, I noticed a line forming. Weird. We kept walking, and it kept winding alongside us.

Right back to our RV.

"Are you seeing this too?" I stopped dead in front of the rental. "I'm not hallucinating, right?"

The RV had been possessed by the spirit of disco. Lights strobed from a hub on top, dancing with the music blasting from hidden speakers. Girlish laughter was piped in to make it seem like a freaking rave on wheels. Thank the goddess, the shades were still lowered.

People in line were drunk or on their way there and looking for a lively way to end the night.

Based on the shouts and red faces, I was guessing they had been waiting for their turns a while.

That meant Clay, who had gone ahead to forage for our dinner, wasn't to blame for the raucous party.

This time.

"We need to get in there." Asa rushed to the driver side. "Before they pry open the doors."

Hot on his heels, I dug in my pocket for my phone. "Where's Clay when you need him?"

To those he loved, he might be a teddy bear, but he was still four hundred pounds of muscle.

No one made a better bouncer than a golem.

"Wait your turn," someone yelled in my face, alcohol hot on his breath. "The line starts back there."

The crowd was turning, and I was quickly growing annoyed with their shoving and pushing, but short of pulling my wand and zapping them individually, I didn't have much recourse without things getting ugly.

You can do whatever you want, the dark core of my soul whispered. *You have the authority now.*

As much as I wanted to blame the grimoire for the intrusive thoughts, they were nothing new.

A part of me would forever be chained in the basement of my mind, thrashing and snarling to get free.

The promotion had simply given it permission to knock and see if I was ready to open the door.

No one can stand against you. You are Hiram Nádasdy's daughter. You are a goddess made flesh.

The word *flesh* conjured a mouthful of hot meat that pulsed between my teeth with a copper aftertaste.

As deputy director, I could kill these humans for the insult of touching me, and no one would bat an eye.

I had the power, and in the supernatural world, that meant I had permission.

"Almost there." Asa reached back for me. "Stay close."

That touch broke the grim spell on my thoughts, yanking me back into myself and away from the precipice I so often walked these days as power nibbled on the moorings I had spent the last ten years building to ground myself.

I wasn't an heir or a legacy.

I was Rue Hollis.

A guardian. A friend. A lover. A cousin.

Asa produced the key, which Clay must have passed to him before he left. Otherwise, it would be at the bottom of the lake. He let us in, and the riot of colors and noises almost bowled me back out the door.

"Colby?" I kicked aside empty boxes and bags. "Where are you?"

No answer.

Heart in my throat, I began a panicked search for her while Asa locked us in and started pushing buttons.

"Colby." I searched high and low, but I couldn't sense her. *"Colby."*

Blessed silence enveloped the bus after Asa punched in the right combination, and darkness followed.

"I can't find her." I rushed up the aisle back to him. "Can you scent her?"

A moment of concentration told me he was attempting to cede control to Blay, who had the better nose for tracking, but he refused to show his face. Even for Colby. He was that afraid of getting in trouble. But Asa was no slouch, and he began a methodical sweep of the premises that ended at the bathroom.

"She came in here." He ran his hand along the ceiling. "She wiggled out through the vent."

"Okay." I gripped the door handle. "So, we wait."

"She knows the protocol." He ran his knuckles along my jaw. "She'll text as soon as she's safe."

Clinging to his words, I hoped he was right. For all of five seconds. "What I said? About waiting? I lied."

Booing sliced through my panic as the crowd registered there would be no free show tonight. Soon, hard smacks from open palms against the side of the bus set it swaying. Dull thuds bouncing off the glass told me they were now throwing rocks. Lovely. These guys weren't taking no for an answer.

"They're trying to tip us over." Asa shot to his feet. "I'll handle it."

"Let me." I was relieved for an excuse to dull my edge. "This ought to do the trick."

Placing my hand flat on the nearest piece of metal, in this case, the doorframe, I shut my eyes and sent a nasty jolt through the exterior of the RV. Yelps and curses rang out, but we quit rocking. One or two shook it off and tried again, but I happily zapped them until they got it through their thick skulls.

With that done, I slumped in my seat and tried calling Colby, since we were stuck in place until the crowd finished dispersing.

A bright ringtone sang out, and Asa lifted the green blanket he knitted for her to reveal her phone on the bench.

Dread coating the back of my throat, I dialed Clay to get him here stat. "Hey—"

"Hey back," he said cheerfully. "You'll never believe what feral creature I spotted in the wild."

Hope coiled in my chest, and my fingers tightened around the phone. "What?"

"Small, white, covered in spiderwebs." He clucked his tongue. "Left her phone behind."

"How did you...?" I stood and peered out the windshield, searching for them. "Where are you?"

She couldn't have gone far covered in gunk, not without risking wing damage, so she must be close.

"Open up." A hard bump against the RV announced their arrival. "My hands are full."

Palm smacking the button, I opened the door on Clay. Asa rushed to help him with a tall metal pot he clutched with handsewn potholders, but I had eyes only for the snarl of moth girl caught in his wavy red-gold wig.

"Colby." I rushed over and picked her out of his hair. "What happened?"

"I was setting up my computer, and the bus went nuts." She held still while I picked spiderweb from her delicate wings and fur. "I tried to shut it down, but it must be on a timer or something." She sneezed as I tickled the end of her proboscis. "All these people showed up and started pounding on the door, so I got out. I planned to wait in the trees until you got back, but there was *so* much gunk in the vent I was too heavy to fly. When I saw Clay, I kind of sailed to him to escape the roof."

As I examined the material, I realized what it was and why it would be in an RV like this one.

"Silly string." I held it up, and it sparkled under the lights. "White silly string."

"The last event must have been a bridal shower." Asa brought a wet cloth from the bathroom. "How did it get in the vents?"

"With enough alcohol, anything is possible." Clay rattled around in the back. "We need to eat fast. I promised Ms. Melchior I would get her pot back to her within the hour."

"Ms. Melchior?" I finished up with Colby and used the cloth to wipe off the sticky remnants.

"She's a sweet old lady staying five slots down. She was sitting on her porch when I smelled her cooking. I went to compliment her, and one thing led to another." He twirled a ratty potholder around his finger. "I bought her Frogmore stew. She made enough to last her all week, so it ought to last me—I mean *us*—tonight."

"Frogmore stew sounds familiar." I turned it over in my head. "Another name for a low country boil?"

"The student has truly become the master." Clay faked wiping a tear that was really condensation. "I'm so proud."

"Women are suckers when it comes to you." I dug into a bag Clay produced from under his arm. "I just don't see it."

"That's why we can be friends." He tweaked my nose. "Otherwise, your pining would ruin what we have."

"Mmm-hmm." I set the heavy-duty foam plates Ms. Melchior had been kind enough to send in a row down one of the benches then Asa piled them high with corncobs, red potatoes, crawfish, and sausage. "Whatever you need to tell yourself."

Colby, cleared for duty, returned to her laptop, muttering about showing them who was boss.

Them, I assumed, was the hacker or hackers who had ruined her day and earned annihilation via moth.

Mouth full of corn, I had to wipe my hands before checking my phone when a text notification chimed for me. Aedan had sent me grinning photos of Arden and Camber with their guests at a parade.

"They look like they're having fun." Asa passed me a bottle of water. "Who are the boys?"

"Friends from high school." I used my fingers to zoom in on Aedan's scowl in the background of the one photo he ended up in next to Arden. "Poor guy."

"Any word on Nolan?"

"He's supposed to show for breakfast." I texted Aedan good night. "Maybe he won't, and the girls can enjoy their trip without him ruining their fun." Possibly with an evil scheme. "But Aedan is point on that. He'll protect them, freeing us up to figure out what's going on with Pontchy."

"And your father?"

"No idea." I lost my appetite. "The missing Garnier witch has his name written all over it, but covens tend to police their own. It's not a Black Hat matter, and he's made it clear he doesn't want my help."

"But it bothers you."

"I feel responsible," I admitted. "If I had laid Mom to rest, he wouldn't be out there kidnapping people."

"We don't know for certain it was him."

He was kind enough not to remind me that, had I tried to help Mom, she might have killed me. The burn of her summoner's compulsion enflamed her, twisting her love, forcing her to act on orders Jai gave her.

"I promised Blay jambalaya with andouille." I lifted the sausage speared on my fork. "Does this count?"

"As much as Clay is feeding us on this trip, I wouldn't worry. Blay will get his jambalaya eventually."

Three meals a day were for amateurs in foodie cities. Between snacks and meals, we were averaging six.

"Listen to this." Clay, who hadn't come up for air since tucking into his meal, read off his laptop screen. "Our body snatcher is moving in a clockwise motion. I emailed the Kellies for a list of morgues, since Colby is out of commission for a bit, and they picked up on the pattern." He crammed a whole potato in his mouth then lifted a finger for us to wait while he chewed. "Now we've got locations for the top two morgues most likely to get hit next."

"We can follow up tomorrow." I grinned when Asa fed me the last bite of his crawfish. "We should rest."

"You're the Double D now," Clay chided. "Tell your minions to check for you."

"That's what I should do." I ought to order Freddie's team to zip their pants and report for duty. "It would save us time."

But there were so many delicate threads crisscrossing this city, I worried a rough hand might snap one.

"I know that tone." Clay slumped in his seat. "We'll be casing the morgues first thing."

"At some point," Asa broke in gently, "you'll have to put your resources to good use."

"I need agents I can trust to manage the ones I can't. Until I have time to make that list, however short it may be, I can't risk it."

That was the fatal flaw in the system. Trust. The lack thereof. Few agents trusted anyone outside their teams, which meant no one wanted to work together. Too many factions with age-old grudges kept them from accepting the truth—that we were all in this together.

Black witch, warg, vampire, fae. It didn't matter. The director owned us. That made us all the same.

"You have to give trust to get trust," Clay said wisely. "And no, that wasn't written on the last fortune cookie I ate." He cleared his throat. "It was the one before that."

"Fine." I held up my hands. "I'll call in the primary team to check the morgue angle for us."

"The light." He pumped his fist. "She's seen it."

"Yeah, yeah." Sticking my tongue out at him, I dug through my bag for clothes. "Dibs on the shower."

As soon as I stepped past Clay, he stuck his leg out in front of Asa to prevent him from following me.

Given the shower was about two feet squared, I didn't kick up a fuss. I sanitized the vent in case Colby needed it again, then washed the lake off me and wondered where Dad was spending the day. And if he had a Garnier witch for company.

9

Much as I hated to admit it, the bunks, while cramped, were oddly cozy. The thin mattresses were comfy, the pillows firm, and the sheets soft. Each cubby included a small TV mounted to the wall and a pair of complimentary earbuds wrapped in plastic rested on every pillow. They even came with cute theater-style curtains for privacy from your fellow sleepers.

Before I faced the day, I checked my phone and found either the Kellies or Clay had looped me into their emails. There were eight missing corpses total, and the humans who worked at the morgue were getting antsy. The problem was quickly growing too large to hide with the wave of a magic wand.

But I had done as Clay suggested and turned the surveillance of the morgues over to Freddie's team.

Light stabbed me in the eyes, and I squinted as a wall of warm, bare skin landed on top of me. "Asa?"

Hips pressing me into the mattress, he bit the side of my neck. "Expecting someone else?"

"Yes." I tossed my phone aside. "Didn't you see the line outside my door last night?"

"That was all for you?" He brushed a trail of kisses down my throat. "I didn't realize you had so many admirers."

"Well, most of the time they don't stand single file. That's why."

"Ah." He rocked against me. "That must be it."

A sigh escaped me, and he fit his hand over my mouth as he did it again, and again, until I bit his palm to hold back the noise trapped in my throat. I hooked a leg over his hip, banging my shin in the process. His groan when I rolled my hips into his I swallowed whole with a kiss that stole his breath.

Lost in the taste of him, I shivered when he hit the right spot to spark starlight behind my eyes.

A ragged breath later, he sighed and went still above me.

"Good morning," I breathed, laughed, really. "I could get used to this."

"Your knee is bleeding." He touched the wound gently. "I have a goose egg on the back of my head."

"And?"

"And nothing."

As I raised my arms to seek out his injury, I noticed him eyeing the bracelet he'd made for me. "Maybe I should make you one, so we match."

"If you made me one, you'd have to make all your admirers one, and then you'd have no hair left."

After murmuring a quick healing spell, I linked my fingers behind his neck. "Good thing I have a friend with a wig obsession." As if Clay would ever let me butcher one. "As an alternative, I have this insane urge to tattoo my name on your forehead."

"It would be cheaper than a wig."

Belonging to someone was new for him, for me too, but love couldn't grow if you kept it chained.

I learned that after reading *The Pitbull and the Piranha*.

Except, in that case, the hero kept the heroine in an aquarium.

Times like this, with Asa and me in our own little cocoon, I wanted to mate the heck out of him. I wanted to reach into his chest and knot the strings of his heart with mine. I wanted to bind him to me so tightly he couldn't escape if he ever woke up and realized who he had fallen into bed with.

"It would ruin your pretty face." I cupped his cheeks in my palms. "And I would probably murder the artist if you so much as flinched."

Footsteps plodded outside the bunks, and we zipped our lips and froze like kids caught reading under the blankets when they should have been sleeping. But the steady thump-thump-thump aimed for the bathroom, and the second the door shut, Asa rolled out from under my curtain.

Sinking back onto my pillow, I snorted at his escape then brought my knee up to examine the cut.

"Ah-ha."

The curtains whooshed open, and I yelped at the sudden invasion. "What is wrong with you?"

"Where is he?" Clay reached in, fluffing the sheet. "I know you're hiding him somewhere."

"You're deranged." I shoved him back. "I was in here minding my own business, like a good little girl."

"I smell him all over you." He tapped the side of his nose. "The stink is what woke me."

"Liar." I planted my foot on his chest. "You're just a killjoy."

Before I could kick him back, he gripped my ankle and tickled the bottom of my foot.

"No," I howled, writhing and thrashing. "I haven't peed yet."

"I'm about to solve that problem for you." He jerked then muttered, "Hey." He spun, half pulling me off my bunk. "What's this?" He twisted again, and my tailbone cracked on the floor. "Betrayal."

"Unhand her, you fiend." Colby dive-bombed him. "Else you'll walk the plank."

"I'm a member of your crew," he protested. "How can you side with this scabby sea bass over me?"

"Scabby sea bass," I echoed. "That sounds offensive."

Expanding to her biggest size, Colby launched herself at Clay's head. Upon which sat the wig from yesterday. A crime of fashion, in his book. He caught her, staggered back, hit the wall, slid to the floor, and rolled around while she giggled herself silly. The brightness of her laugh, paired with the sharpness of her eyes, told on her. On him too.

"You two were up all night, weren't you?"

The pair broke apart and dusted themselves off, both striving for innocence and neither achieving it.

"I was securing my laptop," she said primly, flitting off to her new computer, "if that's what you mean."

"I helped her." Clay got to his feet. "What can I say? I'm a helpful guy who enjoys being helpful."

"All you think about is food." I ignored the rumble in my belly. "You're ninety percent stomach."

"We're in *New Orleans*," he reminded me for the millionth time. "The food is the main attraction."

Once the path was clear, I got out of my bunk, but the bathroom was already locked.

Asa must have snuck in there to clean up after...

Ahem.

"We're here to work, not to eat."

"Blasphemy."

"Truthphemy." I stepped left to get around Clay, and he swerved into my path. "What gives?"

"Nothing." He blocked me to the right then the left again. "Absolutely nothing."

"Your lace hairline is curling—" I pointed above his *shem*, "—right there."

"No, it's not." He reached up anyway. "Nice try."

While he traced his forehead with his fingers, I ducked under his arm and pulled up short. "Oh no."

"It was like that when I got here?" He whirled on me. "The moth made me do it?"

The moth, who very well might have put him up to it, was plugged in and missed him throwing shade.

"Pick an excuse and stick with it." I inspected the nearest stripper pole, which had been crushed in his fists while he was doing goddess only knows what. "Why is the other one leaning?"

"I *might* have gotten a tad enthusiastic during my dance routine and accidentally kicked out on this pole and knocked that one loose from the ceiling." He nudged me away from the damage, guiding me in a circle right back to where I'd started. "You mentioned something about work?"

Seeing as how Colby handled the paperwork, and Colby worshipped Clay, I had no doubt she could find a way to spin the poles' destruction so he wouldn't be held financially responsible for his mess.

They made it. They could clean it up.

Delegation at its finest.

"We've got a bead on Pontchy, on the food supply, and on the method of delivery."

"We need to figure out who's feeding it," Clay pointed out, "and why they brought it here."

"Do you think we can fit in one more errand?" I squinched my toes on the floor. "I want to check up on the missing Garnier witch. Can you get me the files on the coven and on Lazarus witches?"

For the moment, I wasn't sure if Lazarus was a designation within the Garnier coven or a talent that occurred within certain bloodlines.

"Colby can." His eyes glimmered. "She framed a new doorway into the Bureau database last night."

"You'd tell me if she was in over her head, right?" I searched his face. "She's fighting battles for me on a plane of existence I can't see and don't understand. I can't just punch her laptop in the face and make threats if what she discovers hurts her. I'm counting on you to let me know if we need to pull her out."

"Colby is brilliant." He gripped my shoulders. "Give the kid some credit." He shook me gently. "Me too."

Exiting the bathroom on a cloud of steam, Asa toweled his hair dry, a smile on his lips. "Afternoon."

Tracing the droplets running down his chest with my eyes, I asked, "You think you're slick, don't you?"

"Not unless I missed a spot while I was rinsing."

"You two behave." Clay jabbed a finger between us. "And, for the record, no more sleepovers."

As a courtesy, I didn't mention there was no sleep involved. "We need to walk the causeway tonight."

Grumbling under his breath, he flopped down on the bench seat, content to ignore me.

"You need to see more?" Asa raked his fingers through the damp tangle of his hair, but it plastered itself to his chest and back, not that I was standing around transfixed by the simple act of him finger-combing his hair or anything that sappy. "I thought you determined where the deliveries were being made."

"I want to make sure we're not missing something." I cupped his jaw. "Tell Blay to be ready."

Until we caught the delivery boy—or girl—we couldn't begin to piece together the rest of that mystery.

Pontchy had to go, that much was obvious, but we needed to find out why he had been lured here and by whom first if we wanted to avoid Return of the Lake Monster.

"I'm sure he'll cooperate." Asa kissed my palm. "He's not handling his guilt well."

"That brat." I doubted guilt had anything to do with it. Colby explained what grounding meant, and why it happened to her (so often), and now he lived in fear of losing his Mystic Seas privileges. "Let him know I'm not mad, okay?"

"I'll convey it to him." He pulled a comb from his pocket. "Do you mind?"

Of all our rituals, this had become my favorite. Without a chair to sit in, he lowered himself into the aisle. He carried a small bottle of the detangler I'd crafted for him, and each spritz of green apple made me smile. I took the comb and knelt behind him, slicing his part, combing out the knots, and braiding his hair.

"I want to check out the townhouse too. Not where the girls are staying. The one across the street." I finished my work and admired the neat braids. "There must be a reason someone pointed us that way."

Rising, Asa returned to the bathroom. "I don't like that someone knows where the girls are staying."

With the door cracked several inches, I was able to keep the conversation going *and* enjoy him dressing for the day without offending Clay's delicate sensibilities.

"I don't like that someone knows they exist." I hauled myself onto my bunk and sat. "Period."

But allowing them into my life, loving them, meant the blame fell on me.

"Any requests?" Asa opened a carved box holding his jewelry. "I was thinking of the selenite."

The simple studs bore polished selenite cabochons. I bought them for him on a whim from a craft fair in Samford, but they suited him. The crystal was meant to lift darkness on the spirit and bring light on the darkest days. The way our days were going lately, I figured we could use all the light we could get.

"You look good in anything." I watched him switch out his jewelry. "In everything. In nothing."

A flush painted his cheeks as he fought off the embarrassment of knowing I meant every word.

"Hey," Clay called. "You guys might want to stop being disgustingly in love and come see this."

Leaving Asa to put away his things, I finally got to pee then joined Clay on the bench. "Whatcha got?"

Across from us, Colby kept her head down, working away, but she waved a hand for him to carry on.

"That townhouse?" He spun his laptop on his knees. "There was a morgue in the basement."

"Wait." I held up my hand. "How does a building in the Quarter have a basement?"

New Orleans had been built above sea level, originally, but it was sinking. Half the city now sat lower than the ocean. Situated between levees, it created a bowl effect that made getting water out difficult once it leaked in. Basements were *not* a thing here.

"How else?" He rolled his eyes. "Magic."

Ask a stupid question... "Who built the morgue?"

"Believe it or not, wargs. They played critical roles as doctors, nurses, and morticians during the last yellow fever outbreak. Not the 1905 one, the one before that. They were immune to the disease, despite their human half. Anyway, that townhouse was one of five given a basement to use as cold storage for the bodies piling up in the streets."

"One of five." I could see where this was headed. "That one, the girls' townhouse, and three others?"

"They're connected by tunnels. Barely a half mile total, and compact to make it easier to maintain."

"Like the tunnels under Old Candler Hospital in Savannah."

The story goes that a tunnel beneath the hospital, one leading from the morgue, would be stacked with bodies during the day as patients succumbed to yellow fever. Come nightfall, carriages would line up to accept their portion of the grisly accumulation and cart their passengers to their final resting places.

"Except this network forms a five-pointed star."

"Where do you see that?" I flipped through the photos. "I don't see a pentagram."

"Part of the tunnels collapsed," he explained, "and no one repaired them."

"Here." Colby made a flicking motion with her wrist, and a file popped up on his screen. "I highlighted the original routes. That's what I showed Clay earlier."

"Hey." I glanced over at her. "You fling digital files through thin air now?"

"It's a file sharing app." She laughed. "Not magic."

From where I was sitting, it was pretty impressive. "So you say."

"Three of the original five townhouses have suffered structural damage in the last fifty years." Her cheeks flushed from the praise. "The massive foundational shift was blamed on a sinkhole, but they found no evidence to support the theory and elected to repair the homes instead." A bright red X marked each of them. "Those are the areas I believe to be compromised."

"How do we get into the tunnels?" Asa sat beside me, his arm going around my shoulders. "I assume you want to explore them?"

Antennae twitching, she asked, "Why not go in through the girls' townhouse?"

Their weekend accommodations were, of course, in a home marked with a big green X for accessibility.

"Too risky." Clay nixed that idea. "There's a strong chance you picked up your virus there."

"So?" Her forehead scrunched. "Just don't bring any electronics with you."

"If the storage areas don't open into the houses anymore," I cut in on their debate, "I don't want to create new doorways. Especially not there."

"The basements were likely sealed between outbreaks to conserve the magic required to keep them dry and functional," Asa agreed. "Have any of the properties been sold since then?"

"All five properties have changed hands. The last holdout sold ten years ago. Three are now rentals."

"Which means five lucky landowners are living above magically reinforced morgues they may or may not know exist." Had the properties been sold to supernaturals, viable body cold storage would trump curb appeal. "Someone knows, though. They pointed us in this direction."

With Colby's attention split between identifying the hacker and reestablishing her command base, I decided to ask the Kellies for the homeowners' records in case we needed to contact them.

"I vote we alphabetize the townhouses to keep them straight." Clay drummed his fingers on his knee. "The girls can have Townhouse A. The one across the street can be Townhouse B. We'll name C, D, and E going counterclockwise as they appear on the map."

"Works for me." I was all for cutting down on confusion. "Townhouse A-E it is."

"Have you heard from the girls?" Asa read me too easily when I flipped apps to check for updates. "Nolan was supposed to show for breakfast, right?"

"Yeah." I refreshed the screen, as if that would shake out correspondence. "Maybe I should call Aedan?"

"Check on them," he agreed. "Find out their plans."

"Determine if the house will be empty." I read between the lines. "In case we don't have a choice."

The network of tunnels might have been sealed off from the houses entirely, leaving the original exit to act as the only remaining entrance. I couldn't begin to guess where it might open, but Colby had given us the map. We had a search area smaller than, say, the entire city, so that was progress.

Although I didn't trust any invisible hand tossing us breadcrumbs of help, not when we had no idea where they led.

Stepping outside for fresh air, I called Aedan. "How's it going?"

"It's going." His voice was tight. "The girls are getting ready for a parade."

"Did Nolan show?"

"No." He shut a door in the background. "They didn't seem surprised by it either."

"He tends to remember them when it's convenient and forget them when he has better things to do."

"That would explain it." He exhaled. "I should go." He bumped around, opening and shutting drawers. "I need to shower before we leave."

"Okay." I drummed my fingers on my elbow. "Just FYI, we might be dropping in on the townhouse."

Quickly, I explained the morgue network then asked if he had heard about the missing Garnier witch.

"All I've heard is what color lipstick Camber thinks looks best on Arden and what top Arden thinks Camber should wear."

"How are the guys?"

"They're fine," he said flatly. "About what you would expect."

Loud. Drunk. Handsy.

That was what I would expect, seeing as how their roomies were beautiful young women, but I wasn't about to say so. "I'll check in later, okay?"

The call ended with me wishing I could figure out how to toss happily ever afters like beads.

Mulling over our plans for the night, I walked to the pier to check on our AIC.

His berth was empty, his boat gone. As much as he enjoyed fishing, I wasn't surprised, but it did make me wonder how much of his time, if any, he was devoting to the case.

The problem with recruiting people at gunpoint? You had to be ready to pull the trigger to get results.

Most agents did the bare minimum. They had chosen the suit over death, yeah, but that wasn't saying much. At most, Black Hat chained them, preventing them from performing worse atrocities. Perhaps the concept of enforcing justice was too foreign for the agents to grasp. Unless the director motivated his agents, got them invested in the outcomes of their cases, he was doing little more than running a daycare.

And…that wasn't my problem.

I was the deputy director because, like them, I'd had no choice. I had a job to do, and I would do it, but that didn't mean I had to sit around solving the director's problems for him. The title wasn't really mine. It was a placeholder. Or I was. As soon as I got things settled with Dad, I could go back to my real life.

Whatever that meant.

"Ready?"

Lost in thought, I hadn't heard Asa walk up behind me. "Yeah."

"Colby found us a starting point," he reported. "We'll begin there and see where it takes us."

"You finished checking on everyone?" Clay joined us. "You've got that look."

"Whatever you heard troubled you," Asa agreed. "What's wrong?"

"Nothing." I stretched the truth. "Just thinking."

"The next time you want to start a new hobby," Clay said, elbowing me, "try knitting."

"Are you saying thinking is too advanced for me?"

"Well, I'm sure someone tutors in *Thinking for Beginners*."

A text landed before I could give Clay the smackdown he deserved, and I smiled to see it was from Camber.

>>*Aedan looks ready to spit nails.*

>*Oh?*

>>*He caught Wyatt watching Arden change through the keyhole in her room.*

Part of the charm of old homes was a few still used original locks and keys.

>*Then I don't blame him.*

>>*It's fine.*

>*No.*

>*It's not.*

>*In no way, shape, or form.*

>>*No, I mean she handled it. She caught him and stabbed him in the eye with a pen.*

>*That's my girl.*

>*You should still send him home.*

>>*He's heading to the ER. Carter's taking him. I'm packing their bags while they're gone. They'll be waiting on the steps after Wyatt is discharged.*

>>*I didn't think this one through. I thought Wyatt would flirt, Aedan would get jelly, and BOOM. Instant romance. But now Arden feels violated. She was violated. And Aedan is ready to murder Wyatt.*

>*I'm willing to murder Wyatt, if you would prefer.*

>>*That would be great. Care to hop a plane to NO?*

More like call a Swyft for a trip across town. The paranormal ride share app wasn't my favorite mode of transportation—I was too paranoid to put myself at the mercy of strangers on the regular—but it was convenient. No one knew a city better than the people who lived in it.

>*If you guys need me, I'm there.*

>>*We can handle it. I can handle it. It's my mess. I owe it to Arden to fix it. Aedan too.*

A glimmer of warmth filled my chest as it hit me Camber was growing up before my eyes. She was taking responsibility for her own mistake, however well she had intended, and doing what it took to correct it. I would have told her so, but I wasn't her mother, and I didn't want to embarrass myself for being a softy.

"I'm going to rip out his eyes and eat them." Clay snatched my cell. "What the hell was that little shit thinking?" He squeezed until the case popped. "Who does that?"

"Camber wants to handle it." I pried the phone from his hands before he broke it. "If she has any trouble, Aedan will step in." Landing Wyatt in the ER for round two. "He can handle a pervy human." I shoved Clay out of my personal space. "Also? It's rude to read over someone's shoulder uninvited."

"Ace does it all the time," he protested. "You let him get away with it."

"I let him get away with a lot of things you can't." I smiled sweetly. "Would you like a list?"

Plugging his ears with his fingers, he started to hum and wandered toward the SUV.

"Mean." Asa kissed my temple. "I like it."

"One of the many reasons I worry about you." I stuck my head into the RV. "You know the rules, smarty fuzz butt."

"Mmm-hmm."

"On the bright side," I teased, "you cleaned out all the gunk on your escape route last night. You should have a clear path if you need to beat another hasty retreat."

"Mmm-hmm."

"Look out! There's a kraken standing behind you."

"Mmm-hmm."

Eyes fixed on the screen, keyboard clacking a mile a minute, I might as well have not existed.

After locking Colby in, I noticed a familiar bike idling on the main road. "See that?"

Hard to miss the leggy woman astride a motorcycle, her visor up as she stared out at the marina.

"I knew she couldn't resist me." Clay styled his hair with his fingers. "I keep 'em coming back for more."

"She's probably checking on the bus." I pricked his ego. "I doubt she's here to check you out."

Our request must have struck the company as odd, just parking their RV for a week, but we paid upfront for the rental and put down a hefty incident deposit too.

"That hurt." He lowered his arm. "I'm bleeding out. Through my heart. Which you broke."

"Ask the Kellies to dig into the company." I patted his chest. "I want info on the owner and the drivers."

Between that and the list of townhouse owners, we were diving into a sea monster-sized suspect pool.

Good thing we had Freddie's questionable hospitality to keep us afloat.

10

On the drive over to the townhouses, I had an idea about how to get more information on the tunnels. A long shot. But, in all honesty, I had been searching for an excuse to reach out for weeks. This just gave me a valid reason I could fall back on if the whole friendship thing didn't pan out.

Flipping down the visor, I checked my hair and wiped a piece of sleep crust from my eye.

With looks like these, no wonder Asa had been swept off his feet.

"Are you going on a date or something?" Clay leaned forward. "What's with the primping?"

The plan had been to video chat with her, but now I was second-guessing that decision.

"Hush." I pushed him back, screwed up my courage, and dialed the old-fashioned way. "Hey."

"*Rue.*" Marita squealed around a mouthful of something crunchy. "Hey."

Marita Mayhew, wife and mate of Alpha Derry Mayhew, had left an impression on me.

"Yes. Me. Rue." I wiped my damp palm off on my pants. "It's Rue."

"What can I do you for?" She chuckled. "I'm set to referee a cornhole match, so it'll have to be quick."

"Oh." I cringed. "I didn't mean to interrupt your fun. I can call back later…" Or never. Reaching out once had been hard enough, but this felt like a slap on the wrist. Maybe I had been too informal? "I can compensate—"

"I'm not a payphone, Rue. You don't have to drop quarters in to talk to me."

"I didn't mean…" I massaged my forehead. "I'm bad at this."

"If Captain Tightwad had brought you into the fold sooner, like I told him to, then we would already be past this awkwardness. But he was raised different, thanks to Meg's afterlife consultation gig. I try not to hold the nickel-and-diming against him, but I won't lie. His reflex to bill for time costs me friends."

"I am calling for a favor." The tension in my throat eased a few degrees. "It's only fair—"

"I'm not taking your money." She grunted. "What's on your mind?"

"Do you know any packs in New Orleans?"

"I have a cousin in the Metairie pack."

"Would they know about the warg humanitarian efforts made during the yellow fever outbreaks?"

"I doubt it." She took another drink. "Ali married in, so it's not a history she would have grown up with."

"Can she ask around?" I pressed my luck. "If the old morgue tunnels are active again, like I think they are, I could use all the background on them I can get."

"That sounds both creepy and dangerous." She munched with enthusiasm. "Want some company?"

"What?" I blamed her lip-smacking for the misunderstanding. "Company?"

"We're in Bay St. Louis, Mississippi. Yesterday was Uncle Zale's birthday. Anyway, the festivities are mostly over, and the food is gone. We were going to bum around here for the weekend, but spelunking through New Orleans morgue tunnels sounds cooler than painting Aunt Noreen's toenails."

Friendship with me was more fun than watching paint dry. That wasn't saying much, but I would take it.

"You want to spend your weekend here? With us? Hunting a sea monster?"

"Sea monster?" She choked and coughed to clear her throat. "Are you for real?"

"Did I forget to mention that part?"

"Derry will crap his pants over this." Her laughter ran wild down the line. "First Old Man Fang. Now a sea monster. Keep it up, and you'll never get rid of us." A door opened and shut. "Text us where you're staying. We can sleep on the floor. In fur, if necessary. See you soon."

The call ended before I got a handle on what had happened, and I stared at my phone like it was the one to blame before sending over the marina's address. "We're having company."

"I heard." Asa studied me from the corner of his eye. "That was unexpected."

"Aww." Clay formed a heart with his hands. "Rue made a friend."

"I should call her back." I swallowed. "Tell her we don't have anywhere for them to stay."

"We'll make it work." Asa rested a hand on my thigh. "We could use the extra noses."

"Tracking will be a nightmare," Clay agreed. "Too many people, too many competing scents."

"What about Colby?" I shouldn't have made the call. "She can't hide out for a whole weekend."

Expecting her to hole up for three days was too big of an ask. I couldn't do that to her. It wasn't fair.

"What if I claim a bunk?" Clay grew thoughtful. "I don't need the bed, but it would give Colby her own space when the wargs are in-house. I can stay up all night on the bench, and she can hang out in there."

"They'll smell her." I worried my bottom lip. "Or hear her."

"Did you know witches exist?" He tugged the ends of my hair. "I hear they can even cast spells."

"I don't know." I picked at my nails. "I don't want Colby to feel excluded."

"Colby doesn't know you, me, Asa, or Blay exist right now," Clay pointed out. "She's hot on the trail of—wait for it—*The Ferret*."

The hacker was asking for a cheesy nickname with that smoke trick, so I didn't roll my eyes.

Out loud anyway.

"You can seal her in." Asa talked over Clay. "Ward it for protection, spell it for sound, scent, and sight."

"There is a TV..." I let them warm me to the idea. "And she has her new laptop..."

"Good." Clay rebounded. "Then it's settled."

"I've been meaning to ask." Asa stared out the windshield. "How fast can a warg run?"

"Any particular reason why?" I narrowed my eyes on him. "For that matter—who's asking?"

"Blay might be interested in a rematch."

The last time Derry and Blay got together, they broke into a mausoleum, stole an ulna, and played fetch with it. There might have been a race prior, but the graverobbing was what I remembered the most.

"Goddess bless," I muttered, shaking my head. "This is going to be a mess."

We hit congestion earlier than we had yesterday and abandoned the SUV to a public parking lot to walk the rest of the way on foot. The crowds were thick, the music loud, and the rumble of distant thunder promised the humidity would be thick enough to choke on soon.

"Cut through there." Asa gestured toward an alley that required us to walk in single file. "Turn left."

At the end of his directions, I stepped out onto the street facing Townhouse A.

That meant the building beside us was the one The Ferret (good grief) had wanted us to rent.

Hand on the bend of my elbow, Asa drew me back into the shadows before I gave us away.

"How do we get in?" Searching for clues, I checked with Clay. "Where's the nearest entrance?"

"That part wasn't spelled out."

"*Spelled* out?" I pinned him in my sights. "Are you joking with me right now?"

Wargs couldn't perform magic, aside from their single gift of trading forms with their wolf half. There was no point in calling Marita again. Even if her cousin could give us a history lesson, the properties had changed hands, which meant the tunnels had been sealed after the wargs' occupation of the buildings.

An educated guess based on the records the Kellies sent over listing only human buyers and renters over the last ten years. Hmm. Framed that way, I wondered if it had been an intentional effort to avoid paras rediscovering the tunnels and putting them back into use. If so, it was a pity it hadn't gone to plan.

"You are a witch." Clay leaned against the opposite building. "I thought it was funny."

"Of course you did."

"If there's an exterior entrance, it could have sunk lower than street level." Asa ran a palm down the wall. "Do you have the map of the tunnels?"

"Yeah." I handed him my phone. "First pic is the original network. Second shows the collapsed sections."

"The whole point of spelling a basement was to keep the death toll a secret," Clay argued. "I don't see it having street access. Too many people would have noticed bodies going in but not coming out."

Closing my eyes, I placed my hand on the weatherworn brick, listening.

Ba-bump.

Ba-bump.

Ba-bump.

On the other side of this wall, in a house that should have been empty, someone lingered in the dark.

"We should go." I withdrew slowly. "Let's work on identifying the exit rather than the entrances."

The guys didn't question me, and we retraced our route into the chaos of the party spilling out from Bourbon Street.

"What was that?" Clay carved us a path. "What happened back there?"

"Someone was in the house."

"It's for rent." Asa moved to flank me. "It could be the new tenant."

"The lights were out," Clay reminded him, "but it could have been a bedroom for all we know."

"Either way," I settled the debate, "I didn't want them to notice us poking around their place."

The smells of sweat, Old Bay, and sunscreen climbed in my nose and infected my brain with the throbbing cadence of the myriad heartbeats thundering around me in joyful abandon.

"Rue." Asa pulled me to a stop and cradled my face in his hands. "Breathe."

"I'm trying." Clutching his wrists, I did as I was told. "There are just so many..."

Ba-bum. Ba-bum. Ba-bum.

Ba-bum. Ba-bum. Ba-bum.

Ba-bum. Ba-bum. Ba-bum.

The beats filled my soul, music to my ears.

Water pooled in my mouth, and I swallowed convulsively to keep from drooling.

"She's picking up on something powerful." Clay scanned the crowd. "She wouldn't break down like this for a nonmagical source."

New Orleans brimmed with power, and magical practitioners. There was no shortage of temptation.

"I've got it under control." I withdrew from Asa, reclaimed my phone, and began tracing the paths Colby had marked for us, determined to beat this. "Let's try Washington Artillery Park. It's on Decatur Street."

The farther from the closely packed bodies and their salty-sweet vitality, the better.

"This looks promising." Asa kept his eyes on me. "There's direct access to the Mississippi River."

Sure enough, the park sat across from Jackson Square, right along the riverfront.

"Lots of places for a secret entrance." Clay turned a slow circle. "Any ideas where to start?"

"A big red X would make it too easy." I, however, *liked* easy. "Let's begin with the cannon."

A Civil War era replica cannon sat on a raised platform, pointing toward the river, its base shrouded in marble plaques. As far as secret entrances go, it would be a painfully obvious one. But the tunnels predated the park, so the wargs might have had to make do to keep their existing structures in place.

"This one." Asa had barely gotten within six feet of the cannon before he zeroed in on a plaque detailing the purpose of the monument. "There must be a way to open it." He leaned in, filling his lungs. "It smells of death and mold."

From where I stood at the front, where the park's name had been inscribed, three plaques spanned the left and right sides. He was adamant about the right center being our way in, and I trusted his instincts.

"Let me see what I can do to conceal us." I rested a hand on his arm, and the familiar spell sprang to my fingertips. I pushed it out until it enveloped a portion of the monument as well. People would see it, but not us, and not any changes we made. "Can you scent any concentrated magic? Or is there a mechanism?"

"I can't tell." He shook his head. "It's too faint."

Crouching beside him, I traced the thick edges of the plaque with my wand, dowsing for a lock or hinge. I made three passes, whispering an unlocking spell as I went, and a subtle *click* was my reward. The plaque slid out an inch, enough for me to dig in my fingertips, and I pulled it toward me on a metal track.

"Must be original," I murmured, noticing a latch so well hidden in the design, we missed it entirely. "Mechanical so the wargs could operate it."

The entire section holding the plaque, marble and all, folded flat, creating a thick step. The first of many. A metal staircase disappeared below us into the dark. The hole was big enough for me to climb in with ease. Asa could make it if he wedged his shoulders just right. Clay? Not so much.

"Clay, you're the lookout." I willed the tip of my wand to brightness. "Asa, care for a moonlit stroll?"

Minus the moon, which would disappear within a few feet of the dank opening.

"I would be delighted." His lips hitched to one side. "Shall I lead?"

Fingers closing over one of his braids, I gave it a hard tug. "Don't think I don't know what you're doing."

"I'm a better tracker than you." He tapped the side of his nose then went ahead. "That's all."

Had I not enjoyed the view so much, I might have argued more, but I did, so I didn't.

"I don't like this." Clay leaned against the monument. "Cramped quarters make using magic dangerous."

Ricochet wasn't just for bullets, but I had plenty of combat experience. Not as a gray witch, but still.

"I have Asa and Blay." I patted his hand. "I'll be okay."

"You better be," he grumbled. "I would have to strip and lube myself to squeeze in that tiny hole."

"I don't need those kinds of details about your sex life."

"You *wish* I shared details."

"Keep telling yourself that." I plugged my ears with my fingers. "Just don't keep telling *me*."

Eager to make my escape before he scarred me for life, I began the descent. Twenty-five steps later, I stood in a tunnel the height and width of a generous door. Already, I regretted brushing off Clay's warning about close quarters. *Close* was one thing. This was downright claustrophobic.

Asa stood a few feet ahead, scenting the air. He gave me a nod and set out, leaving me to follow him. By unspoken mutual agreement, we kept quiet as we padded around and around the mildew-rich labyrinth.

"Beeswax," he said softly. "Someone was burning candles."

"Do you hear that?" I cocked my head, and what I heard urged me forward. "Over there."

Instinct guided me deeper into the maze until a glimmer of light pulled me up short.

"Rue Hollis," said the woman who delivered our RV. "It's a pleasure to formally meet you."

"How did you know where to find us?"

"Nan has done everything short of knock on your door, take you by the hand, and lead you here." Her laugh was as cold and flat as her eyes. "I didn't find you. You finally found me."

"Nan is The Ferret."

"The Ferret?" Amusement curved her red lips. "Oh, she won't like that. Her signature is a mink."

Minks were vicious, aggressive, and ruthless. Not a bad choice of emblem for a black witch.

"The Kellies didn't find my backdoor, did they?" I studied her, curious if she would react to the name of the Black Hat hacker duo. "Nan did."

As usual, she gave nothing away, but I didn't see the harm in naming the Kellies when she had to be a rogue agent herself. Even if by some miracle she wasn't Bureau, Nan would have told her who they were up against.

"You don't have a backdoor. You have *a* door, one down a long and winding hallway."

That sounded...bad. Very, very bad. Even for a computer illiterate like me.

Nan must have infected Colby via the Kellies rather than through the security system on Townhouse A.

All she had to do was wait for us to arrive, activate her protocol, and alert her coconspirator.

"The RV delivery was, what, for funsies? Do you know how embarrassing it is to stay in that eyesore?"

"Had you rented the townhouse, you wouldn't have that problem. Nan even created a custom listing for you on your rental site of choice."

That explained why VacayNStay got hit, but it was a clumsy effort. The lack of subtlety screamed *trap*.

"When that didn't work, your second choice was the Strippermobile?"

"The Toussaints have a fleet of them, so they were eager to lend Nan one for her personal use while she was in town." Her smile grew sharper. "The hotel situation is rather dismal this time of year."

"The Toussaints had no idea you were charging us exorbitant rent for that crime against RVs."

"The party bus was a stopgap measure to earn me an introduction to you and your team. You recognize me now. You all do. The bus gave me a plausible excuse for visiting the marina. That recognition, that plausibility, would have made you hesitate before you killed me. Those extra seconds were all I needed if I had to bring this conversation to your doorstep."

"Any particular reason why you were in a rush for an introduction?"

A rustling noise confirmed the second heartbeat that led me to them, and a thin girl with dark skin and a vibrant scarf wrapped around her head stepped forward. Heavy cuffs made from vines bound her wrists, the thorns digging into her skin. She swayed on her bare dirty feet, and her soft brown eyes were blurry.

"This is Tibby Garnier." The woman gripped her shoulder to steady her. "She's the last living Lazarus."

There was only one reason I could fathom for this unexpected meeting, and I was bitter to find myself as much a pawn as Mom had ever been.

Thanks, Gramps.

Airing our family's dirty laundry had kicked up a stink that clung to me like black magic. "And you are?"

"Call me Luca." At long last, her cold expression matched her empty eyes. "I'm here to broker a trade."

Luca.

The woman who saved Dad.

The woman who foolishly believed she owned him now.

The woman who was about to get a brutal wake-up call if she cost Dad that witch.

"Of course you are." Dread curdled my stomach. "What did you have in mind?"

"Your father wants Tibby. He can have her, *after* he's fulfilled his promise."

There was no *after* in that scenario for Dad. Once he killed the director, the animus vow would take his life. He wouldn't have a use for Tibby then. Just as he had no use for Luca now.

"Why does he want her?" I was curious if she knew why he defected. "What can a Lazarus do?"

Playing dumb wasn't that hard when I had bare-bones information on that designation.

"What she can or can't do is immaterial," she demurred. "Your father has made it known he wants her."

That sounded a whole lot like she didn't see the big picture. Or maybe she was okay with having blind spots as long as she got what she wanted.

Leverage was leverage.

"I'll give your father twenty-four hours to contact me. He knows how." She lifted her wand and drilled it into Tibby's neck, and the faint light caught on her distinctive bracelet. "After that, I'll kill her, and neither of us will get what we want."

"I'll pass along the information, but I have no part in your bargain, and I have no stake in the outcome."

Dad made his choice the day he spoke the words that ensured he would die to avenge Mom.

And it wasn't me.

"Twenty-four hours," she repeated, backing away. "Not one second longer."

Asa made as if to follow her, but I held out my hand to give her a head start.

"She came primed for a confrontation." I set a five-minute timer. "We need to be smart about this."

Anything she set up in advance could be activated with a word as she ran past, and I didn't want to find out she rigged the tunnel to collapse by it falling on our heads.

Lowering my arm, I thought back on what I had seen. "Did you notice her bracelet?"

"No."

"The charm was a pottery shard. I recognized the design. It was the same as the smashed vase from the mausoleum. The one the summoning circle kept in their homes and on their persons to hide the smell of their magic."

No wonder we hadn't scented anything peculiar about her when she dropped off the RV. And why Nan had kept her distance. Only the card Luca gave Clay with transference tipped us off to their true natures.

"Do you think Luca is the one who supplied the Boo Brothers?"

"That would make her a major player in a seriously long game, and complicit in the desecration of Mom's remains." I wish I had gotten a better look at the shard. "We have no way of knowing how long ago the vase was broken, or if all the pieces were accounted for prior to the case. She could have come by her charm another way."

Like through Jai Parish, who set the summoning circle in motion.

Or through the Bureau, after the shards were collected and logged into evidence.

For all we knew, she could have been the one who smashed it in the first place.

Goddess, could this get any more complicated?

"Perhaps." Asa crouched where the Lazarus had stood. "Luca has excellent timing."

"I'm willing to bet she was the heartbeat on the other side of Townhouse B's wall. Since we didn't invite ourselves in, she probably hit the tunnels after we left, then waited for us to find her."

"That means there's tunnel access through Townhouse B."

"The townhouse her buddy, The Ferret, attempted to trick us into booking."

"Do you think they've staked out the other four as well?"

"Depends," I decided, "on whether those have tunnel access. I doubt she was simply guiding us to the only vacant home in the network."

The house directly across the street from my very human friends.

How did Camber and Arden—and Nolan—tie into the tunnels, the sea monster, and the Garnier witch? The girls had no value to supernatural factions, except as bait. For me. And wasn't that a comforting thought?

"Your dad, Nolan, the girls, and us, all in one place at one time." Asa wiped dust off his cheek. "That's no coincidence."

"Don't forget Pontchy. Tibby is mixed up in this too, which

means the Garnier coven has a stake in what's going on." I sneezed into the bend of my arm. "They say New Orleans is a melting pot." I rubbed my ticklish nose. "Guess that makes us the ingredients."

If we returned the girl, the Garniers might back down, but that potential fix hinged on Dad cooperating, and I didn't see that happening if Tibby had the power to work miracles.

Luca might not have concrete proof Dad wanted Tibby for Mom's sake, but this convinced me she suspected it. She didn't have to know Mom was a manifested spirit to conclude his rebellion involved searching for a means to reunite with his wife.

The timer pinged, and I blew out a breath, hoping I was equal to the task.

"We better get started." I focused on the path ahead. "Clay will be getting antsy."

What should have taken maybe twenty minutes from end to end took us three times that. Aside from one ensnarement charm, meant to bind our legs together at the ankles, Luca didn't waste time or magic on seeding her escape route. That worked great for her, as far as strategies go, but not so much for us.

Hers was a quick getaway, but I couldn't be certain she hadn't booby-trapped the entire network, so I had to proceed as if she had or risk the consequences.

"Text Clay." I hit the end, at least one of them. "Tell him to stand his ground."

It would be embarrassing if Luca ran a loop around us then shot out the back door while we were inching along.

"Luca passed through there." Asa reached over my shoulder, phone in hand, to point out an alcove. "I can scent her and Tibby, but neither smell like black magic." He eased in front of me. "The rot I scented at the entrance isn't here either, so there must be at least two active routes."

This one, which we assumed led to Townhouse B.

The other, which must be used for the storage and transportation of bodies.

"You might as well go on ahead." I shoved his backside, and not just as an excuse to touch his butt. "You're already halfway there."

The smile he cast over his shoulder was feline in its pleasure.

I blame fascination for my confusion over whether he was happy to guide the way or happy I copped a feel.

The climb out was gradual, more what you would expect from stairs leading from a basement into a house. About the time my thighs began to protest, Asa quit walking and placed his palm on the underside of a wooden rectangle set into what must be the floor above us.

"There's a door here, but it's got no hardware."

"Let me squeeze by you." I slid with my back against the wall, splinters tearing at my shirt. "A spell was used to lock it." I could tell that much from holding my palm above the panel. "Do you smell that?" I breathed in. "Vetiver, green grass, and vanilla beans."

"Luca has no signature," Asa said, no doubt thinking of the shard. "Do you think Tibby did this?"

"Luca is hiding her power for a reason. I could see her using Tibby for small magics to avoid cluing us in."

Except, she knew I was—or had been—a black witch. Dad too. Why hide that from us?

Unless her secret was bigger than we gave her credit for.

"There are no dark undertones to Tibby's scent." Asa filled his lungs. "How can that be?"

"Maybe she hasn't been trained yet?"

Unlike necromancers who resuscitated dead humans, resulting in vampires, Lazarus witches brought the dead back exactly as they had been. Just with more sand topping off the hourglass of their lives.

That was how the dossier the Kellies pieced together from fragments of lore framed it anyway.

News of a practicing Lazarus witch in New Orleans would get around, and necromancers would come for her. They would kill her, and anyone who got in their way, in order to secure their power base.

Until she was old enough and powerful enough to hold her own, her coven was wise to hide her and her abilities.

Or they had been, until Mr. Garnier decided to spread word of her talent as leverage to get her back.

"Wouldn't Luca verify her skill set before abducting her?"

"As long as Dad doesn't know Tibby can't help him, she still has value to Luca."

Drawing magic from Colby, I spread power through my fingers into the wood until a hinge groaned with the weight of the door attached to it, and the whole thing crashed open with a bang I'm sure folks heard on the next block over. Above me, blackness loomed, dark and endless.

Wand in hand, I prepared for an attack, in case Luca had decided to wait around, but as soon as my head cleared the hatch, I was sucked into a vortex and spat out into an empty bedroom on unsteady legs.

Seconds later, Asa appeared with barely a hitch in his stride on his way to check on me.

"Whoever glamoured this place is a master." I examined the smooth wall behind us. "There's no seam."

A portal woven in the ether had hurled us anywhere from seven to ten feet through solid earth.

"How did we get here?" He ran his hand over the plaster. "A teleportation charm?"

"If the charm is original to the time period, then the tunnels were never connected to the houses via mundane means. Magic bridged the gap the whole time."

The mystery of the pentagram shape was solved, if my theory was correct.

"What does that mean for the wargs?"

"Either white witches were working in concert with the wargs during the outbreaks, or they were acting as gatekeepers." I left the room to wander the space. "The wargs couldn't have gotten from the houses into the tunnels with the bodies without help." I checked the fridge and found takeout containers from where Luca had been squatting in the house. "Though I'll admit, I don't see how they got dead bodies..."

"Patients," he finished the thought for me. "To lower the number of deaths reported in hospitals, they could have taken the infected poor off the street to treat them."

In 1853, the worst plague year on record, eight thousand or more people died, earning New Orleans the grim nickname Necropolis: City of the Dead.

"Except there is no treatment. It's wait, hope, and see."

And if the worst happened, which it often did, they stored the bodies under the houses then carried them out the tunnel to the river where they were taken to a mass grave on a barge. That was my new working theory, based on what we had learned so far. Too bad learning the past wouldn't help us in the present.

A soft buzz had Asa fishing his phone from his pocket. "Clay is demanding an update."

"Tell him to shut the hatch and make sure it seals. We don't want people wandering around down there. The illusion will fade within a few minutes of him leaving, so he doesn't have to worry about that part."

A text lit up my screen, and I thought for a second Clay must have gotten impatient.

>>*Boys have been sent home.*
>>*Except Aedan.*
>*I'm sorry it didn't work out like you hoped.*
>>*The weekend's not over yet.*
>>*Cupid might have one last arrow in her quiver.*
>*Good luck.*

If her aim was true, then we would all need it.

11

With the clock ticking, we needed to locate Dad. *Fast*. But I didn't have the bottle with me, and it was an oddly faithful servant to Aedan. That left me with one option before I got the type of magic involved that Dad would see coming and, no doubt, evade in order to avoid the confrontation that came along with it.

"Clear," Asa called on his way down from the second floor of Townhouse B.

Until Clay arrived, we might as well be productive. That meant Asa searching the residence for evidence and me updating Colby on everything Luca told us.

"The scent path leads from the bedroom to the kitchen and from the bedroom to the front door. There's nothing on the stairs or in the rooms on the other two floors."

Without magic to track, he was reduced to the human options of deodorant, soap, lotion, or perfume.

"Luca is using this as an entry point to the tunnels, not as a base. Or she was. I doubt she comes back."

True to her word, she had been waiting here for us to get with the program, nothing more.

"That leaves us one other potential basement that must be where the corpses are kept." He glanced back the way we came in. "Luca might have kept Tibby down there too."

"We would have to explore those tunnels to be sure."

"I can do that while you touch base with Aedan."

"You're going to let Blay run amuck down there, aren't you?"

"We need to bait him to the surface if you're ever going to confront him."

"*Confront* is a harsh word. I want him to know I forgive him, but if he ever does it again, I will delete his Mystic Realms *and* Mystic Seas profiles and make him start over from scratch using a freebie account."

"Cruel and unusual punishment indeed." He sounded approving. "We'll be back."

"I'll be here." I took a seat near the door. "You didn't think I was going to leave you two alone, did you?"

The smile growing on his face told me that yes, he would have expected it. From anyone else. But not from me. He was learning to trust I was his safety net. To believe I would catch him or break myself trying, no matter how far the fall.

Battling his inner daemon, Asa returned to the tunnels with his phone in hand to begin mapping.

Dread coiling in my stomach, I forced myself to relax before dialing Aedan. "Hey, coz."

"You heard about the boys?"

"I did." A swell of pride filled my chest. "The girls handled it well."

"Better than I would have," he agreed, an edge of violence in his voice. "What's up?"

"I don't suppose you brought the secret message bottle with you?"

"I wasn't sure if you would need it, so yes, I did."

"I knew you were my favorite cousin for a reason."

"The only other cousin you've met tried to kill you…"

"Minor detail," I assured him. "Any ideas on how to send it? Sink? Bathtub? Toilet?"

"I was thinking more along the lines of the lake or the river. They're more creeklike than a toilet bowl."

"Dad would probably appreciate it more too."

"What's the message?"

To guarantee his immediate response, I had to risk sharing information that might prove dangerous.

"Tell him I found his Lazarus, but she's only available for twenty-two hours." I touched the pendant at my throat, my palms going damp. "He'll know how to find me."

The note, he might ignore to avoid a confrontation.

The grimoire, and its boundless magic, he would not.

Raised voices in the background interrupted our conversation as the girls found where he had gone.

"Party time," Camber yelled as Arden laughed and plastic beads clacked near the phone.

"I'll let you know how it goes," Aedan said under his breath then ended the call.

A hard rap on the door kept me from stewing over the Luca problem, and I shot to my feet. Careful not to make a noise, I crept to the door and peered through its peephole to find a glowering golem. With a sigh, I opened the door and let him in.

"Good thing you're so stealthy." I crossed my arms. "Otherwise, people might think we broke in."

"It's a rental," he countered. "Neighbors are used to strangers traipsing in and out." He scanned behind me. "Where's Ace?"

"Blay is in the tunnels." I gestured toward the bedroom with the portal. "He's mapping them."

"Still hiding from you?"

"Yup."

"Smart man." He chuckled. "Remember that time I hid from you for a whole week?"

"I still haven't figured out how you did it." I leaned against the wall. "We were sharing a hotel room. You were there. I saw the takeout containers. You even baked apology cruffins. Cinnamon ones."

"Ah, cruffins." His eyes grew wistful. "The love child of muffins and croissants."

"All that drama because you mixed a bleach kit for your wig in my shampoo bottle and left it in the shower."

"I lost the little squirty thing that came in the kit, okay?" He huffed. "I didn't mean to turn you blonde."

"You should have thrown it away when you were done with it."

"I didn't want to toss it until I was sure I had the color right."

Usually, our bickering soothed me in a way few things did. Clay was one of the constants in my life. He had been the only thing I could count on for a long time. But I was being yanked in so many directions, I didn't have the energy to be snarky.

After a moment of silence, Clay dragged us back onto the real topic. "He's not going to be happy."

"If that witch is a dud? No. He's not."

"I meant with Luca for approaching you. She'll be lucky if he doesn't kill her."

"She didn't threaten me." I heard the throb of hurt in my voice. "She threatened his wife."

Even if she didn't grasp the nuances of Mom's condition, her actions put Mom at risk of a more final death than her current state. That was how Dad would see it. And if Luca cost him the opportunity, no matter how slim, to bring Mom back to life, Dad would kill her. Of that, I had no doubt.

"Rue…"

"Let's check on Blay." I shoved to my feet. "See if he needs help."

Before Clay could assure me Dad cared about me too, I brushed past him to the bedroom and used a spell to pry the unmarked doorway open. Expecting a cyclone to slurp me up, I was surprised by the stairs I was given instead.

Clearly, there were different rules for entering versus exiting the tunnels.

Far below me, Blay sat on the lowest step, elbows on his knees, staring at the grungy floor.

"How long have you been waiting?" I took the stairs at a clip. "Did you need help getting back in?"

"Blay sorry." He curved his shoulders inward. "Rue mad at Blay?"

Joining him on the cold concrete, I rested my head on his shoulder. "No, I'm not."

"Rue screamed." He glanced over at me. "A *lot*."

"I was surprised." I looped my arm through his. "I would appreciate if you didn't trick me like that again. I might have agreed to the jump, if you had asked." Probably not. "But you didn't, and it scared me."

"Blay sorry." He nuzzled the top of my head. "Rue forgive?"

"Of course I do, big guy." I petted him without prompting to show we were good. "Did you have any luck?"

"Yes." He stood in a rush. "Room there." He pointed down the tunnel. "Stinks like death."

"We're already down here." Clay weighed in from behind us. "We might as well check it out."

A hesitant smile on his lips, Blay offered me a hand up, which I took.

The fit would be tight for Clay, but if Blay could squeeze through, then he could too.

"Rue pet more." He passed me a section of his hair. "Blay lead."

For this, I had no one to blame but myself. "Did you pick up on anything else?"

"Magic." He nodded. "Black magic but not. Death magic but not."

These days, it was a given that black magic would pop up in our cases. I was the specialist, after all. Promotion or not, it made sense for me to be here. Even if I suspected the director had dispatched me for other reasons. Namely to track down his son.

That made two people who expected me to deliver Dad to them with a cherry on top.

But a face-off with the director would end with the director dead, and the animus vow killing Dad.

And a meeting with Luca would only accomplish the same thing, if in a more roundabout way.

"Luca didn't mention the bodies or Pontchy." I should have pressed her harder. "Any guesses how they tie in?"

"The bodies are a handy food source." Clay mirrored my thoughts. "I'm shocked she's going through the effort of stealing when she could just kill someone." He caught my look and frowned. "What? I didn't say I condoned murder for a pet's raw diet, just that it's a lot of extra work for a black witch."

"We don't know that Luca is a black witch," I reminded him. "The Ferret might be the practitioner."

Between the two of them, it made more sense she was the cause of the occasional stink we encountered, given Luca carried a shard with her.

"This it." Blay stepped into the rectangular chamber. "Bodies go there."

Inside the cramped room, I caught a whiff of formaldehyde, but there was no lingering decay odor.

Unless Pontchy was like a tiger shark, known as trash cans of the sea, preserved bodies would give it an upset stomach. If not outright kill it. Likely the chemical remnants came from storage in the morgue.

"The bodies don't spend much time here." Clay walked the perimeter. "The scent is too faint."

"They're fresh," I reminded him, "and the temperature down here has to be mid-sixties."

"What do you think, Blayer the Slayer?"

I ought to have known that along with a name came a plethora of, often terrible, nicknames from Clay.

"Few hours," he decided. "Not long."

"When only the freshest corpses will do." I sighed. "Any trace of Luca's BO or whatever you're tracking?"

"No Luca." He shook his head. "She not come here."

"The Ferret is her underling." Clay wrinkled his nose. "She probably lets her deal with the fish food."

"Makes sense," I had to agree. "She's the likeliest suspect for tampering with the morgues' feeds."

However, our single glimpse of her slight build made me doubt she was the one hauling bodies on her thin shoulders. There was a third accomplice. There must be. The math didn't add up otherwise. But who? A Toussaint witch? Or someone—some*thing*—else?

"You've got that look." Clay studied me. "You think we're missing something."

"Aren't we always?"

"That's why we're lucky so many of our suspects end up trying to kill us."

"Remind me how that's a good thing again?"

"It gives them time to launch into their villain—or *villainess*—monologue and fill in the blanks."

Hard to argue with that logic. Bad guys liked to hear themselves talk.

"To really be successful at our jobs, we need to get to the *fill in the blanks* part without almost dying."

"You know who does that? Sherlock Holmes. Last I checked, he's a fictional character. And he did a *lot* of cocaine."

Fictional or not, sympathy for Holmes welled in me. I was all too familiar with the power of addiction.

"Okay, okay. You win." I rolled my eyes. "We'll keep getting almost murdered for clues instead."

Spreading his hands, he graciously accepted the win. "That's all I ask."

"Blay." I backed out into the tunnel. "Did you find the entrance?"

"Door that way." He pointed over my shoulder. "Locked with magic."

"Good work." I stepped up to inspect it and found it identical to the first. A door without hardware that opened on a jump through space. "Any idea what's up there?"

"Here map." Blay passed over Asa's phone. "Check notes."

"You're under a souvenir shop now," Colby said, her voice tinny. "There's a deli behind it."

That…was not what I expected on either count. The location or the speaker.

For that to be true, this tunnel must have been rerouted to a more convenient location.

But convenient for whom? Luca and Nan? Or their mysterious accomplice?

"Colby?" I swallowed my surprise. "You've been listening in the whole time?"

"What?" Her voice warped and twisted with white noise. "I can't hear you."

"Colby tell Blay where to go," he explained. "Help track Blay's position."

"Has the signal been weak the whole time?" I held the phone higher, searching for a better signal, but the bars didn't budge. "Can she hear us at all?"

"She talk." He flashed the highlighted speaker button. "Blay listen."

"Okay." That smoothed my ruffled feathers a bit. "At least we've got that much to go on."

"A deli and a souvenir shop are both super public." Clay ruffled dust from his wig. "Do we really want to appear in the middle of either?"

"As much as I want to believe the low sobriety factor would work in our favor, you're right. We either go up and check them out as customers through the front door, or we wait until they close and sneak in after hours."

Offering me his hair, Blay suggested, "Glamour?"

"The portal might strip it off us." Sidestepping his silent request for pets, I touched the rotting hatch, which was definitely original. "Hard to say when we don't know what we're walking into or why this hatch was diverted to a new location."

Unless it was a necessary redirect after the collapse of so much of the underground system.

"Nothing ventured, nothing gained." Clay rubbed his hands together. "Let's do this."

"All right." I fed magic into the unseen lock until it clicked open. "Here goes nothing."

The portal inhaled me off the step then sneezed me out into a deli where I stumbled forward right into a chip display, which crashed to the tiles beneath me with a booming clatter and crunch.

Seconds later, Clay appeared behind me and whipped out his phone.

"I'll be saving this to the Rue blackmail file." He snapped a picture. "Too bad you're the boss. Otherwise, I could email this to the boss and tell them you fell down on the job. Literally."

"I could point out the reason you weren't flung is because you're *four hundred pounds*, but I won't."

Before Clay retaliated, Asa knocked into him, sending him careening toward the restaurant's front door.

"I can't tell if you're drunk or I am," said the man behind the counter. "Did y'all walk through a wall?"

"We came through the door." I indicated the one behind us. "I tripped and fell over the display, and they stumbled over me." I got to my feet and held out a bag of chips like I meant to buy them. "How much?"

As our fingers brushed, I pushed a little magic his way, enough to make his eyelids go heavy and his voice slur when he told me, "It's on the housh." A bubbling laugh escaped him. "I mean housh." He sat on the stool behind the counter. "No, no." He wiped a hand across his mouth. "*Housh.*"

"Why don't you take your break?" I wove suggestion into my words. "We can wait."

"Yeah." He leaned against the wall and shut his eyes. "Yeah."

As soon as I was sure he was out cold, I turned my attention back to the others.

"Storing a corpse in a deli can't be sanitary," Clay lamented. "His muffulettas looked good too."

Until he mentioned the possibility, I figured Luca's accomplice was using this as a shortcut, not a pit stop.

"I'll check the back." Asa cut behind the counter, careful not to bump the clerk. "See if they have a walk-in fridge or freezer."

"They don't," Colby informed us. "I checked earlier."

A beat later, I realized the line was static free, that we could talk to her.

"So, Luca—or her henchman—is just passing through."

"Hench*woman*," Clay countered. "No need to be sexist. Women can hench just as good as men."

A giggle bubbled out of Colby, but then she fell silent. "I hear something."

"Colby?" Blood turned to ice in my veins. *"Colby?"*

"Someone is here," she whispered before the call ended.

12

The drive to the marina, thwarted by traffic at every turn, was one of the longest of my life. I kept dialing Colby, and she kept not answering. Frustrated, I threw the phone, and it bounced across the floorboard.

"She got out once." Asa reached for my hand. "She can do it again."

"There was no music, and she didn't mention the strobes. She would have told me if it was that simple."

"What if another line formed?" Clay tossed out the idea. "After how rowdy it got last time, I could see her bailing to avoid it."

"Why would they come back?" Asa rubbed my knuckles. "We made it clear the bus was off-limits."

"Alcohol shortens memory spans." Clay was having no luck on the phone either. "Can't you go faster?"

Gaze finding Clay's in the rearview mirror, Asa said, "If you want me to run down tourists, then yes."

"He's doing the best he can," I defended while secretly agreeing with Clay. "The traffic is a nightmare."

When my phone rang, I didn't check the screen before answering with a breathless, "Yes?"

"Two wargs are prowling around your bus," Freddie reported. "Just thought you'd want to know."

Relief attempted to wash through me, but I held back the tide. "Male and female?"

"Aye," he confirmed. "They smell like mates." He paused. "And barbecue sauce."

Our wonky connection to Colby in the tunnels meant I hadn't warned her about Marita and Derry. I had so much else bouncing around in my head, I hadn't remembered to mention it after the signal cleared. It was my fault she got spooked, but at least she was safe from her unexpected guests.

"I appreciate the heads-up. We're on our way now."

"Do you require assistance?" A twinge of longing filled his voice. "They're already marinated."

"They're allies." I gripped Asa harder. "Don't harm them."

"As you like."

Texting the alpha warg and his mate, I checked with the guys. "You heard?"

"Marita and Derry?" Asa's lips twitched. "They didn't waste time getting here."

"Who eats barbeque in New Orleans?" Clay twisted his mouth. "A waste of Creole cuisine, in my book."

"You love barbeque." I slanted him a look, wishing the Mayhews would answer their phones. "It's one of your top five foods."

"Not in New Orleans during Mardi Gras." He sat back, the tension melting off him. "I should write a guide."

"The Grumpy Golem's Guide to Gastropubs?"

"I'm insulted by your word choice." He meshed his hands behind his head. "I might also steal that."

"Clay's Quest for Creole Cuisine."

"Okay, that one's good too." Clay brought his watch to his mouth. "I should be notating these."

"You could do a guidebook for every city we visit, telling other foodies where to find the best meals."

"It's a saturated market." He slumped, a shiny idea gone dull. "Probably a waste of time."

"How about set up one of those photo only social media accounts with a catchy title and post food pics there? You can build a following and then decide on the writing part."

"I'll think about it." He fiddled with his watch face. "I might be persuaded to try."

The thing about Clay was, he loved picking up new hobbies. Usually, they dovetailed with what we liked. Or what he thought we would like. It was his way of caring for those he loved, by engaging their interests. His last big obsession was Mystic Realms, but he passed that mantle on to Blay. It was time he was selfish and picked something that mattered to *him*, a way to express his creative side.

The distraction of hashing out the food guide worked, and soon we were pulling into the marina.

Sure enough, I spotted Marita and Derry sitting on the tailgate of his pickup, sharing a beer.

Wargs had to work hard to get drunk, and it didn't last long. Their metabolisms were too fast. But that didn't mean they didn't enjoy trying.

We parked behind them, and I got out, wiping my sweaty palms on my jeans.

"Hey." I waved, like a dork. "You're here."

Hopping down from the tailgate, Marita aimed for me with a spring in her step. As if she was happy to see me. I realized, when she got in touching distance, how glad I was to see her too.

"Rue." She picked me up like I was a feather and twirled me. "We're going to have *so* much fun."

"Asa." Derry leapt down and fired a football straight at his face. "Catch."

He did, seconds before it would have smashed into his nose, a smile stretching his cheeks.

"That all you got?" Clay inserted himself into the game, moving it away from the RV. I hoped that meant he had Colby in his sights and was providing cover for her to climb back in. "My granny can throw better than that."

"I'm just warming up." Derry stretched his arms. "You're gonna be crying for your granny soon."

Their easy camaraderie made me curious if Derry had been indoctrinated into the Mystic Realms cult.

"Bite me." Clay stole the ball from Asa and rocketed it into Derry's gut. "Or not. I wouldn't want to turn into a hairball under the full moon."

"I've showered after him," Marita called. "Full moons aren't a requirement."

"Keep talking," Derry countered, "and I'll show you a full moon."

"Derry requires no encouragement to drop his drawers, so unless you want an eyeful of my man's junk, I suggest we leave the boys to their game and find more ladylike entertainment." Marita opened the bag slung over her shoulder to reveal a selection of wine coolers. "Let's go be elegant somewhere else."

"The last time she broke out that bag," Derry warned, "she got drunk and fell off the roof."

"I thought I was a griffin, okay?" She threw a bottle at his head. "I saw my paws and got confused."

While the guys used the distraction to pummel each other in the head, we sneaked off to the pier.

As much as Colby loved her tech, I might turn to magic to give her a secondary means of communicating. I didn't want to suffocate her or baby her, but it was too stressful losing touch in times of crisis.

Gah.

Not-exactly-parenting was hard.

"A griffin, huh?" I couldn't hold in my laugh as we sat. "Thought you could fly?"

"A witch we do business with brews what she calls Downward

Dog. It's the only alcohol that sticks with a shifter. It's godawful tasting, but one can later, you forget your name. Too bad no one told me that before I tossed back four." She sat beside me. "Never again." She pulled out a solid black can with a grinning canine logo. "*After* tonight."

"Impressive." I accepted the piña colada she handed me. "I didn't know that was a thing."

"It's not available for sale. Only trade." She cracked her bad idea open. "For the novelty factor, mostly." Wincing, she gulped it down and tossed it. "We're basically her guinea pigs, and I'm okay with that."

"I'm more of an eater than a drinker." I picked at my label. "Loss of control isn't a great idea for me."

"I'm the same way during my time of the month." Humming, she chose a sangria next. "I crave raw meat like you wouldn't believe. If I don't eat enough, I start picturing everyone as bloody steaks with tiny arms and scrawny legs."

A laugh caught in my throat, gratitude for her not judging me making it hard to swallow.

"Tell me about this monster." She drained her bottle in three draws. "Have you seen it yet?"

Pointing toward the causeway, I explained what we knew so far. "Want to watch the show tonight?"

"Yes, please." She dipped a toe in the water. "Can we also ditch Derry?"

"Competitive much?"

"He got to see Old Man Fang, and I didn't. I need the boost to my street cred."

"Understood." I scanned the lake for signs of Freddie, but he was gone again. "I don't see our ride."

"Do we need a boat?" She lifted the hem of her shirt to reveal a swimsuit. "It's not that far to swim."

For a warg with her muscle definition, I imagine it was an invigorating lap.

An idea occurred to me as I debated how to get out there, and I could have smacked myself.

"I can fly." I set aside the drink. "I know a spell, I mean. For wings. But I've only used it once."

Other than flapping them in the director's face to cover for Dad, I hadn't put them to much use.

"I can't think of a better way to test them than with a nice monster-infested lake beneath you."

"True." I kicked off my shoes. "We have an hour before the dinner bell rings."

Marita shot to her feet and stripped out of her shorts and tee. "Let's do this."

"Aren't you worried about swimming with a *sea monster*? His name is Pontchy, by the way."

"From what you've told me, he's a scavenger." She tied her hair in a bun. "I'm a predator."

"Hey, predator," Derry called, his arm hooked around Clay's throat. "Remember your noodle."

"Noodle?"

"Not the best swimmer." She held up a finger. "Be right back."

The opening gave me a chance to try Colby again.

>*Answer me or suffer the consequences.*

>>*Back in the bus. Phew. That was a workout.*

>*Sorry I didn't warn you ahead of time. I didn't think they would be here so soon.*

>>*Text me when I need to get scarce.*

>*Touch base with Clay. He has an idea for you.*

>>*Will do.*

With that weight off my mind, I returned my attention to Marita, who had pillaged their truck bed and was now lugging an armful of floats, noodles, and foam boards to our spot.

"I'll bring a board for you," she decided, "in case I need to swim you back to shore."

Hands cupping his mouth, Derry yelled, "Don't you mean *noodle* her back to shore?"

"Shut it, Derriere." She shook her butt at him then sighed at me. "Mates, am I right?"

"I'm not mated yet."

"Next best thing." She pulled on cartoon flamingo water wings. "Oh, I spoke to Ali. She dug up a few stories, but nothing concrete." She checked their fit. "Want me to ask for more dirt?"

"Thanks, but I don't think it will help us as much as I hoped it would when I called you."

"Okay." She shook out her arms. "Let me know if you change your mind."

"Are those goggles?" I swallowed a laugh. "And a nose clip?"

"I know what you're thinking." She presented her noodle, slung with a hammock-like seat. "Where does she get her toys?" She selected a board for me. "The answer is—the dollar store."

"Are you sure about this?" I admired her arsenal. "You aren't going to drown, are you?"

"I haven't yet." She produced a noodle duct-taped into a circle with a mesh shopping bag zip tied around the edge. She dumped her drinks in before it hit me I was looking at a floating cooler. "Let's pray that trend continues."

Uncertainty twisted my stomach at the thought of leaving her unsupervised—and drinking—in water.

"I can practice flying later." I took a noodle hammock from her stash instead. "Let's go float."

For years, the lake had been too polluted from shell-dredging and urban runoff for swimmers. But it had since been cleared for recreational use. Thank the goddess too, since I had already drunk gallons of it on this trip.

"Don't forget your drink," she sang as she slipped into the warm water. "You might work up a thirst."

I wish I had a bottle of water, but I didn't want Marita to think I was lame if I ran into the RV to get one like a lightweight. I hadn't gotten around to ordering Blay's swim trunks, and I didn't have a swimsuit yet either. When packing for this trip, I hadn't anticipated me getting in the water with Pontchy. Or Marita.

Still, friends don't let friends drink and noodle. I don't think. I wasn't entirely sure, since it had never come up before, but it seemed like a good rule of thumb. Like something Clay would say.

Wriggling out of my jeans, I kicked them to dry ground and pulled my shirt over my head, leaving me in a peach-tone underwear set. From a distance, it might pass for a bikini. Marita didn't care, so I tried my best not to either.

We drifted leisurely toward the causeway, moving into position for the body drop.

The bizarreness of the whole situation was enough to make me smile. "I'm glad you guys could make it."

"Derry has a man crush on Asa." She kicked her feet. "Or maybe on the daemon?"

"Why not both?" I flicked water at her like I would have with Clay. "What's with that look?"

"The truth?" She sipped her drink. "Derry has wanted to meet you forever. Your mom and Meg are pack legends. Meg warned him off you for the longest time, but I figured it was because the reminder of your mom, after everything that happened, was too painful for you."

More likely, Meg had been protecting her descendants.

From me.

An unasked question lingered in the silence, making me wonder how much she knew about my past.

"Meg was right to keep the pack away from me." I rolled the bottle between my palms. "I was a black witch. A powerful one. A nasty one." I glanced up to see how she had taken the admission. "You wouldn't have liked me much back then, so it's for the best we just met."

"I heard the rumors." She stared at me. "But you also keep in regular contact with Meg, so…"

"So?"

"I knew we'd be here, one day."

"On the lake, in noodle hammocks, about to watch someone feed a sea monster a dead body?"

"Honestly?" She cracked a smile. "Not surprised at all."

"That makes one of us." Kicking my legs, I spun in a circle, and my head kept on spinning. "This is nice."

"You and Clay throw off hardcore bestie vibes," she observed, "but sometimes you need to cut the testosterone with some estrogen."

Thinking on Camber and Arden, how much I enjoyed spending time with them, I had to agree. "Yeah."

For years, they had scratched the natural witch itch to have a coven surrounding me.

"We should vacation together in the summer or something," she tossed out casually. "It could be fun."

As much as I would love to, I had a confession to make first. "I have a familiar."

One I couldn't exclude for three months out of the year without breaking her heart, and mine.

"Bring it. I don't care." She dipped her head back. "If it's a cat, I promise we won't chase it."

"She's a very special familiar." I lowered my voice to ensure it didn't carry. "People would kill for her."

And if Marita betrayed my tipsy confidence, she would learn firsthand how far I would go to protect Colby.

"Okay." Marita's frown deepened. "What am I missing?"

The alcohol spun my thoughts out like ripples across the water, reminding me why I avoided drinking.

"She's like a daughter to me." I hadn't expected Colby to be so hard to explain. "She's not an animal. She isn't that kind of familiar. She is—*was*—a fae girl." The halting story cut its way free of my throat, and an odd sense of peace swept over me that was, probably, not from the slight buzz. "You can't tell anyone."

"I understand."

"Cliché as it is, I'm going to say it anyway." I let her glimpse the old me, the rotten core beneath a glossy red apple skin. "I will kill you if you hurt her, or if your actions result in harm coming to her. That goes for you and anyone you tell. No one who raises a hand against her is permitted to live."

"Wargs protect their pups above all else. Even our mates." She extended her hand, pinky up. "If I hurt your little girl, you won't have to come for me. I'll turn myself in."

Had Clay not made me pinky promises before, I would have been stumped as to what the gesture meant. I owed him thanks for teaching me the basics of friendship. I wasn't a pro, but I wasn't as awkward with her as I had been with him. He had tamed a feral beast. All Marita had to do was avoid any sudden movements that might get her bitten.

We made our promise, and I checked the time. "Not long now."

"Do you smell that?" She wrinkled her nose. "Like warm moss and fresh earth."

"I smell fishy water, but that's about it."

"Meat." She leaned forward in her hammock. "Sour meat."

Whatever Marita picked up on, I couldn't help her identify. I was little more than human when out bobbing in the water. Which seriously made me question why I agreed to go swimming in the first place.

Oh.

Right.

Peer pressure.

"Look." She pointed toward the causeway. "Something's moving up there."

"How can you tell?" I leaned forward, squinting at the bridge spans. "I don't see anything."

"Fun fact." Her incisors grew long in her mouth. "I'm wearing a charm to help me see through glamour."

The sting was instant, the rush of guilt that she thought I would hurt or trick her left me raw. "I see."

"This has nothing to do with you." She grew animated. "No, listen." She hooked her fingers through the mesh of my seat. "Glamour would explain why no one has seen the sea monster, right? It's aquatic. So, it makes sense it's got some natural camouflage. That's why I bought it." She reeled me in. "Okay, Derry bought it." She extended her arm and shook the fishbone bracelet on her wrist. "But I stole it from his pocket while copping a feel fair and square."

"It actually works?" I was too stunned to break the news that I had seen Pontchy. "That's...wow."

Not only was she sitting low in the water, but her hand had been submerged most of that time.

"There's a tactical witch coven out of Georgia who specializes in waterproof magic. Their main source of income is search and rescue, but they've gotten into the salvage business in the last year or two. Anyway. They use Meg for their stickier contracts. That's how I know about them."

Despite what I paid Meg, I hadn't realized how lucrative her afterlife business was for the pack in terms of trading favors and establishing working relationships within echelons of the paranormal community.

"I've never heard of a coven with that specialization."

"Rumor has it they interbred with freshwater mermaids to temper their powers, but they smell like witches to me." She tossed back the rest of her drink and reached for a strawberry daiquiri. "Although, if you're going to fabricate a backstory, then merwitch is pretty badass."

Mermaids were murderous, carnivorous, and malicious. With the best PR department in the entire paranormal world, in my opinion. Otherwise, *The Little Mermaid* wouldn't be a classic fairy tale. It would be a cautionary tale.

"Can I touch it?" I wanted to read its power level. "I wonder if it would work for me."

"Sure." She held out her arm. "Grope away."

A charm I hadn't noticed earlier dangled from the fishbones. A gold doubloon the size of my thumbnail. I couldn't tell if it was authentic or only decorative, a nod to how that coven earned its living. I sensed no magic when I pinched it between my fingers, but when I glanced at the causeway, I almost dropped my bottle in the lake.

A grayish figure built like a gorilla swung hand to meaty hand under the bridge with the agility of a spider monkey.

"I need to get me one of these." I kept my hold light so as not to damage it. "What is that?"

Even with the illusion ripped off, the creature blended with the aged concrete, and my vision wasn't a match for Marita's lupine eyes.

"Based on the smell?" She pursed her lips. "I would guess a troll."

"Stone troll." That seemed most likely. "Makes sense."

"You want to borrow the bracelet?" She shook her wrist. "You could fly up and take a closer look."

"That's not a bad idea." I measured the distance to the pilings. "Keep your bracelet, though. Just in case."

With no time to waste, I flopped out of my hammock and swam hard to beat the troll to the high point.

Blay made climbing the concrete seem easy, but I cursed under my breath as I dragged myself out of the water. Had I been sober, it would have been tough. Fuzzy around the edges, I was *not* having much luck.

Drawing a thread of power from Colby, hoping it would perk me up, I began murmuring the wing spell.

For the longest time, nothing happened, but then rancid shadows exploded from my back. Moments later, they lightened to a shimmering gray that carried faint notes of hydrangea.

Unsure how to work the things, I pictured Dad's easy mastery of flight and did my best to imitate him. It wasn't pretty, but I did get airborne. Eventually. Hoping for the best now that I wasn't as waterlogged, I cast a spell to see past the troll's glamour.

Strapped to its back was a lump wrapped in a white sheet and bound with twine. That must be dinner.

As I rose, I began to hear it humming under its breath, which gave me hope for a civil conversation.

"Hi there." I struggled to get near him but out of reach. "Are you the one feeding the sea monster?"

The troll locked gazes with me, sniffed the air, then yelped like a scalded cat. It hurled the body at me, tagging my left arm and spinning me out. During the seconds it took me to find my balance, it pivoted and ran. Well, swung. Whatever. It made its getaway, leaving me to fly after it.

And by fly, I mean claw at the sky and try not to splatter on the water.

13

"I just want to talk," I called after it. "I'm not going to hurt you."

"Black witch, black witch," he sang under his breath, and it was a male voice. "Not gonna catch me."

"Slow down." I struggled for more speed. "I'll pay you for your help."

"Already got a job, black witch." His humming reached a fever pitch. "Don't need another."

"Who hired you?" I was falling behind. "Luca?"

Several yards ahead, his hand closed over a portion of causeway that made him hiss. Must have been iron. His momentum worked against him. He was already mid-swing and nursing his curled fingers in a tight fist when he slipped and plummeted toward the water.

Again, my inexperience cost me the opportunity to catch him. I would have dislocated a shoulder if I offered him a hand, and he would have dragged me under with him if he had taken it, but I still tried.

"Don't bother," Marita called, paddling toward me. "He sank like a stone."

The joke would have made Clay laugh. Me too. Under different circumstances.

"He'll drown." I glanced around, wishing for Freddie and his rustbucket to appear, half convinced he was hiding under his glamour, watching the show and cackling. "We can't leave him down there."

Sticking bottle caps to her face, she laughed at my panic. "Did you see the lichen on his cheeks?"

"I was distracted by the corpse he hurled at my head."

"Take it from me. He spends a lot of time in water for them to grow in such a distinctive pattern."

"So, what? He'll sink to the bottom then walk out of the lake?"

"That's my guess—" Marita's eyes rounded. "Rue?"

"Yeah."

"I don't want to swim anymore." She reached for me like a child asking for its mother. "Starting now."

"What's wrong?" A slow ripple arrowed toward where Marita floated, and I understood. "The body."

We had gotten too close to the feeding grounds. Dinner was in the water, and so was she. The loud splash of the rock troll smacking the surface had as good as slapped the sea monster in the face.

It was here, and it was hungry.

"It touched my leg." Marita grabbed my noodle and ripped the hammock off, wielding it like a sword. "It's touching me." She wiggled and flailed. "Oh, God, Rue. Tell Derry I love him, and to suck it."

"Uh, okay." I locked forearms with her, muscles straining with each wingbeat. "Do I want to know why?"

"If I get eaten by a sea monster, I will go down in pack history. Nothing he does will ever top that."

Already exhausted, I barely tugged her knees clear of the water. "Are you serious?"

"Rue," she gasped. "Its tentacle is climbing up the inside of my leg."

With one final heave, I yanked her clear, only to squint against a splash behind her. "What the...?"

Laughter rang out across the lake as a suddenly lighter Marita clung to me, wrapping her legs around my waist. We pivoted to look down and found Derry, spluttering and breathless. And right behind him, Blay popped his head out of the water, his horns glistening.

"Blay not prank Rue," he told me solemnly. "Derry prank Marita."

"I'm going to kill you." Marita kicked off me, launching herself at her mate. "You idiot."

"You should have seen your face." He caught her and reeled her in for a kiss. "You thought it had you."

"Derry not nice to Marita," Blay tacked on, eager to distance himself from Derry. "Blay nice to Rue."

"Mmm-hmm."

Hovering required more energy than I had left after my flying lesson. I released the spell and dropped next to Blay, who plucked me out of the water and set me on his shoulders. I slumped against him, totally spent. I was about to check on Marita when I realized the wet noises had gone from violent to...well...slightly less violent. Wherever that "tentacle" had been heading, I didn't want to stick around and find out.

"Let's go." I gripped his horns like reins. "I'm done with water."

"Rue pet." He slapped me in the face with a hank of soaked hair. "Blay swim."

"I'll take that deal." I glanced over my shoulder then promptly wished I hadn't. "You guys realize there's still a body in the lake. And a sea monster."

Neither quit sucking face long enough to answer, but I had warned them. That counted in my book.

Back on shore, Clay fished me out and set me on the dock. "Those two might be worse than you two."

"They're willing to risk life and limb for a make-out session."

After Blay allowed Asa to surface, Asa climbed out, breathless from his exertion.

"They've been mated for decades," he panted, "and still find joy in one another."

"Joy in *tormenting* one another." I wavered my hand. "Slight difference."

"They're keeping the spark alive," Clay weighed in. "You should take notes."

There was no possible future I could imagine where I lacked a spark with Asa. There were still times, after a long day, that I glanced at the clock and realized I had lost minutes to staring at him rather than engrossed in my current book. Knitting, working, or just existing. I couldn't take my eyes off him. I wasn't afraid he would disappear, exactly. More like he would wake up, realize who he was with, and finally see he could do so much better.

A waft of carrion rode the breeze, and I tensed as a dark figure landed heavily on a nearby picnic table.

"Rue," he said gruffly. "I got your message."

"Dad." I ignored the uptick in my pulse, the throb of hurt at seeing him. "We need to talk."

The guys would overhear us, but I moved as if to pull Dad off to the side for this private conversation.

Except Dad didn't follow, forcing me to rock back into place. "You want to do this here? Fine."

"Why are you in New Orleans?"

"A case."

"You tracked me here using the bottle. There was a chip of some kind in the cork."

So much for sneaking that past him. "I did."

Note to self: Dad might be as clueless about modern tech as me, but I inherited my paranoia from him.

"Then a case fell into your lap, one involving the same city, and you didn't question it?"

"I questioned it, but you—" I bit the inside of my cheek. "I'm worried about you."

"Are you speaking as my daughter or as the deputy director of Black Hat?"

A slap across the face would have hurt less, but of course he knew about the promotion.

"You made a mess with Parish." A thread of anger wove through my words. "You left me to clean it up."

The spark of my temper disarmed him. "I am sorry for that."

"Not half as sorry as I am, believe me." I studied the empty space around him. "Where is she?"

As tight as my throat was right now, I wasn't sure I could get out her name or if I should speak it here.

"Safe," he said softly. "You mentioned the Lazarus witch?"

That he didn't trust me with Mom's location shouldn't have come as a shock. I hadn't told him about Colby either. Based on our father/daughter track record, I doubted I would ever introduce them. The alcohol that tipped me toward confiding in Marita wasn't nearly enough to loosen my tongue around him. Rather, his presence was sobering.

"That's why you're here, right?" I searched his face, hoping to find answers there. "To bring her back."

His gaze landed on Asa then slid to Clay before spearing out across the water to the splashing wargs.

Oh, sure. Now he wanted privacy. Too bad I didn't care what he wanted at this point.

Seeming to sense that, he let his voice go cold. "Where is the witch?"

"Ask your buddy Luca. She's the one holding Tibby hostage contingent upon your return to service."

An emotion spread across his face I couldn't read, one so bitter and furious maybe it had no name.

Clay might label it soul-quenching fury and blame it on her involving me as the cause, but I knew better.

"I'll make the arrangements." He spread his wings. "Thank you for playing intermediary."

"Let me help." I hadn't given the words permission, but they escaped all the same. "For Mom."

The ice cracked then, and he crossed to me, cupping my cheek. "You lie as badly as your mother."

"She deserves peace." I gripped his wrist. "It's what she wanted, what she asked me to give her."

"She *deserves* to be here." He broke my hold. "We *deserve* to be a family again."

"We don't always get what we deserve."

The director alive and plotting against us while Mom lay cold, in pieces, in unmarked graves was proof of that.

"Your mother is fading." He wiped a hand over his mouth like that might erase the words he had spoken. "We'll revisit this when she's better."

"She's dead," I said, hating the cruel edge his selfishness brought out in me. "She won't recover from that."

"I failed to save her once." His shoulders twitched. "I won't again."

Without another word, he launched into the sky, and I watched him go.

As much as it hurt, I was getting used to him leaving me.

"Are you all right?" Asa brushed a tear I hadn't given permission to fall off my cheek. "That couldn't have been easy."

"I'm as good as I'm going to get." I reached into my back pocket. "Give me a minute, and we can go."

"Go?" He followed me to the picnic table. "What did I miss?"

"I hit him with a tracking spell." I fixed a smile on my mouth. "He was too wound up to notice."

The contact he initiated had given me the perfect opportunity to affix a quick bit of magic to him.

As usual, Asa saw too much. "That's why you picked a fight?"

"I wanted to say those things. I meant them. They just happened to serve a purpose."

A tattered map worked as my focal, and Asa was nice enough to hold its curling edges flat while I dug in my kit for the crystal pendulum I used for locator spells. I wound its silver chain around my index finger then moved the tip over New Orleans and waited for its swaying to snap into a focused location.

"What did we miss?" Marita padded over to me, adjusting her swimsuit top. "Who are we looking for?"

"Trouble," Clay answered with a smile. "Have a nice swim?"

"It would have been better if we saw Pontchy." Derry shook water from his hair. "We, uh, missed the show."

"With all that splashing, I worried Marita was drowning." Clay lifted his eyebrows. "That's what you were doing, right? Saving her?"

"Yes," Derry said slowly, and Marita punched him in the arm hard enough to rock him back a step.

"Got it." I circled the spot where the pendulum stilled with a marker. "Let's go."

"Are we invited?" Marita shucked her water wings. "I'm willing to lend my nose to the cause."

"That gives me an idea." I texted a quick pic to Colby. "Feel like hunting down a rock troll?"

"Rock troll?" Derry rubbed his hands together. "Sounds like fun."

"You say that now," Marita teased, "but it swung like Donkey Kong under the causeway."

"If it's too hard for you..." I spread my hands. "I totally understand."

"A rock troll is too hard," Clay snickered. "Oh, Rue, you bring me such joy."

The sad thing was, after hanging around with Clay for so many years, I didn't catch half the bad jokes I made on reflex before they escaped my mouth. We had been partners for too long. His warped sense of humor had infected me.

"Challenge accepted." Marita stuck out her pinky. "I'll find the troll, even if I have to throw Derry off the bridge to do it."

Slapping his hand over ours to break the promise, he asked, "What does one thing have to do with the other?"

"You know payback's coming for the stunt you pulled." Her eyes glittered. "Just giving you a few ideas to stew over in the night." She sauntered up to him, stopping when their chests bumped. "When you're sleeping next to me, dead to the world."

"You're insane." He lowered his head, capturing her lips. "I love that about you."

"Yes, well, if you were married to you then you would have gone crazy by now too."

"I prefer to believe crazy attracts crazy." He grinned down at her, eyes golden. "And I am *very* attracted right now."

"We'll handle the troll." Marita shoved her man back. "You guys do what you've got to do."

"Be careful." I glanced between them. "Meg would kill me if I got you hurt."

"Whatever happens, it's not your fault." Derry waved off my concern. "We volunteered."

People really ought to stop telling me that when, if it wasn't for me, they wouldn't be in danger in the first place.

Sliding his hand into mine, Asa pulled me away before I could waste what little time we had before Dad found Luca and things got ugly. I let him guide me to the SUV, knowing I had to pinpoint our destination before we got there, but hating we were leaving friends behind. Even if they could fend for themselves.

"Focus." Asa started the engine while Clay settled in. "The wargs can call on pack if they need help."

"Yet another reason why Black Hat is broken." I ground my knuckles into my thigh. "We ought to be able to call for backup without worrying our fellow agents will maim, eat, or kill us."

"File a complaint with the deputy director." A smile flirted with his mouth. "Let her figure it out."

"Funny." I elbowed him. "I didn't accept the job to fix the system. I did it to protect Samford."

The GPS pinged as Colby remotely fed it our destination based on the photo I sent her.

"Sure you did." Clay patted my head. "That's why you started a to-do list in your notebook."

"That's not a to-do list." I swatted him away. "That's the kill list you suggested I write."

"Oh." He cleared his throat. "Well, then, this is awkward."

\>\>Nan is Nanette Bakersfield.

\>You can give directions and perform background checks at the same time?

\>\>I'm a moth of many talents.

\>You don't have to tell me twice.

\>\>She hacked the security system in Townhouse A. She had eyes on the girls.

\>Ugh.

\>Wait. She had *eyes*?

\>\>I poked them out.

\>That's my girl.

\>\>She had feelers in the RV too. Another magi-virus. I recognized a string of code and compared it to what she used at Townhouse A. They're identical. That makes her responsible for our rave, but I don't think she meant to throw us a party. Whatever she was planning, your magic protected us from her intentions.

Ready to get this show on the road, I settled in to pinpoint where Dad had gone to meet Luca.

"The monument." I recognized the area. "They're meeting there."

Their rendezvous point was a five-minute walk to Bourbon Street, which partied hard until dawn.

An excess of humans in a public space meant they would both, in theory, be on their best behavior. But I had my doubts. Dad had already proven himself willing to break supernatural law in pursuit of his goals.

Traffic moved at a crawl, but we finally reached a point in walking distance and parked on the street.

One foot out the door, heart pounding with the hunt, I growled when my phone rang. "Hollis."

"The girls are missing," Aedan rushed out. "They were right beside me, and then they were gone."

"Okay." I pressed a hand to my chest, over my pounding heart. "Do you think they ditched you?"

As much as Arden enjoyed Aedan's company, she and Camber had wanted a girls' trip. I was the one who forced a chaperone on them. With the recent boy trouble, they might have decided a night alone was just what the doctor ordered to shake off those bad vibes.

"It's possible," he admitted. "I searched for ten minutes before I called you."

"I assume they're not answering their phones."

"That was the first thing I tried, but it's so loud. Even on vibrate, it's hard to tell when it's ringing."

Between the teeth-jarring speakers, the jostling crowd, and the sensory overload, I could believe it.

"I'll send backup." I had two perfect candidates. "Marita and Derry Mayhew. They're friends of mine."

"Black Hat?"

"No." I almost laughed at the idea of trusting my fellow agents with the girls. "Meg's relatives."

"Wargs," he said thoughtfully. "Good timing on their visit."

"They came to hunt Pontchy, but I'm sure they won't mind pitching in."

"Tell Clay just because he named it doesn't mean he can keep it."

"Will do." I rubbed my breastbone. "Hang in there, okay? We'll find them."

The second he hung up, I dialed Marita.

"Done already?" She whistled soft and low. "We're barely on the bridge."

"Can you help track someone else?"

"Depends." She sounded willing to be persuaded. "Are we talking better than a rock troll?"

"The two human girls who work in my shop are here, and they've gone missing." Already counting on her agreement, I texted her photos of the girls and Aedan. "I was hoping you could meet up with my cousin in the Quarter. He was with them when they disappeared."

"We'll be right there," she promised, tone solemn. "Family first."

"Family first," I agreed, and the line went dead. "Guys..." Framed that way, I had trouble pushing myself onward. "Those girls are more family to me than my parents." I faced Asa and Clay. "What do I do?"

"Take Clay." Asa squeezed my shoulder. "I'll help Aedan and the Mayhews."

"We'll join them as soon as we're finished with Saint and Luca." Clay took my elbow. "Come on, or we'll miss the epic showdown."

A sour taste flooded the back of my throat, but I let Asa go and tried to focus on locating our targets. With the monument off the Quarter, we didn't have far to go, and neither did he. "There they are."

Dad stood with his back to us, Luca across from him. Tibby wasn't present, but she must be nearby.

If Luca meant to honor her bargain after Dad had broken his.

Twisting my fingers in the wind, I wove a spell that carried their voices to us.

"You gave your word." Luca's tone cracked over us like a whip. "I honored my half of the bargain, Hiram. I set you free."

"I need time." He held his ground, his expression as empty as hers. "And that witch."

"Your wife has been dead for a long time."

A beat of silence lapsed, and I held my breath, half expecting him to kill her for daring to speak of Mom.

"I'm aware," he said coldly, "but thank you for the reminder."

"Do you really believe the Garnier witch can conjure your Vonda out of thin air?"

Mom wasn't thin air so much as semisolid goop, but still. The point held. Even if Luca didn't know it.

"What I want with the witch is my business." His fingers tapped against the outside of his thigh in a pattern that convinced me he was readying a defensive spell in case he needed one. "I will keep my word, but I have unfinished business that needs to be settled before I declare outright war on my father."

"That wasn't part of our agreement."

"Agreements change."

"I'm on a bit of a schedule myself." Her temper sparked again. "Events have been set into motion."

Hard as it was to tear myself away from them, I tuned out their conversation to focus on the heartbeats in the area. There were many. So, so many. Deafening when I let myself linger for too long. But at last, I singled out an oddly muffled one near where they were standing.

"Come on." Nails biting into Clay's arm, I led him away from their confrontation. "We don't have long."

"Long for what?" He glanced over his shoulder. "We're going to miss the smackdown."

As soon as we were clear, I broke into a run toward Townhouse B, and Clay kept pace with ease.

"The Garnier witch is in the tunnel." I bounded up the stairs to the front door. "We have to—"

"Rue?"

Crushing my eyes closed, I banged my forehead against the polished wood. "This isn't happening."

"What are you doing here?" Arden called from behind us. "When did you arrive?"

There was no use pretending I didn't hear her. She had caught me out, fair and square.

"Did you follow us?" Camber crowded me on the steps. "Seriously?"

"Did you ditch Aedan?" I spun the accusatory tone around on her. "Seriously?"

"You rented the house across from ours?" Camber didn't back down. "Don't you trust us?"

"I don't have time for this." I heard how bad it sounded, but I couldn't take back the words. "Call Aedan right now. He's terrified something happened to you." I sent magic through my palm to unlock the door. "We'll discuss this later."

"We have an emergency." Clay, who had kept his distance, spoke up for me. "Just call Aedan, okay?"

"Everything is an emergency with you lately." Arden crossed her arms over her chest. "We've worked for you for years, we've been running the shop alone for months, but you're treating us like children."

"You're acting like children." I held my temper in check. "You could have asked Aedan to wait for you at the townhouse. You didn't have to get him out in public then run off and hide from him without a word. He was terrified something happened to you. We all were."

As usual, I had said the wrong thing. As always, it was too late to take it back.

"You sent Aedan to spy on us." Camber climbed another step. "Is that why he's working with us too?"

"I'm sorry, I really am." I turned away from them. "But I can't do this right now."

Leaving them on the stoop felt like the first step down a short road leading to a dead end. Tears stung the backs of my eyes, but I had known this would happen. Eventually. I just hadn't expected it tonight.

"They'll be fine." Clay locked up behind us to keep them out. "You can fix this later."

The problem with *later* was how rarely it came around.

"I'm not sure I can." I wiped my cheeks dry with my hands. Stupid feelings. Stupid heartache. Stupid *me*. "From their perspective, it's pretty damning."

Checking ahead to ensure Luca had set no traps since our last visit, I ignored Clay breathing down my neck to focus on any changes within the house. I found none.

"Tell them you worried when you heard Nolan flaked."

"Then drove in and rented a house across the street to spy on them instead of knocking on their door?"

"It does sound bad when you put it like that..."

"More lies won't fix this." I relocated the hidden doorway and used the unlocking spell to access the stairs. "Maybe nothing will."

More than hurt feelings were at stake here. Tibby's life was on the line, and I had to prioritize.

Whatever her coven's sins, she didn't deserve to be a pawn in Luca's match against my father.

The staircase appeared, and we took the steps down into the smoke-and-herb murk of the tunnels.

Thanks to Blay, we only had to check our phones to orient ourselves. As we crept toward the monument where Dad and Luca quarreled, I identified the same heartbeat from above and followed it to its source.

Tibby sat with her knees drawn to her chest in an antechamber, where she kept a bundled corpse not yet on the menu company. Her simple cotton dress was muddy, and tears flowed down her sharp cheeks. Her fragile wrists had been rubbed raw, her blood a steady trickle, and a single candle held the darkness at bay.

"Hey." Hands up to show they were empty, I crept toward her. "We're going to get you out of here."

Until her gaze swung up to mine, I had pegged her as mid to late twenties. Her heavily lined features, courtesy of the filth caked on her face, had convinced me she was older. Up close? She was a teenager. I was sure of it.

"I remember you from the meeting." She sniffled, unable to wipe her nose. "You work for Luca."

"I don't, but my dad does." I shifted my attention toward the monument. "That's who Luca is meeting with now." I indicated Clay. "We'd like to get you out of here before that becomes a complication."

"How can I trust you don't want to use me too?"

"We're getting you out." I rested a hand on her shoulder, and she recoiled from my touch. "Then we're setting you free."

"Your father…"

"…wants you to resurrect my mother with a handful of bones and her spirit."

"I can't do that." She wet her lips, her eyes shining. "I haven't come into those powers yet."

That confirmed why there was no hint of decay to her magic. "Does Luca know?"

"Y-y-yes." She trembled as fear settled in. "I told her, but she didn't care."

Luca had known, just as I did, that Dad wouldn't believe Tibby wasn't the solution to his problems sight unseen.

Gripping her elbows, I helped her rise. "Your family can protect you?"

"Luca caught us unaware." She took a steadying breath. "It won't happen again."

"Good." I shuffled her beside me. "I'm going to try to free you on the run."

Or, in her case, a hobbling power walk that left me concerned for her overall health.

"Okay." She thrust out her bound hands, chest pumping to keep up with me. "I'm game."

Fingers circling her thin wrists, I pulled magic from Colby and fed it through to the manacles.

Nothing happened.

Intuition told me to draw from myself instead, from my gray magic, allowing the black to seep through.

On the next push, the sharp vines cracked and crumbled and fell away.

"T-t-thank you." A sob of relief tore through her. "You're really going to let me go?"

"We really are," I promised her. "As soon as we get out of here."

"They're coming." Clay pressed a hand into my back. "We need to move, Dollface."

"She's doing the best she can." I heard, seconds later, what had set him on edge. Heavy footsteps thundering toward us. "Do you mind if he carries you?"

"I guess not?" She raised her slight arms with what strength she had left. "I just want out of here."

"Piggyback is the only way that works," he warned. "The walls are too close for anything else."

"O-o-kay?" She cleared her throat. "Okay. Yes. I can do that."

To get in front, Clay wedged himself between us and the wall. Even then, I had to suck in my stomach and turn my head to give him enough room to squeeze past.

Now I knew how dough felt as it was threaded through a pasta maker.

Clay hit one knee, and I lifted Tibby—who was light as a feather—onto his back. Hands folding against her chest, she pressed her face into the valley between his shoulder blades. He stood slowly, his grip on her twiglike legs gentle. Afraid for her balance, I pinned her to him with a palm on her knobby spine.

"Let's go." I popped his flank. "Move it."

Working together, we cleared the tunnels and returned to the hatch leading to the deli.

Hand pressing to the aged wood, I sank into my magic. "Here goes nothing."

Familiarity with the process enabled me to open the portal faster than ever, and I stumbled into the same metal stand of potato chips. A quick sidestep prevented me from knocking it over, but I didn't get out of Clay's way fast enough. He smashed into it, and it crashed, spilling snacks across the linoleum.

There must be a trick to avoiding the blasted thing, if this was an active route, but I had yet to find it.

"You're not real." The same clerk as yesterday stood behind the counter. "Nope. Nope. Nope." He made himself a sandwich, locked himself in the break room, and yelled through the door, "I expect you to be gone when I get back in twenty."

"We will be," I promised him with a cringe. "Enjoy your dinner."

Poor guy was going to need therapy after this.

Then again, if I didn't work through my daddy issues soon, I might be right there with him.

14

After settling Tibby into a booth, Clay knelt at her feet and reached into his pocket.

Meanwhile, I cast a barrier spell over the wall to keep anyone from following us.

"Here." Clay handed her his phone. "Call your people, and let's get you home."

Fingers clumsy on the buttons, she made her call, bursting into tears when a strained voice answered.

"Papa," she breathed. "I'm out. I'm safe. I need you to come get me."

Mr. Garnier asked a few questions, which Tibby required help to answer, then ended the conversation.

With her coven on the way, I exchanged the phone for a business card with my name and number on it.

"If they come after you again, call me." I indicated her ravaged wrists. "Do you mind?"

"You can heal?" A faint blush warmed her cheeks. "I smell the black magic on you."

"I identify as a gray witch."

Gently, I held her trembling hands and summoned Colby's magic to heal the worst of her injuries. Since she was too drained to do it herself, I used a spell to scour the area clean of her blood to ensure it couldn't be used to track her down again.

The whole process took about twenty minutes, and I was wiped at the end of it, so I sat in the booth across from her to catch my breath. "Do you know anything about the sea monster in the lake?"

"There's a sea monster in the lake?" Her eyes snapped open wide. "Are you sure?"

"I've seen it." I judged her shock to be authentic. "Do you know what happens to the corpses like the one who kept you company?"

Before she could answer, a warm breeze swirled through the shop as an older man with silver-black hair stepped inside the deli.

"Papa." Tibby struggled to get to her feet, but she made it on her own. "You're here."

Mr. Garnier escorted her outside, cutting short my interrogation, but we hung back, giving her a chance to vouch for us before we ended up crammed in a deli full of mad witches demanding what role we played in her abduction.

After five minutes, I stepped outside to find her burrowed against her dad's side, who held on tight.

Must be nice to have that bond. To know if you called, he came running.

"You brought her back to us." Mr. Garnier rubbed her arms, soothing her. "How can I ever thank you?"

The wind carried a hint of cologne, and the familiar scent of the black magic I had expected on Tibby.

"Get her out of here." I glanced over my shoulder. "You don't have long to reach safety."

A man stepped forward to lift Tibby, tsking at her weight, then loaded her into the waiting car.

Mr. Garnier slid onto the seat next to her, smiling. As the car sped off, I waved goodbye to Tibby.

"What do we do now?" Clay rested a hand on my shoulder. "Wait for your dad or find the others?"

"Dad will come for us when he figures out what happened." I stepped onto the street, texting a meeting point for our searchers. "We need to handle the situation with the girls before then."

We didn't have to wait long for Aedan to arrive with a scowl cutting his mouth.

Clay, reading his expression, made his excuses to hit a nearby vendor selling dirty rice with shrimp.

"They took my key." Aedan unslung a backpack from his shoulder. "And they dumped my clothes in the road."

Townhouse A was far enough from Bourbon Street, I wasn't worried they had landed in pee, but it was still in the area where the streets were washed nightly, and there was always vomit around this time of year.

"How about we burn all that and buy new?"

"Give me a second." He retrieved his ID and a few other items then scanned the crowd. "Excuse me, sir."

A man with dark skin and graying hair slowed his walk. He wore a tight purple crop top over the tattered remains of a Mardi Gras flag he had fashioned into a skirt. The gold ballcap he wore bore the Saints logo, and it was pristine. The man stood taller for wearing it, and I wondered if tourists had dropped it earlier.

When he set eyes on Aedan, and then me, he clutched the handle of his shopping cart until his swollen knuckles turned white.

"What?" He shook the cart, rattling it loudly, trying to spook us. "You got something to say to me?"

"I have some clothes here. They're not all clean, but they're in good shape." Aedan held out the backpack. "Do you know anyone who can use them? I'd hate to throw them away just because I don't need them anymore."

"I might know someone." He crept forward slowly then snatched the bag lightning fast. "Thanks."

"No problem."

Once the man had rolled away, I smiled at Aedan. "That was nice of you."

"Yeah, well, this black witch I know taught me to pay it forward."

Tears pricking the backs of my eyes, I knew exactly how the Grinch felt when his heart grew three sizes.

"Gray witch," I corrected him, voice wobbly. "Maybe if I use it enough, it'll catch on?"

"Or maybe you're one of a kind."

A fist clenched around my throat and squeezed until I couldn't breathe for a second. "Maybe."

"I called around to some hotels." He switched topics before I was reduced to a blubbering mess. "Still no vacancies. Are you sure you need me?"

The wound the girls had dealt his pride, Arden's jab in particular, was as tender as fresh bruises.

"You can stay with us." I did my best to make the RV sound ritzy, but what really sold him was the access to the water. "We still have to relocate Pontchy. Know any aquatic daemons with herding experience?"

Wildlife relocation was the job I blurted out when pressed for why he was staying with me, and like most of my lies told in Samford, it had stuck.

Thankfully, locals only asked for his help with squirrels, raccoons, and possums. Things he could handle without breaking a sweat.

"I might know a guy." A smile crept across his face. "Let me know when you need me."

There was an entire speech I had to give him about why he didn't want to work with or for Black Hat, but I was starting to see that wasn't the appeal. He wanted to help me. Not the organization. He was determined to pull his own weight, as if he would wear out his welcome otherwise, or like I wouldn't claim him as family if he couldn't keep up with the rest of us. Arden-specific tasks aside, I suspected that was why he was so quick to volunteer for any assignment, no matter how dangerous.

"It's your choice." I slid my arm through his. "You don't have to do it."

"The creature might be innocent in this," he countered. "Plus, after talking to Derry and Marita, I worry they're going to get eaten. They're betting who can ride it the longest. Like it's a bronco that will buck them off. Instead of, you know, swallowing them whole."

Humans must be to Pontchy what a raw leg of lamb was to a dog.

A tasty treat.

Even if the corpses weighed two hundred pounds each, that might account for one fifth of the food it required daily. The only reason I could see for the creature jumping through so many hoops, or lakes, in this case, wasn't the lure of free food but of a delicacy.

"They're crazy," I agreed, thinking back to their aquatic aerobics, "but I like them."

"Me too." He gave my arm a squeeze, encouraging me like I was the kid always standing alone on the playground and a peer was finally showing interest in me. "I've heard some of the stories about your mom and Meg. After meeting her descendant, I can definitely see how Meg got her into so much trouble." He burst out laughing. "Marita and Derry have so many *bad* ideas."

"A veritable bad idea factory," Clay mouthed around a spoon behind us. "They truly are kindred spirits."

"They're something all right." I jumped when a hand landed on my shoulder, but I scented the cherry tobacco scent of Asa twined with green apple undercurrents before I turned my head. "Hey."

"The Mayhews are on their way." Asa fell back to walk with Clay. "They should be here in five."

Despite the show of deference, Aedan untangled from me quickly, still wary fascination might get his butt handed to him. I wanted to reassure him that Asa and I had that under control, but I would be lying.

Big time.

Much as it pained me to admit, Asa wasn't the one to look out for. No. That honor fell to me.

"Hurricane for the lady." Marita appeared before me like magic. "Drink up while it's still cold."

"Thanks." I accepted the hourglass-shaped cup that must have been three feet tall. "I think."

"Rum, passion fruit syrup, and lemon juice." She had several tucked under her arm and gave one to Clay and Asa, leaving her with three. "They're delish."

Five minutes later, Derry found us and passed out shrimp po' boys, holding back four each for him and Marita.

I won't lie.

I was impressed.

Both by their generosity and their appetites.

We ate on the run, my team and I, but we disposed of the alcohol before reaching the SUV.

And by *disposed of*, I mean Marita drank a gallon of hurricane in the span of two blocks.

Despite the brew in her system, she didn't even wobble. She must have been serious about giving up the Downward Dog after Derry used her tipsiness to scare her silly in the lake.

With a full SUV, Aedan ended up sitting with Clay in the backseat, I rode shotgun, and the wargs cuddled in the cargo area. At least I hoped that was all they were doing back there.

"Well, you've managed to piss off Luca and your dad." Clay got comfy. "What's next on your agenda?"

"The Mayhews go back to tracking the troll, we set up surveillance on Townhouse A to watch the girls, and then we figure out what role Pontchy plays in all this."

No sooner had we parked at the marina than I caught a whiff of trouble.

"I'll handle this." I got out, shut the others in, and went to join Dad at the picnic table. "Hello again."

"Do you have any idea what you've done?" He sat on the bench, back to the table, staring across the water. He didn't, or couldn't stand to, look at me. "You set her free, didn't you?"

"She's a scared kid who hasn't come into her powers." I lowered myself across from him. "She couldn't help you."

"She manipulated you." His laughter was rough and tired. "Those thorn manacles? Luca didn't put them on her. Her own coven did that."

A bitter taste flooded my mouth. "Her family…"

"*Not* her family." He put his head in his hands. "She called the Toussaint patriarch. That's who you gave her to, and now there's no stopping what comes next."

Toussaint.

I should have known that incident with the Toussaints would come back to bite me on the butt.

Now that I thought about it, her "papa" hadn't introduced himself as Amaury Garnier. I had assumed, and he rolled with it to avoid another tumble with Black Hat like the one that killed his predecessor.

I had let too much slip through the cracks on this case. I had too many personal ties to keep a level head. The trick Tibby played on us shouldn't have worked, but it did, because I failed my team.

Oh, how the Toussaints must have laughed all the way home knowing they got one over on Black Hat.

"Care to enlighten me?"

"The Toussaints hired the rock troll to do the heavy lifting and the technomancer to cover its trail. They're responsible for the morgue thefts."

A technomancer. Lovely. Colby would have a conniption when I told her.

"What does that have to do with Tibby?"

"The beast is the sacrifice required for any Lazarus witch to ascend. She must cut out its heart and consume it to unlock her powers."

More lost than ever, I didn't know what to say. "Isn't that what you want?"

"I did, yes, but she's too young. I didn't realize my mistake until after I arrived." His despair was genuine, though I was more than a little surprised he let her age thwart him. "I would have left none the wiser to Luca's scheming if you hadn't contacted me."

"How did Luca know what you were after?"

"I wasn't as careful with my inquiries as I should have been. There wasn't—*isn't*—time for subterfuge."

"What does that have to do with the Toussaints? Why did Tibby call them of all people?"

"She was dating the patriarch's eldest heir. Eliza. That was how Tibby ended up in chains."

"Do the Toussaints know their technomancer acquired Tibby for Luca and not them?"

By hiring Nan, the Toussaints had unwittingly granted Luca access to their coven. Through Nan, Luca could track their progress in locating Tibby, beat them to the punch, then hand her over to Dad.

"The Toussaints have no idea who Luca is or how she's involved in their current plight. She's careful to always keep her hands clean. That's why she travels with Nan, so she leaves no trace behind. Father would crucify her if he caught her."

Knowing the director, it was a safe bet Dad meant that literally.

"I thought I was saving Tibby from you." That wasn't entirely true. "I thought I was saving *Mom* from you."

If I hurt or offended him, he didn't show it. His focus was too singular to allow for me to dent him with my doubts.

"Tibby will never come into her full power if she accepts the mantle too early. She'll burn out within days."

Ah.

There it was.

The reason he marked her off his list.

Not because Tibby's premature awakening meant she would die

after depleting her nascent reserves, but because it meant she was too weak to trade a life for a life. Her death served no purpose. For him.

Always, it was about him.

"Why destroy a weapon that powerful, if she's already in their pocket?"

For decades, the Toussaints had been running things, but a functional Lazarus would tip those scales. People would come from all over with their dead and beg her to bring them back. They would offer her tribute, and her coven would grow wealthy off her labors. But if she was with them of her own free will, they would be the benefactors.

"Tibby is the last, and she's young. Eliza won't be her last fling, and she wasn't her first love. Tommy Far, a warlock from Metairie, was her boyfriend for over a year."

"The Toussaints worry the girls will break up, and Tibby will end up with a boy."

One who could get her pregnant if the young lovers weren't careful, thus passing on her rare gift. A boon to her family, but not so for the Toussaints.

"They're more worried the Garniers will steal her back and breed her to beef up their stock after she ascends, or she might fall into the hands of other covens who would use her to enrich their blood, but yours is a kinder version of her potential futures, yes." He rose with painful slowness, or perhaps regret. "Her life is, and always has been, destined for betrayal and misery."

"You're leaving?" I hopped up and ran to face him. "You're just going to let them get away with it?"

"I did what I could for her. She's no longer my concern." He summoned his wings. "I advise you to let the local covens govern their own."

"What did you do?" I saw red at his claims. "Except stand there and trade insults with Luca—"

"—while my daughter freed Tibby." He took credit for her

escape, as if he had planned it. "Any debt between her and me is paid. Her life is her own, and I won't interfere again."

"Unbelievable." I stared up at him, willing myself to be wrong, but I was exactly right. "You really don't care about anything except Mom."

"Rue..."

"I might have lost two of the most important relationships of my life by coming here." Camber and Arden might never speak to me again. Or worse. They might cut me out of their lives except for work, forcing me to be on the outside of their friendship for eight hours a day until they moved on or I did. "I could drop everything and fix it, or try to, but people's lives are at stake. I have to do what's right. Not only what's right for me."

"You're so much like her," he said softly, his voice catching.

"If that were true, then you would listen to me. You would stay. You would *help*."

"I'm not a good man, Rue. I never meant for you to believe otherwise."

Jaw clenched so tight my teeth squeaked against one another, I gritted out, "You should go."

"Leave Black Hat." He spread his wings. "If you don't, it will scoop out your goodness until you're hollow."

"Her potential isn't finite," Asa said as he stepped up beside me. "It's infinite."

"You were born into Black Hat. You witnessed the corruption firsthand," Clay piled on, coming to stand on my other side, "and you ran rather than face it. You created a new life, a new identity. You became a different person. A better one. But that new you never looked back, did he? And when Vonda died, you decided to let the world burn." He took my hand. "Including your daughter."

The gentle click of paws on concrete told me the Mayhews had gotten tired of waiting in the car too.

Marita padded over to me and sat on my right. Derry positioned himself on my left.

Hackles raised, they growled low in their throats, warning Dad away from me.

"You truly are your mother's daughter," he rasped then thrust his wings.

Launching himself into the sky, he left me.

Again.

Just like he always would.

15

The next night, Clay hunted Freddie down and strong-armed him into cooperating with the investigation. That gave us a ride to the middle of the lake, kept me dry to cast spells, and provided us with a base of operations if the Toussaints accelerated their timetable. They had only so long before word got back to the Garniers that Tibby was free and shacking up with their enemy.

Tonight, tomorrow at the latest, we might be able to end this.

What that meant for Tibby, I didn't know, and it bothered me that her potential could mean her death.

>>*Nan accepted a payout from the Toussaints.*

Armed with a name and access point, Colby was hounding Nan across the far reaches of the internet. Now that Colby had caught her scent, there was nowhere Nan could run that Colby couldn't find her.

With any luck, that meant Colby could track Luca's movements through her as well.

>*They hired her to black out the morgue cameras for them?*
>>*That's my guess.*
>*Good job, smarty fuzz butt.*

"The troll might not come tonight." I put away my phone and gripped the rope railing. "The Toussaints will want Pontchy hungry."

Aedan sat with his legs hanging in the water, his expression a million miles away. Swimming around him, a soft glow about them, was a swarm of moon jellies. They were our canaries in a coal mine. They would alert us when a predator appeared in range that we might not otherwise detect in the darkness below.

"You okay?" I sat beside him, and he startled, noticing me for the first time. "Is this about Arden?"

"She kicked me out." He stared at nothing. "That proves she never saw me as anything but a babysitter."

"I wouldn't say that." I dipped my toes in the water, careful to avoid his new friends. "She's hurting—both girls are—and you're an easy target." I bumped my shoulder against his. "I'm sorry for making this more complicated for you."

"It was always going to happen eventually." He looked at me then. "Nolan never did show."

"Pretty sure he has no clue the girls are here."

Texts and emails could be hacked if you knew what you were doing, and Nan had preternatural skill.

The goodies left in the girls' rooms, the brand-new camera equipment, were all props on a larger stage.

A crinkle gathered across his forehead. "Someone lured you here."

"Story of my life." I scrunched my toes. "The question is, who baited me this time?"

"Let's talk it out." He leaned back on his palms. "Pontchy was the reason you came."

Anything was better than mooning over Arden. I got that. We had avoidance of that topic in common.

"Yes, but the director assigned me the case shortly *after* we learned Dad was in the area."

Odds were good I would have found my way here via Luca even without the sea monster.

"Who else could have known where Saint had gone and why?"

"Dad told me he wasn't as careful as he should have been with his inquiries." I heard the *tick-tick-ticking* of a clock counting down every time I looked at him. "He came searching for the Lazarus heir, maybe let himself be identified to expedite matters. His return from the dead—paired with his quest—would have been hot gossip in witching circles. Luca would have had an easy time finding him."

"The Garnier and Toussaint covens were already feuding over Tibby."

"The Garniers locked Tibby up to keep her from Eliza, then Luca stole Tibby from the Garniers."

"The Toussaints had a lot of faith they would get her back. They were confident enough to begin taming Pontchy. I don't see them inviting that much scrutiny into their affairs without certain assurances."

The appearance of a giant man-eater in a public lake guaranteed top tier Black Hat involvement.

Humans couldn't be allowed to discover Pontchy, or any of the other factions fighting over him.

As per usual, the fate of our hidden world hung in precarious balance with humanity.

"You think they struck a deal?" I watched the jellies bobbing happily. "With who? For what?"

"A traitor inside the Garnier coven with access to Tibby?" He shrugged. "For money, power, revenge."

"A classic combo," I had to agree. "Where do Camber and Arden come in?"

"The Toussaints know you're Director Nádasdy's granddaughter." Asa, who had been conversing with Freddie in his language since we set out, had come to check on me. "That Hiram Nádasdy is your father."

"Saint made no secret of falling out with his father." Clay, who was allergic to being excluded, joined us. "The Toussaints couldn't gamble on that, with you being raised by the director and now acting as his Deputy Director, you hadn't taken your grandfather's side in their feud. They needed a more direct link to you to ensure your cooperation in wrangling your father."

"You mean a weakness to exploit." I had so many these days. "I led them straight to Samford."

"Rue," Marita called from the front of the boat. "We've got company."

Magic required more effort on the water, even when I was bone dry, so I waited until she gave me the signal to activate the charm I'd premade—another way to conserve magic—so that I could see the troll.

High above us, I blinked his rapid path into clarity. "Here we go."

Aedan released his human glamour, allowing the vibrant turquoise scales covering his skin to show. "I'll head on down."

"Get in position." I caught him before he dropped in. "Wait for my signal."

With barely a ripple, he disappeared beneath the black surface and began his hunt for Pontchy.

"Testing," he murmured, his voice filling my head. "One, two, three."

"I hear you." A slight echo accompanied my words. "Plenty loud, but not so clear. I'll tweak it before we use it again."

His comms charm was a dupe of the one Clay wore at work, but I was fresh out of Rolexes.

A pebble I found on the lakeshore would have to do. Hopefully, that tie to the area would make the spell stick long enough to get us through the next hour or two before water eroded its power. So far, so good.

Once I perfected an all-weather version, I could charm something superlight for Colby. Maybe I ought to take a page out of Asa's book and use a few threads of my hair to make her a lightweight bracelet.

"We drive Pontchy back out to sea," I reminded them of the plan, "and we save Tibby."

Without its heart, she couldn't complete her ritual. That would make her safe. For now.

Thanks to the Kellies, we had full dossiers on the Garnier and Toussaint covens. With photos.

I wouldn't screw up a second time. If I did, Tibby might not survive it.

"You make it sound so easy." Marita came around the corner. "How are we going to steer it?"

"The old carrot and stick." I tugged my hair into a ponytail. "How else?"

"Wait." Derry held up a hand. "You brought corpses?"

"I had a few here and there I was done with," Freddie told them. "Seemed a pity to waste them."

The wargs slid their gazes toward the door to his boathouse.

"If you have the grub," Marita wondered, "then why are we waiting on the body drop to get started?"

"We need to intercept the body before it hits the water." I was dreading that part. "They've spent days acclimating Pontchy to a feeding schedule. We can use that to our advantage."

"Personally, I never get full on appetizers." She patted her belly. "I'm more of a main course kind of girl."

"He's learned there's one treat per night. We need to time it right, so he knows there's more where that came from." Marita nodded, so I continued. "Once we guide Pontchy out of the lake, I can ward the inlets to prevent him from coming back in." A magic expenditure of that size would leave me weak as a kitten without Colby as a lifeline. Even with her, it would be brutal. "He ought to take the hint and move on once he bumps off the magic a few times."

"If he's smart enough to train," Clay agreed, "he's smart enough to untrain."

Above us, the troll was almost in position, which meant I had to get my butt in gear. "Showtime."

With a roll of my shoulders, I shook out my wings, thrust downward, and achieved liftoff.

"That's so badass." Marita clapped. "Your form is already improving."

Recalling my last attempt, I laughed. "I have nowhere to go but up."

"Literally." She punched the air. "Unless you splat, but hey! That's why we have a safety net."

Not as comforting to hear as she maybe thought it would be, but I appreciated the effort.

As I gained altitude, I checked on my cousin. "Aedan, you copy?"

"Pontchy is already circling. Not close enough for me to see. But I feel him."

"You didn't say copy."

"Do people really say copy?"

"Maybe I'm thinking about over, over?"

"Do you see the troll, over?"

"I'm airborne and moving to intercept, over."

"Be careful up there, over."

"Be careful down there, under."

With his laughter in my ears, I focused on the troll and his burden. If I timed this right, I could catch the body and avoid an altercation with the troll altogether. That would be ideal. We had no fight with him. Unless he left us no choice.

As I was thinking it, the troll reached the apex and flung the body, pivoting to leave.

Arms outstretched, I swooped in to catch the bundle and got a swift and painful introduction to Force, and his BFF Velocity.

I had dipped too far, and the body smacked me in the face. The plan had been to pluck it from the air. Like a daisy in a field. Except decomposing, and not in a field. So, maybe not like a daisy at all.

Impact stunned me, and the extra weight knocked me lower, until I saw my reflection below me.

"Pontchy's here," Aedan reported. "Do you have the body?"

"The body has me." A burn ignited between my shoulder blades. "I'm falling."

"Do not touch down, Rue. I repeat. Do *not* touch down."

"I may not have a choice." I couldn't beat my wings fast enough to recover. "I'm almost treading water."

Splashing drew my attention down in time to lock glowing gazes with Pontchy, who noticed the bundle in my arms and concluded dinner was getting hand-delivered tonight. Its jaw unhinged to reveal wide rows of razor-sharp teeth more at home in a predator's mouth.

"Crap, crap, crap," I chanted through the charm to Aedan. "Do I drop it or let it drop me?"

"Dump it then get out of there." Aedan didn't hesitate. "We can try again later."

"There might not be a later." I trembled with strain, hating to give up now. "The Toussaints—"

"Drop it," he repeated. "It's not worth losing you."

Pretty sure with all the black magic still in my system, Pontchy wouldn't be interested in my bitter taste. Then again, he was a scavenger, so he was used to rot and decay. Just not of the moral variety.

A series of splashes convinced me Pontchy was about to breach and swallow me whole, but when I dared to look, I almost wished I hadn't. What I saw was so much worse than what I imagined.

Determination in his golden eyes, Derry swam, leather straps clamped between his teeth.

"Backup has arrived," Derry growled. "This is going to be *fun*."

"Aedan, are you seeing this?"

"How do you think he reached you so fast?" He scoffed at my surprise. "Give me a minute, okay?"

"Okay," I wheezed, magic and muscles straining. "Take your time."

The temptation must have proved too great for Pontchy. Unhappy that his regularly scheduled meal was postponed, he stuck his head clear of the surface for the first time, but I had no chance to admire him.

Derry seized the opportunity, outfitting Pontchy with a length of chain that worked like a bit in a horse's mouth. The leather straps I saw earlier must be the reins.

Now that he had a means of directing Pontchy, Derry was attempting to climb on his back while Aedan soothed the creature with words I couldn't understand. One wrong move and Derry could be dinner. Pontchy might prefer an easy meal, but he could procure his own. His teeth told me that. I couldn't believe Marita let him do this.

Okay, so, maybe I could. But not alone. Water wings and all, I expected her to be right beside him.

Using gills for handholds, Derry swung himself onto Pontchy's back, and Aedan passed him the reins.

"Get the body to Freddie," Aedan told me. "He knows what to do."

Easier said than done.

Aedan vanished beneath the surface, rippling arrows of current pointing out his direction.

"Yeehaw." Derry, grinning from ear to ear, dug in his heels. "Giddyup, pardner."

Pontchy emitted a shrill, gurgling cry and thrashed beneath Derry, desperate to buck him off.

Lungs aching, muscles spasming, I hit my limit. I had no choice but to ease into the water with the body.

I've never been a strong swimmer, but I'm pretty sure I could have medaled if anyone had timed me.

"Freddie." I grasped the rope railing to keep my head above water. "Aedan said you know what to do."

"Aye." He held up a bucket. "Get ahead of them and drop breadcrumbs for the beast to follow."

Upon closer inspection, I could tell the *breadcrumbs* were hands and feet with other chunks mixed in.

Lovely.

The sunbaked innards were enough to turn a girl off eating raw hearts forever.

Or at least for the rest of the weekend.

Thumping the bucket onto the deck, he wandered off and left me floating with the corpse.

"Here." Marita fisted her hands in the damp fabric bundling it. "Let me help."

"Thanks," I panted, breathless. "You're a lifesaver."

Once she hauled the body onboard, I dragged myself out of the water, grateful to be on solid footing.

"Did you see Derry out there?" Marita rolled the body away from the edge. "What the hell was he thinking?" Her tirade veered from concern to indignation. "There was plenty of room for both of us."

Unable to spare the oxygen, I shook my head and focused on breathing, until I noticed who was missing. "Where are Asa and Clay?"

"They were here a second ago." Marita straightened. "Sorry, Rue. I dropped the ball. I got so butthurt over Derry ditching me, I wasn't paying attention." She got to her feet. "Let's ask Freddie."

Hand on the wall to brace myself, I made my way back up front. "Where are they?"

"Your daemon friend is bringing up the rear." Freddie winked. "In case the beast needs a bit of prodding."

More than likely, Derry and Blay cooked up that bright idea. After I left. "And Clay?"

"He's standing watch on the bridge pilings, so we have eyes on the shore and the causeway."

Sure enough, when I fumbled to the back, I spied Clay and Blay at their posts. "Goddess bless."

The only way he could have gotten there was if he pulled a rock troll and sank then walked over.

"Are those..." Marita looped an arm through mine to steady me, "...*my noodles?*"

"Where did Blay hide them?" I hadn't noticed them smuggled aboard. "He's straddling six."

Even with that much help, he sat dangerously low in the water, but he bobbed and waved at me, not at all concerned with the possibility of imminent death. His joy made me regret never getting around to buying us bathing suits, but he didn't seem to care as long as he got to swim.

The overwhelming stink of rotten flesh in the bucket made my eyes water, but I had a job to do.

"Here goes nothing." I reached in and pulled out a man's foot. "This had better work."

Though unpleasant, I had stuck my hand in worse things, which said a lot about who I used to be.

Soon Derry cut in front of Blay, and he blew a kiss to Marita from Pontchy's back. She caught it, crushed it in her fist, then hurled it in the lake.

"Let me help." She pulled the bucket to her side. "High five, Derriere."

The severed hand she pitched smacked him in the face, and she cackled with delight.

"Maybe I should handle this part." I drew the bait back to my side. "Asa and Blay are back there."

Already the scent of food had Pontchy writhing to locate the snack that overshot the mark, which left Derry holding on for dear life while the beast whipped its head back and forth.

Lucky for us, Aedan was there to dive for it and toss it into Pontchy's mouth.

"Sorry about that." Marita tucked her hands under her thighs. "Poor impulse control."

"Really?" I took over feeding with a snort. "I never would have guessed that about you."

"He punctured my water wings. He knows I don't go anywhere without them."

"Resist the urge to murder him, and I'll buy you a new set."

Our procession made good time crossing Pontchartrain to the Rigolets strait, which we followed into nearby Lake Borgne. Coastal erosion had washed away its original boundaries, leaving it open to the Gulf of Mexico. Now that we had Pontchy where we wanted him, we just had to make sure he stayed there.

Just north of Rabbit Island, before we hit Old Pearl River, Freddie guided the boat close to shore.

I kicked off my shoes, hit the waist-deep water, then waded onto dry land, ready to cast my magical net.

Through Marita, I had brokered a deal with the water witches for a temporary containment spell. It ought to hold Pontchy for a few hours. The coven itself was en route to put permanent measures in place, and I was happy to leave them to it.

Pretty sure that earned me a gold star in delegation. I was getting the hang of this management thing.

Digging my bare feet into the rich soil on the shore, I drew my athame from my kit and sliced across my palm. Crimson ran through my fingers, dripping onto the moist earth and mixing with the current. Scooping a handful of warm liquid, I whispered to that which flowed over, around, and through the creature.

The ward snapped into place like a kick to my chest, a mesh of power stringing itself across the gap.

Binding the wound before I hit the water, I waded back to the boat and Marita pulled me onboard.

Using the comms charm, I reached out to Aedan. "We're going to circle back and hit Chef Pass."

"Toss the body over before you go," he advised. "We don't want Pontchy to follow the food."

Now that we had whet his appetite, he ought to be ready for the main course.

"Good idea." I rolled the corpse under the railing, and it hit with a splash. "See you on the other side."

The white sheet turned dark as saturation drew the remains down, its scent teasing out toward Pontchy.

Hopefully, that would be enough to keep Pontchy busy while we made our escape.

Head angling toward Derry, still astride Pontchy, Marita asked, "Can Aedan get through that?"

"The witches told me it won't stop anything smaller than a bull shark."

"There are sharks in the lake?" Marita inched closer. "It's a *lake*."

Great whites had been known to visit New Orleans's waterways too, but I kept that to myself.

"You're afraid of sharks, but you're fine with a sea monster?"

"Afraid is a strong word, but yes. Sharks are cool, but they're so mundane. I want to die epically."

No wonder she was hanging out with me. She had a death wish. An *epic* one.

Times like this, I wondered if she wasn't the one related to Meg.

Derry was something else, but she was next level.

"They're more of a summer problem. They move on to the Gulf in the fall and winter."

"You get that we're basically in the Gulf now, and you were bleeding all over the place."

"Good thing Pontchy's still around to spook any smaller predators."

"Girl, you might be just as crazy as I am." Marita slung an arm around my neck, almost choking me when she yanked me against her side. "I knew there was a reason I liked you."

"Other than I bring you on all the good monster hunts?"

"Yes."

"And I spend a fortune on consultation fees?"

"Yes."

"And—"

"Shh." Marita pressed a finger to my lips. "Your crazy complements my crazy. We're meant to be."

A fist of emotion crushed my lungs, but for once, I didn't mind. "You sure about that?"

"Yup." She planted a smacking kiss on my cheek. "Now, let's shake a leg." She cut a path to Frederick. "I brought water balloons, and I'm itching for an excuse to hurl objects at my mate's face. The sooner we tie this up, the sooner we can tie off enough balloons to make him regret puncturing my water wings."

"Take us to Chef Pass," I told Freddie. "We're ready to wrap up this little adventure."

Humming a tune, he guided us down the coast, past Alligator Bend, then up into Chef Pass.

Just shy of Fort Macomb, we repeated the process, but this time, Marita came with me. Good thing too. I wouldn't have reached the boat without her help. I had overextended myself, magically and physically.

"Are we done?" Freddie reached into the bucket and pulled out a finger. "Or do we have another stop?"

"Get us back to Pontchartrain." I didn't flinch when he crunched down. "We'll wait for the others there."

Forty-five minutes of drifting later, the guys still hadn't returned, and we were getting antsy.

"Aedan?"

No response.

"Aedan?"

A whooshing crackle filled my ears as the comms charm coughed up his voice.

"Derry is posing with Pontchy." Aedan sighed. "We might be a minute."

"Then we'll head on in." The spell wheezed its last. "Freddie, we need to get back."

With the Toussaints and the Garniers guaranteed to show at some point, I wanted to return to Colby.

A quick check of the pilings revealed Clay had climbed them until he stood on the bridge.

That was a problem easily solved by a text. Those were my favorites.

Except my phone was as dead as a doornail since I had forgotten to take it out of my back pocket before sloshing around in the shallows. Thankfully, Marita's was fine, and she let me borrow hers to message him.

>>*Rue here.*

>>*Grab a Swyft back to the marina.*

>*Sure thing, Dollface.*

"All right." Freddie stooped and came up with a toe. "Afterward, if you don't mind, I'll take my leave."

"Get us to shore, and you're free to go."

Eager to be rid of us, he wasted no time returning to the marina and dumping us at the dock.

Shoulder to shoulder, Marita and I watched him check his supplies, grunt at his bait, then set out again.

"That guy really likes to fish." Her expression turned thoughtful. "And murder people."

"In my line of work, everyone is a killer. Of fish or people or fill in the blank."

She made commiserating noises that left me wondering, not for the first time, about her dietary choices.

"Hey, I know a place that serves *the best* grilled gator with dirty rice." She rubbed her stomach, the topic of murder sparking her hunger. "They do an out of this world bananas Foster. Heavy on the rum. It burns all the way down." She linked arms with me. "Let's go stuff our faces."

"Shouldn't we wait on the guys?"

"If they hurry, they can catch us. If they don't, they can smell our breath later and regret their life choices."

No wonder Marita's shoulders were so muscular. The woman knew how to carry a grudge.

"I hope Asa and I are still crazy about each other after we've been together as long as you guys."

"Stay petty," she advised. "Petty leads to fights, which leads to makeup sex, which leads to happiness."

"I don't understand," a broken voice carried to me from the shore.

No, no, no.

This was not happening.

Arden, who must have been hidden behind an RV, walked out with glazed eyes that had seen too much. Camber trailed a step behind her, close enough for Arden to reach back and take her hand.

"Hey." I sent Marita ahead to give us privacy. "What are you two doing here?"

"We got your text with the address." Arden cringed away from Marita. "You told us where to meet you."

A ball of anger burned in my gut so hot I wouldn't have been surprised if smoke curled from my nostrils or I breathed flames on my exhale.

Nan had done this. On Luca's orders. This was payback for stealing Tibby.

And no one could convince me otherwise.

"We wanted to see what you were doing that was so much more important than us." Camber's breaths came faster. "What was that thing? It was red as a crawfish. With horns. And long black hair."

Nothing.

That should have been the answer.

They shouldn't have seen through the *don't look here*.

But Nan was a technomancer. She cast spells through technology. She sent those texts, which meant she could have imbedded spells that activated upon opening them. One to rip the blinders from their eyes. One to distract me when I could least afford to let down my guard. One to destroy their lives...and mine.

There were too many secrets in play, too much danger afoot, to hash this out now.

This marina would become ground zero as soon as the Toussaints made their move.

Which meant I had to hurt the girls. Again. To get them to leave.

They must have been waiting here for hours to confront me, desperate for me to prove their eyes had deceived them.

"Horns?" I tugged on my old skin, the one that lied so well. "How much did you have to drink?"

"We know what we saw." Arden's lips thinned. "Is it cosplay? Some kind of kink? Was Asa under there?"

She had no idea.

"You partied too hard." I swear I felt my heart cracking. "You're seeing things that aren't there."

"You're gaslighting her, and I have proof." Camber almost dropped her phone when she raised it like a shield between us. "It's in the cloud, by the way, and my mom combs through my uploads with me every month in the name of bonding."

As far as threats go, I didn't have the heart to break it to them that it wasn't one. Colby would erase the video the moment I texted her. From there, it depended on how far they wanted to push this.

"Show me." I waved them over. "I want to see."

Neither girl budged, and that hurt. Oh, it hurt. But Arden cued the video, held her phone facing me, and hit play. On the screen, I watched Blay riding his noodles and Clay scaling the pilings with preternatural grace in the background behind him.

The only small mercy was they had been so gobsmacked by Blay, they missed the sea monster rodeo. That, or the spell cast on them had its limits. Mostly, they had filmed Blay splashing and laughing, and I ached at how quick they were to reduce him to a *thing*, to an *it*.

"Explain." Arden stiffened her spine, forgetting her own fear as she reacted to Camber's. "We're listening."

"Let's go to my RV." I stepped forward, but they took healthy steps back "We can talk there."

Water sloshed behind me, and I screwed my eyes shut, knowing this was about to get so much worse.

"We're back," Aedan announced from the water, his human glamour in place. "Pontchy is…"

"They can see through glamour," I blurted, forced to watch his face crumple. "I'm sorry."

"You're one of them too." Arden stumbled back, seeing the scales beneath his illusion. "A monster."

"Yeah." Aedan rose slowly, as if his legs no longer wanted to bear his weight. "I am."

"Did you know, Rue?" Camber's nails bit into her palms, and I smelled blood. "Of course you knew."

"Are you one of them too?" Arden's gaze flicked between us. "Is Asa? What about Clay?"

"I'm not a daemon." I hesitated. "Well, I'm not *all* daemon. More like a quarter."

"I don't understand." Camber's teeth began to chatter. "W-w-what are you then?"

Her conscious mind might not remember what happened to her and Arden that night at Tadpole Swim, but her subconscious was screaming at her to *run, run, run.* And never, ever look back. No matter what.

"A witch." I reached out to help steady her, but she recoiled from me. "Let's go somewhere private."

"No." Arden wrapped an arm around Camber's waist. "I don't think we will."

"You can't tell anyone." Aedan kept his tone neutral, but the warning was plain. "Lives are at stake."

Theirs.

Black Hat had policies for dealing with humans who peered into our world then fled screaming from it.

"I can't believe you didn't tell us." Arden addressed me but locked gazes with Aedan. "You lied to us."

"We did it to keep you safe," I pled my case. "That doesn't make it right, but that's why."

"Safe from you?" Camber was hyperventilating like she hadn't in months. "Safe from him?" Her gaze slid over my shoulder, in the direction Blay had swum. "Safe from that *thing*?"

"You're afraid, I don't blame you, but we're not the bad guys."

For the most part.

But they didn't want to hear that. They wanted someone to blame.

That person should be me and me alone.

As much as I loved them, I was still very much in fascination with Asa, and their insults stoked my anger. Words aside, I wasn't mad at them. I was furious with myself. This had been a long time coming. I should have been ready. I should have had a plan. They shouldn't have found out like this.

"How do you want to play this?" Marita stepped up behind them. "It's your call."

"What's that supposed to mean?" Camber demanded of me. "Will you kill us now that we know?"

Shock she would even ask knifed through me. "I would never hurt either of you."

"Too late," Arden muttered. "Just let us go, and we'll pack for home."

They had waited and hoped for a miracle, but this was my reality, and I couldn't spare them from it.

"It doesn't work that way," Marita said with sympathy. "Rue loves you girls, but you're liabilities."

Frantic, Camber dropped her jaw on a scream, forcing me to act before she alerted the whole marina.

Lunging forward, I gripped both girls by their shoulders and willed them to sleep.

Marita dove for Camber while I caught Arden, both girls as limp as overcooked spaghetti noodles.

"Let's put them in the RV." I lifted her gently. "They can rest in the bunks."

"We see this a lot." Marita swung Camber into her arms. "Wargs fall for humans, wargs reveal their true selves, and then the humans smack face first into a wall we like to call *reality*."

"How does that usually go?"

"About how you'd expect." She readjusted Camber's weight. "There's screaming, cursing, throwing stuff. That's the reaction you want, honestly. The ones who get mad? They get over it. Eventually. It's the ones who can't shake their fear that can't adapt. We bring in a witch for them, to wipe their memories."

"You know the girls." I pivoted toward Aedan. "What do you think?"

"They work for you. They live in your town. Everyone knows you're all close. They can't magically forget you exist or block out chunks of their pasts, or everyone will panic it's delayed-onset PTSD from the kidnapping." He kept staring at his hands, at the delicate webbing between them even now. "You're too much a part of their lives to be erased."

"You're voting we initiate them?" I searched his tormented expression. "That might not go so well."

"Can it go any worse?" His voice came out raw. "She called me a monster, Rue."

Like me, Aedan might have braced for the rejection in a *maybe someday* kind of way, but it was different to have her look him in the eyes and say things that would echo in his head for the rest of his life.

"We get that a lot too." Marita tried to smile. "You have to cut them slack for how they act the moment they realize how big the world they've been living in is, and how small they are in it."

"Yeah." He couldn't keep his eyes off Arden. "Sure."

"Text Shorty," I told him. "Tell her to assume the position."

"Cryptic." Marita chuckled. "I like it."

An apologetic smile was all the explanation I could offer her until after her formal introduction to Colby.

Used to the drill, Colby wouldn't take long to hide, so we continued to the RV and got the girls inside.

Sensing I needed a moment alone with them, Marita left to sit at the end of the dock and wait for Derry and Blay to quit goofing off and come ashore.

"I texted you when I saw them." Colby peeked out beyond the curtain on her bunk. "I didn't know what else to do."

"It's not your fault." I smoothed a thumb down her cheek. "I got my phone wet. It's brain-dead."

Otherwise, I would have known the girls had sneaked into the marina after that damning text.

"Clay went to get food." Colby worried her hands together. "He'll be back soon."

"Can you do me a favor and keep an eye on Camber and Arden for me?"

"Sure thing." She flitted up, squeezed my neck, then slid back into her cave. "I'll call Clay if they wake."

"Thanks."

Once I finished fussing over the girls, I set the wards on Colby's bunk. I hadn't had time to before the Mayhews arrived, and then I hadn't seen much point in hiding her when I had already told Marita she existed. The bigger concern, for the moment, was protecting Colby from Camber and Arden.

People tended to react to bugs with swatting, stomping, screaming, or a combo of the three.

A giant bug would garner an even bigger reaction, especially if she spoke to defend herself.

Exiting the RV, I ran into Aedan, who was pretending not to stare past me for a glimpse of Arden.

"However this goes," I promised him, "you'll always have me."

"Same goes for you." He raked his damp hair off his forehead. "So, the Toussaints didn't show tonight."

Again, he was locking me out. And again, I was grateful for it. Neither of us were ready to face the music.

"We can expect them tomorrow, if not sooner. Depends on how closely they monitor Pontchy."

"The troll will tell them you interfered again."

"Will it?" I had been wondering this very thing. "Fae tend to honor their bargains to the letter. If the troll agreed to fetch one body per night from the tunnels, take it to the causeway, and drop it in the lake, as long as those exact requirements were met, it might consider its bargain fulfilled."

"You don't think it told the Toussaints about your first confrontation?"

Behind him, Derry and Asa waded out of the lake with huge grins and noodles tucked under their arms.

Marita, still fuming, snatched one from Asa and began chasing Derry down the shoreline while beating him over the head with it.

As much as I enjoyed the domestic drama, I reeled my attention back to my conversation with Aedan.

"With so much riding on Pontchy, I would have expected security after our first encounter, but there was none."

With Asa's timely arrival, I was able to put the question to him, and luckily, he agreed with me.

"Rock trolls are simple folk." He wore soaked boxers. "They wouldn't go above and beyond the agreed upon service. It's not in their nature. They're best hired for simple tasks with few steps between them."

"So, more than likely, they'll realize Pontchy is gone when his next feeding ends in a no-show."

Or, if the troll didn't notice, when fishermen discovered days' worth of corpses floating in the lake.

"That gives us time to sleep." Asa shoved his long hair off his shoulders, and it smacked against his back. "You're dead on your feet." He embraced me, perhaps sensing how very much I needed someone to tell me it was going to be okay without words that might turn into a lie. "We'll focus on Tibby tomorrow."

"Dad really screwed up this time." I mashed my face into Asa's chest. "He was seen. He spoke to people. The director must already suspect we're in contact, but now? How do I cover for him this time?"

The little girl in me, abandoned and hurting, wanted him to suffer the consequences of his rash actions. He was picking at the threads that bound Black Hat together, and one day, they just might snap. But...

...he was my dad.

"Your father chose his side." Asa ran his hands up and down my back. "Now you have to choose yours."

"You knew this would happen." I craned my neck to stare up at him. "That after I got promoted, I would feel responsible. For the agents. The Bureau." I smacked my open palm against his slick chest. "You saw it coming, and you let it blindside me."

"Rue." He captured my wrist. "You've been atoning for your past crimes since I met you."

"Key word *your*." I jerked back. "As in *mine*." I honed my glare. "Not everyone else's."

"This didn't blindside you," he said gently. "You don't want it to be true, but you know it is. You don't want to care about the Bureau, or its people, but you do. Samford taught you there's strength in community, the girls taught you there's power in shared dreams, and Colby taught you—"

"—that life is cruel, and it ends too fast."

"—that there's purpose to be found in caring for others."

"I can't handle power." The darkness in me wanted it too much. "I'm not that strong."

"You're doing fine so far."

"It's only been a few weeks." I hadn't even worn a dent in my seat cushion. "I spent most of that time stuck behind a desk, bored out of my mind and plotting my assistant's imminent demise."

He laughed, which I enjoyed, but I wasn't convinced I had been joking.

"The girls are safe—"

"They're magically roofied and stashed in a bunk until I have time to deal with them."

"What's the alternative? Erase their memories? Return them to their townhouse? Leave them alone and exposed? Stasis isn't ideal, but we have no good options. The marina will become a war zone when the Toussaints and the Garniers clash, and I don't want the girls to become casualties."

"You're right, I know you're right, but it still feels like betrayal."

Or cowardice.

Yeah.

That.

"As I was saying..." He took my hand. "The girls are safe, Colby is plugged in, fueled by rage and sugar water. Clay is keeping an eye on her bunk. The Mayhews can share the third, and we'll take yours."

"What about Aedan?"

"He chose to spend the night in the lake."

A fresh crack fizzled across my heart. "I wish I could fix this for him."

"I know." Asa pressed his lips to my forehead, my cheek, my chin. "I know you do."

While I was in a confessional mood, I might as well tell him the decision the wine cooler made for me.

"I *might* have told Marita about Colby." I caved to his touch. "Not everything, but enough."

"Colby will be thrilled." He dragged me toward the RV. "She loves expanding her community."

Between her gamer friends and me, we had been her entire social circle. She deserved the chance to make friends IRL and explore as much as the rest of us. And, it warmed me to realize, that was why I had told Marita. She was a friend. She told me so. But I had known it earlier, hadn't I? That was why I called her and not Derry or my usual contact with the pack.

Maybe I wasn't as hopeless at this friendship stuff as I first thought.

Unlike Clay, who had chipped away for years to get through to me, Marita waltzed down the path he already carved and slipped behind my defenses. Maybe this was my way of honoring Mom. Maybe it was Marita's connection to Meg that made her feel safe. Or maybe I was tired of hiding who I was, and Marita made it easier to skip the getting-to-know-you parts, since her mate's family shared so much history with mine.

"I should have asked her first." I opened the door. "She deserves to make that choice."

"Colby won't mind," he assured me. Again. "You can always ask her permission going forward."

"One more thing." I flexed my palm, unnerved by how quickly I had healed the deep cuts. "I need to ward the RV to hide our magic signatures."

"In case the Toussaints are up and about before we are," he realized. "Do you have the strength?"

"Not even close." I drew my wand anyway. "Good thing I have a fully charged familiar."

The spell was clumsy, and it wouldn't have solidified without Colby's bright power giving it substance.

"That will hold for twenty-four hours." I leaned against the hood. "Then we'll reevaluate."

Dead on my feet, I let him lead me into the RV, guide me to the bathroom, and strip me for bed. He tugged one of his tees over my head, and somehow my panties got lost in the mix.

Tired I might be, but I was willing to put off sleep for a bit longer.

Or so I told myself seconds before my head hit the pillow.

16

A warm hand palming my breast woke me, and I arched against Asa, who took the opportunity to nibble my ear while I cast a privacy spell over our bunk. The purpose behind yesterday's lack of underwear became clear as he slid his hand between my thighs and hooked my leg over his hip.

Spreading me wide, he cupped my core with a possessive growl that curled my toes. His clever fingers, long and slender, found me wet and ready. He eased them inside me, pumping slowly until I bit my lip to stop from crying out.

"Now." I grabbed his wrist to keep him from pushing me over the edge. "I want you *now*."

Warm breath fanning my ear, he bit the delicate shell as the hard length of him teased me. "Are you sure?"

"I will end you," I snarled, fisting his hair and hauling his mouth down to mine.

"Hmm." Teeth raking my jaw, his erection hot and insistent, he entered me with an achingly slow glide that almost cost him the silky hair knotted around my fist. "Better?"

Shifting against him, my heart pounding, I gasped, "No."

"This?" His fingers dug into my hip, holding us together, forcing me to hold still. "Is this better?"

"Understand that I say this with love—" I pried his fingers off and ground down on him, "—if you don't start moving, I'm going to finish while you watch then laugh in your face as your balls turn blue and fall off. I might even bake them into a blueberry pie."

"Vicious creature," he breathed, his palm roaming higher, until he pinched my nipple. "It's your own fault."

Sheets tangling around my feet, I kept my pace, climbing higher. "What?"

"You taught me everything I know." He growled into my ear. "You have only yourself to blame."

With that, he cinched his arm around my middle, clamping my elbows down at my sides, and thrust harder and faster, until I bumped my head on the wall with each pump of his hips.

"Rue..."

Snaking my foot around his calf, I snarled, "Don't. You. Dare. Stop."

Quiet laughter carried me to my peak, and I shuddered around him as he spilled into me.

Several minutes later, I attempted to move then groaned at the pins and needles sensation in my palm.

"My hand's asleep." I nudged him back with my butt. "Let go so I can turn over."

"Keep wiggling," he threatened, his teeth on my throat. "See what happens."

I put more roll into my hips, and I didn't regret what happened next.

Not one bit.

"No sign of the troll." Colby tapped on her keyboard. "His magic reads different than a spell."

The kid was taking a break from hunting The Ferret to run a program she was writing.

For identifying creatures using glamour on security footage.

How? I mean, really. *How?*

I was starting to believe my little moth girl was a budding technomancer, not unlike The Ferret.

Sentient familiars could develop their own skill set separate from their witch, but it was rare. Super rare. Then again, Colby wasn't your average familiar either. She was a *loinnir*, and she had been fae.

"Keep at it." I tousled her fuzzy head. "Innate magics are tricky."

"I doubt he comes back." Clay tossed voodoo-flavored potato chips in his mouth. "He's done his part."

How does voodoo taste, you ask? According to the manufacturer, like salt, vinegar, barbecue, and jalapeños.

"The Toussaints might handle this last feeding themselves," I agreed. "To better control the outcome."

At sundown, Derry and Marita had returned to the tunnels to get Tibby's scent. It had been a long shot, picking up her trail in the Quarter. The Toussaints would have secured her until the time came for the ceremony, so I wasn't surprised when Derry texted Asa to say they were packing it in.

"The Mayhews are circling back," I told the others. "Keep an eye out."

"When do I get to meet them?" Colby's antennae quivered. "They sound so cool."

"They are so cool, and soon. Maybe tonight, if everything goes well."

"I still can't believe Derry rode Pontchy." Her dark eyes glittered. "Blay and I defeated a kraken in Mystic Seas, but it's not the same as battling a real sea monster. I wish I had been there to see it."

"I saw the whole thing," Clay grumbled, unhappy with her adoration. "There was no battle."

A musical pinging noise interrupted her next question, and she focused on her laptop screen.

One of the extra purchases she and Clay made alongside her new laptop was an antennalike camera they mounted on the roof to prevent more ugly surprises like the one we had last night.

"We've got company." A furrow cut across her brow. "Two black SUVs parked on the main road."

Black SUVs always put me in mind of Black Hat, but the truth was, every organization and their mammas used them for official business. The whole reason the Bureau had adopted the most common color, make, and model was to blend in.

Scooching next to Colby on the bench, I studied the first person to exit the rear of the SUV.

"That's 'papa.'" I asked her to zoom in. "Laurent Toussaint."

Satisfied the way was clear, thanks to our hidden powers, he lifted a hand. The driver of the second SUV jumped out, rushed to the passenger side, and opened the rear door. Tibby stepped out, washed and in fresh clothes. The girl who slid out next, the one whose hand she was holding, must be Eliza Toussaint.

"This is the girl we want." I indicated Tibby. "We need to get her away from the others."

Laptop under his arm, Asa appeared from the back. "How long do we have?"

"About two hours until the body drop." I made room for him to sit next to me. "They're cutting it close."

"Have we learned anything else about the ceremony?"

"No." I kicked out my feet and crossed them at the ankles. "All we know is what Dad told us."

"Well..." Colby switched off the surveillance screen to a scanned document, yellowed with age. "There is a vague reference in another case file in the Black Hat database that *might* be about Pontchy."

"When did you find that, Shorty?" Clay polished off his chips. "Last night, you were hitting a wall."

"The search parameters were giving me grief," she agreed. "The problem is—Pontchy isn't a plesiosaur."

"Hey," Clay protested. "Wait just a cotton-picking minute."

"He's not a bakunawa either."

Mollified they were both wrong, Clay reined in his outrage. "What is it then?"

"A giant electric eel, basically."

"I did not see that coming." I studied the photo, but it was grainy and black-and-white. "Eels are…gross."

"An eel heart." Clay tilted his head. "It just doesn't have the same ring to it."

"Except the creature is the *magical equivalent*. A normal electric eel can generate up to six hundred and fifty volts. That's like sticking a fork in an outlet times five. Pontchy?" Her wings twitched with excitement as she told Clay. "Best guess on a reading is one hundred thousand amps."

"I can't tell if you gave us that reading in two different values to scare us or not, but it's working."

"Why didn't the creature attack Derry?" Asa reminded us, "He climbed on its back, and it ignored him."

"They're like honeybees." Her smile faded. "One sting—or charge in this case—and they're done."

"Why am I picturing Tibby as Frankenstein's monster?" Metal platform rising to the open ceiling, rain pouring in, thunder booming, and lightning striking. "Is that how Lazarus witches work?"

"There's no definitive answer in the database. Not much is known about them. So few of them are born, and even less survive to maturity. The ones who do are killed by necromancers or competitive covens." Colby scrunched up her face. "But, if I had to guess, their powers are like…supernatural defibrillators."

"Pontchy wouldn't have discharged until Tibby attempted to strike a death blow, a last line of defense." I was glad we helped the poor icky thing escape. "Does that mean Lazarus witches absorb magic?"

"Can they absorb any magic," Asa countered, "or only that of lower life-forms?"

"The creatures are critically endangered," Colby told us. "The Lazarus witches hunted them almost to extinction."

"Lazarus witches must have evolved to prey on it alone." Clay rubbed his chin. "Wonder if that's why so few of them are born these days?"

"Correlation or causation?"

Asa made a good point, but with so little information to go on, we had no firm answers.

An alert on Colby's laptop had her switching back to the surveillance feed to check on the Toussaints.

"I'm giving Marita a heads-up that it's go time." I reached for my cell but came up empty. I had forgotten it was in a jar of rice in the back. Turning to Asa, I told him, "Text Derry. I want them back ASAP."

Jittery with anticipation, I paced the length of the bus while Colby monitored the coven for movement.

Only after the Toussaints strode to the water's edge did Asa steer me to the front seats.

"What will you do with Tibby?" He sat behind the wheel, and I beside him. "Return her to the Garniers?"

"If I do, they'll chain her again. Or worse." I flipped the armrest up and down. "She'll rebel as long as her girlfriend is out there." I gave up and left it alone. "Young love, you know?"

"That doesn't leave you many options that aren't...permanent."

"There's only one way I can see clear of this, and I hate even thinking it again so soon."

"You're going to recruit her."

"I'm offended you didn't even *pretend* I was hinting at killing her. Sheesh. Have I totally lost my edge?"

Angling his chin to hide most of his smile, he hit on the problem. "What about the director?"

He would love to have his own Lazarus witch, and he would be willing to wait for her to mature.

"I can't arm him with that kind of weapon."

"Without Pontchy," he ruminated, "or another of his kind, he can't use her."

"She's years away from maturity, which works in our favor. I'll convince him to spend the time searching for a Pontchy to sacrifice while doing everything in my power to ensure he never gets his hands on one."

"Do you think Tibby will agree?"

"Hard to say." She didn't know her *papa* was killing her. "Black Hat might be the safest place for her."

And wasn't that saying something?

The alternative, her declining our invitation, wasn't a possibility I wanted to entertain.

The rule of thumb with recruiting was *join or die* for the simple reason the candidates were problems to be solved. Tibby held the potential to cause us major headaches down the line, but she hadn't earned an invitation based on her actions. This was more of a mercy hire. Except there was no carrot for the stick. The best offer I could make her was stick, stick, or more stick.

"What will you do about Camber and Arden?"

"No clue." I rested my head in my hands. "Keep them unconscious forever?"

"Sleeping beauties?" His lips quirked. "I doubt that would win you any favors when they woke."

"Bad enough they know monsters exist. If they wake in thirty years, or however long it takes me to work up the courage to face them, they would kill me." I groaned through my fingers. "And I'd deserve it."

"How's Aedan?" He pried my hands loose. "I haven't seen him tonight."

"Still in the lake." I stared out at the water. "He's running point on Tibby retrieval."

After I set him up with a new comms charm at dusk, he left to avoid a potential run-in with Arden.

"Tibby is stepping out of her clothes," Colby announced. "She's wearing some type of chain mail."

Probably the supernatural equivalent of a woven stainless-steel shark suit.

"Most rites of passage require a solo effort." I shifted to keep the patriarch in sight. "She ought to go in the water alone. Give her time to get into position away from shore, then we'll move on the coven."

"How do you want to handle them?" Clay cracked his knuckles. "They won't let her go easily."

"We're watching attempted murder live. The intent is there. The Toussaints have no idea we've removed the danger."

"That's not an answer." Asa rubbed my back. "Can you take them out with a sleep spell?"

Without meaning to, I turned my head toward the bunk where the girls would rest until I could spare a moment to decide their fates. "Another witch wouldn't let me get that close."

Spells like that required stealth...or worse...a level of trust. Neither of which applied here.

"Um." Colby fluttered to me. "We got problems."

"Only on days that end in Y." I was quickly adopting that as our team motto. "What's up?"

"Three more SUVs just parked on the main road, boxing in the Toussaints. Six witches per vehicle."

"What do you bet the Garnier coven just figured out where to find their lost witch?" I checked my kit and my wand then turned to Colby. "Protect the girls, okay?"

"I will." Her sweet face hardened with grim determination. "I won't let them get hurt."

"I'll redirect the Mayhews to you, so you're not alone. If this turns into a brawl, you might need them to drive you someplace safer." I kissed her forehead then checked to make sure Asa had left the keys in the ignition. "Can you handle introductions?"

Left and right, I was failing the girls in my life who looked to me for guidance and protection.

"Do me a favor and tell them I'm a bug?" Her complexion paled. "I don't want to get swatted."

"You're not a bug." I adopted a stern tone. "You're a Colby."

"And if they swat you," Clay said, voice low, "it'll be the last thing they do."

Flittering over to him, she kissed him on the cheek. "Thanks, BFF."

"You're welcome, BFF." He shooed her toward her computer. "Eyes on the monitor, Shorty."

"Will do." She waved to me then settled in to monitor the battle. "Be safe."

To preserve magic, I skipped the glamour, and we exited the RV. We slinked behind the other vehicles to hide, tracking the covens' movements, waiting for our opening.

"The marina is packed." Clay crouched beside me. "How do we shield all these people?"

Earlier, I counted twenty-five RVs and six boats in residence. Not a single one had left yet.

"I can secure the area within maybe four yards of the shore." More than that, and it would erode too quickly. "That gives them access to the water, which isn't ideal, but it will trap them between the lake and the ward. It will keep them, and their magic, away from the humans. But it won't conceal them."

That required a second spell not worth casting until the first was locked in place.

"Okay." He shifted his weight. "How do we maneuver the covens into place behind your barrier without getting caught in the middle?"

"I don't think that will be a problem," Asa observed. "The Toussaints have noticed the Garniers."

Counting the drivers, the Toussaints brought six people total. They were grossly outnumbered. Or they would have been, if they weren't the more powerful coven. The Garniers were playing a numbers game, and I doubted even that would help them win in a magical confrontation.

"Tibby," an older man with silver-streaked hair called out. "Come home, or face the repercussions."

That was the real Amaury Garnier.

"You chained me to a wall," she seethed. "You left me with a bucket to piss in and straw to sleep on."

That popped my eyebrows high. Talk about your retro imprisonments. That was downright medieval.

"Don't take that tone with me," he warned. "You chose that girl over your family. You gave me no other option."

"You could have left us alone." Tears blurred her eyes. "You could have let us be in love."

"Child." He hung his head, pity in every line on his face. "Eliza doesn't care about you. The Toussaints are using you. *She* is using you. Why else would they be pushing for you to perform your rite when you know it isn't safe yet?"

"After it's done, I'll have the power to protect myself. You won't be able to touch me."

"After it's done, you'll be dead, and no one—not even your pretty girlfriend—will ever touch you again."

Beside her, Eliza sucked in a sharp breath. "Papa?"

That explained where Tibby picked up the nickname for Mr. Toussaint.

"He lies," the Toussaint patriarch said smoothly. "He would say anything to keep his daughter from aligning with us." He gentled his voice for the girls. "You saw how they treated Tibby. Her wrists are scarred beyond the help of magic after so many months of abuse. She's lucky to be alive."

Had Luca not intervened, I was starting to wonder if Tibby would have survived this long.

Hard to believe Luca might have done a good deed, however inadvertent, while attempting to entrap my father.

"You know the truth," the Garnier patriarch bellowed. "Your scheming will kill her, just as you planned."

"It's my choice." Tibby lifted her chin. "I want the power."

"Tibs..." Eliza gripped her bony elbows. "Are you sure this is the right call?"

"What else can I do?" She kissed Eliza softly. "It's the only way I can make us safe."

In that horrible moment of clarity, I realized Garnier was wrong. Eliza did care about Tibby. Very much. Maybe it had started as a con that grew into something more. Or maybe Toussaint merely capitalized on his daughter's attachment to a valuable resource. Either way, Eliza might be the only person here who genuinely cared what happened to her girlfriend, and that saddened me.

However the next few minutes unfurled, I saw no happily ever after in the cards for them.

Breaking from Eliza, Tibby dove into the water, and both men turned to watch her determined swim.

Eyes full of unshed tears, Eliza began a prayer under her breath that didn't quite carry to me.

"On my signal," I ordered Asa, folding into lotus position on the grass, "secure Eliza."

"I'm on Rue duty," Clay informed me. "You need someone to watch your back while you cast."

Both guys stared at me, waiting for my protest, but I held up my hands. "I surrender."

With Clay on guard duty, I could sink into my magic and let the rest fade into the background.

Threading my power with Colby's, I wove the wards before the witches noticed they were being caged in our magic. I took only the bare minimum through the familiar bond, aware I might need more juice once the dueling patriarchs noticed me and what I had done.

Frustrated screams rang out as Asa restrained Eliza to keep her from harming herself, or him, to reach Tibby. But she was on the wrong side of the spell. Her coven couldn't hear her, but our neighbors would.

Palms bracing on the earth, I began casting a murky glamour to conceal the covens from human sight.

Laurent noticed Eliza's absence first, though he couldn't have heard her protests through the barrier. He pounded his fists against the membrane and spat out spells or curses or both.

Meanwhile, Garnier used the distraction to bolt for the water and dive in after his daughter.

As much as I wished it was a show of fatherly affection, barely leashed fury powered his every stroke.

Noticing Garnier, Toussaint snarled his lip and began yelling words I couldn't hear.

"Got her," Aedan reported in my ear. "Where do you want me to bring her?"

With Tibby secure in Aedan's custody, safe from fulfilling her destiny, I could breathe easier.

"Her dad is in the water. Toussaint might be going in. Take her the scenic route to get back here."

With that, he cut out and sped off to secret away our prize.

Poor word choice on my part.

Viewing the girl as a prize was what landed us all in this mess in the first place.

Future employee had a much nicer ring to it. Kind of. But not really.

"Rue." Asa wrestled with Eliza, who bit, scratched, and clawed him. "I could use assistance."

The request wasn't made for himself but for me. I wouldn't react well if she hurt him, and he knew it.

There was also the matter of the *y'nai*, who lived for moments when people got handsy with his hair.

"I've got this." I nudged Clay's shoe with my foot. "Go help him wrangle Eliza."

An engine rumbled a few rows over, and my stomach bottomed

out as the RV sped out of the lot. I was grateful the Mayhews had arrived and taken measures to protect the sleeping girls, but the farther I was from Colby, the thinner our tether stretched. I was slinging a lot of magic I couldn't otherwise tap into without her.

"You're trembling." Asa knelt beside me. "How can I help?"

Past him, Clay had bound and gagged Eliza, which would get us in trouble with humans fast.

"You can't." I ached with the raw power required to hold so many witches at bay. "It's too much."

Hearing my rough admission, Clay came running with Eliza tossed over his shoulder. "Dollface?"

"Call Derry. Get Eliza in the RV. They can't be far. Maybe you can catch them at the main road."

"Don't ask me to leave." He glanced around us. "I can stash her under an RV or something."

"…kill…witch…"

"…death…slow…wish…"

Jerking my head up, I got an eyeful of the hole the Toussaint patriarch had burned through my defenses. I didn't have to imagine what he was spouting anymore. I heard him, his voice growing clearer as the tear ripped wider.

"Go." I rose to my feet. "Asa and I can manage."

Neither of them believed me, I could tell, but they let the lie stand to save time we would have otherwise spent arguing.

A snarl of pain left me when I flung a rudimentary glamour over Clay and Eliza to conceal their escape.

"You have to stop." Asa stood in front of me. "You're burning out."

"I don't like our odds against that many witches." I bent double as another cramp twisted my insides. "I can hold on while you—"

"I won't leave you," he said simply. "We're in this together."

"I have to let go." I fought back tears. "Can Blay run defense while I cover him?"

After a sharp nod, crackling fire consumed Asa. Blay emerged, ready to rumble, and flashed me a grin.

"On three," I gritted out from between my teeth. "One... two...three."

Time slowed as the ward fell. Fingers cramping on the pendant, I summoned the grimoire into my hand. Its joy at being free lasted the five seconds it took me to force it back into its cage with the little magic I had left. But this time, instead of its hold on me snapping as the choker dampened its malice, a sticky sensation cobwebbed the back of my mind, one I couldn't brush away.

Come on, Dad. If you ever loved me, even a little bit, help me. You're the only one who can.

The flare of power from the book was a beacon, an SOS, one I hoped he would answer.

A bone-rattling battle cry shook me from my stupor as Blay charged past the illusion's watery barrier and began doing what he did best. The cracking noise as spines broke and moist suction as heads wrenched off shoulders soured my stomach.

I really was going soft if all it required was a few beheadings for queasiness to grab hold of me.

Oh no.

This couldn't be happening. Not now. Not when our enemies swarmed yards away from us.

Gratuitous murder wasn't the problem. This wasn't a crisis of conscience. This was...a disaster.

The more power I reached for, the faster it slid through my fingers, until I grasped at nothing.

The utter hollow of my stomach as my magic hit rock bottom had spots dancing in my vision, but I held a shield over Blay as he wiped out the bloodthirsty witches. Mass slaughter of my enemies wasn't an ideal start to my tenure as deputy director, but it was one my fellow agents would understand and respect.

A wobble began in my thighs and spread to my knees, which buckled, landing me in the dirt. The sticky sensation returned twofold, gumming my thoughts together, gluing me in place. Copper flooded my mouth, but I kept Blay safe as he waded through the brawling covens.

As if a giant hand had squeezed my lungs in a vise, I collapsed with a wheeze.

And then there was only fire.

"Rue."

I swatted the buzzing at my ear and curled against the warm body cradling mine.

"*Rue.*"

"Five more minutes," I mumbled, mouth parched. "Then I'll wake up."

"Open your eyes." Asa cradled my jaw between his palms. "Look at me."

With great effort, I pried open my eyes...

...and beheld a post-apocalyptic wasteland.

Scorched earth fanned out from where I lay, a good dozen feet from the water. "What happened?"

"You happened."

A grim figure swathed in darkness strode into my line of sight.

Dad.

"What did you do?" I struggled until Asa sat me upright. "Where is everyone?"

"Baby, your father didn't do this." Mom eased up on my other side. "You did." She knelt beside me, smoothing sweat-sticky hairs off my face. "We came as soon as we felt the blast."

The slimy texture of her skin should have made me recoil, but I pressed my face into her touch.

"The...blast?" I swallowed, coughed, my throat dry as dust. "What blast?"

A steady growl rumbled through Asa's chest, vibrating through my head where it rested against him.

"The compulsion to harm her died with my summoner," Mom assured him. "I won't hurt her."

Asa remained tense under me, and I was relieved he was there, allowing me to feel rather than think.

"You cast a spell," Dad explained. "It burned fifteen witches alive and incinerated several more corpses."

"No." I managed to hold my head up on my own. "I didn't—" I coughed into my fist. "I *wouldn't* do that."

"I know that spell." He pegged me with a stern look I might have feared, if I was still seven. "I created it."

Beside me, Mom kept stroking my cheeks and playing with my hair, as if she couldn't believe I was real.

Or, a more chilling possibility, she couldn't believe I had survived the scope of what I had done.

"I only wrote it down once." Dad began pacing. "That means you've seen the Maudit Grimoire."

Hot relief prickled through me that he suspected I had learned his spell through study and not...

What, exactly, had happened?

I remember putting the grimoire back where it came from after summoning it, hoping Dad would sense the flare of its power and follow it to me, but I hadn't cracked its cover in ages. I had given the thing up as a lost cause, was content entombing it within the pendant until I discovered a more permanent solution.

"The important thing is you're all right." Mom kissed my forehead. "I was so worried."

"*How* are you all right?" Dad swept his gaze over me. "You were burnt black when we arrived."

The hot metal singeing the skin at my throat gave me a good idea how I had survived the blast.

Holding my hands in front of my face, I studied the smooth, unblemished skin. "Burnouts aren't literal."

"They are when you stand within the blast radius of your own spell without shielding." Shadows whirled in his eyes when he shifted his focus to Asa. "You chose to protect him rather than yourself."

"I didn't *choose* anything." I scratched an inch on my side. "What is...?"

Crunchy fabric bunched under my hand, and dirt crumbled between my fingers. I glanced down to find I had been wrapped in a moldy fabric tarp Asa must have dug up somewhere. Otherwise, I didn't have on a stitch of clothing. Only the pendant and its protective chain remained, both of them sooty.

Both of them, thankfully, hidden.

But my kit...and my wand...were ash.

The wand had been a length of twisted wood resembling a crooked finger. I cut it from the magnolia tree that grew above Mom's empty grave.

Now it was gone. Soon, she would be too. And I had no idea what to do about either.

"Come with us." Mom gathered my hands in hers. "I would love to spend what time I have left with you both."

"Bring the grimoire." Dad kicked crunchy grass. "Unless it's a pile of dust too."

The frustration in his tone might have irked me yesterday. Today I was too grateful that, while he had tracked me by the grimoire's flare, he couldn't tell it was still on me. Though, now that I thought about it, he hadn't mentioned it. Either Mom didn't know that was what alerted him, or I was wrong about it.

Maybe the grimoire wasn't summoning him so much as...

What?

Fatherly intuition?

I snorted at the thought then covered it with a mild coughing fit that soon became real.

"Saint," Mom chastised. "That's not the reason I invited her."

"She ought to help if she can." His gaze softened. "That book might hold a solution to our problem."

"I'm dead," she said gently, but he still flinched. "This isn't a problem you can solve."

Balanced on the line between truth and lies, I gave them some of each.

"I want to help," I said, voice cracking, "but I don't know where I got that spell or how I cast it."

All I could figure was the choker had stolen from the grimoire what it required to protect me.

Stolen might be the wrong word, and that possibility terrified me. Almost as much as the subtle rot I detected in my scent that hadn't been there before I detonated inside a black magic curse.

If the chain could wrest control away and obliterate threats to me, I was in trouble.

If the book could wrest control away and obliterate threats to it, I was in trouble.

The pendant was a receptacle of magic. It hadn't been aware when I added it to my collection years ago, but then it had been empty. Now it had a houseguest in the grimoire. And an amplifier in the chain. Who knew what that would do to it? To any of the individual items?

"We should go." Dad reached for Mom's hand to help her stand. "Black Hat will be here soon."

As my thoughts cleared, I choked on a gasp and pawed at Asa. "Where is...?"

Colby.

"At the RV with the others." Asa kissed my fingertips. "Everyone is okay."

Aware I sounded like a frightened child asking for her favorite plushie, I pressed him. "Clay?"

"On his way here."

"I'm so glad my little girl found you." Mom patted Asa's cheek. "You complement one another."

"Careful of the hair," I warned her. "You should be safe, but I wouldn't bet on it."

"You're family," Asa agreed, "but your present state of existence might put you in danger."

"The *y'nai* act like they're auditioning to be the next *Iron Chef*."

"Rue." Dad drew Mom against his side. "Can you get the grimoire?"

"Did you come for me or for the book?"

Brows slanting down, Dad took a step forward. "What kind of question is that?"

One he didn't answer, which explained why I couldn't help twisting the knife.

"You knew I intended to save the girl. You could have been here. You could have helped me."

Then, black witches or not, maybe all those lives would have been spared.

"I warned you I wouldn't intervene in her life again, and I won't."

"This might have always been the path she was going to walk. Those covens might have always intended to rip her apart, but they each grabbed an arm and started pulling sooner because *you* wanted her."

"As I said, she isn't my responsibility."

"Then whose is she?" I held myself upright. "Her parents? They locked her up and threw away the key. The Toussaints? They want her dead to maintain their stranglehold on the magic users in this city." The fire in my belly threatened to consume me. "They have no right to treat their child that way."

"They have no right," he repeated slowly. "But you do?"

"What good is being deputy director if I can't use that power to make a difference?"

"Do you know who you sound like when you assume that might makes right?"

Don't say it. Don't say it. Don't say it.

"Like Father." He said it. Actually said it And he meant it. "Always keen to do what's right—in his eyes."

"Do *not* compare us." Clutching the musty tarp, I rose, or tried to anyway. Asa braced my elbows and got me on my feet, where my knees quivered with strain. "I'm nothing like him, and I'm nothing like you."

"Saint," Mom warned under her breath. "Think before you speak."

The spark in her eyes made her realer than she had been, and I had to ask myself if Dad noticed she was a pale echo of the spitfire he fell in love with. From the stories I heard of her, I expected Mom to see how he was treating me then smack some sense into him. Instead, she meekly let him walk all over her, as if there wasn't enough left of her soul—her *self*—to push back. That, more than anything, gutted me.

"You're the deputy director of the Black Hat Bureau." Dad drew no quarter. "The perfect heir."

"That's enough." Asa stood beside me. "Unlike the rest of her family, Rue has a genuine interest in helping others. You would know that, if you knew her at all."

"Rue has all the time in the world," Dad growled. "Howl has only what moments I can steal for her."

"Life doesn't work that way." Asa slid his arm around my waist to steady me. "People don't wait until it's convenient for someone to love them. They live, with or without you. Either you show up and put in the work, no matter how hard it is or how tired you are, or you get left behind."

"Are you threatening me?" Darkness swirled around Dad. "Are you trying to keep her from me?"

"Keep her from you?" Asa frowned. "As far as I can tell, you haven't tried to see her. Except when it's benefited you. Even now, you're here. Too late to help. You haven't hugged your daughter or told her you're grateful she's alive. You only asked for the book that gave her the power to cause such harm."

"He's right." Mom stepped between us, her palms on Dad's chest. "Even if you don't want to admit it."

"You know its power." He studied her face. "It might be our last hope."

"We gave the book to a keeper so that it would never be used. By writing down those spells, you tore them from yourself. It was the only thing that saved you—and the others. Pick it up now, and you'll damn yourself all over again."

This was a story I hadn't heard, one I scarcely dared to believe.

The magic in the grimoire was so toxic Dad ripped it out of himself?

Static whined in my head, so loud I missed the conversations happening around me.

"You could stay." I wasn't sure which parent I addressed. "I could help."

"Baby." Mom wrapped me up tight. "You don't have to make yourself useful to be welcome."

"You've already made up your mind." I dismissed the regret in her tone. "You're leaving. With Dad."

"You can come with us." She peered up at Dad. "You'll behave, won't you?"

"I'm sorry, Rue. For all I've said. All I've done." He dragged a hand down his face. "Having hope is worse than having none." He aged before my eyes. "If you come with us, I won't ask anything of you. I swear it."

As much as I wanted to clutch his offer with both hands, I couldn't help but ask, "What about Asa?"

And Colby.

And Clay.

And Aedan.

"We must travel light." Dad kept his tone gentle but weary. "Otherwise, we'll be too easy to spot."

"I can't leave him." I wouldn't cut ties with the others either, but

Asa was the safest ground for me to stand on before him. "I can't choose between my parents and my family."

"We understand," Mom assured me. "Of course we do."

"Do me a favor?" I waited for her nod. "Come see me before..."

"If it's at all possible," she promised, bringing me in for a hug, "I'll find you."

"I'll get her to you," Dad said roughly. "No matter the cost."

"Thank you," I told them both then hesitated. "What about Luca?"

"Luca can wait for me," Dad said, "or she can proceed without me."

No doubt that squared things in Dad's mind. In Luca's? Not so much. Anyone willing to kidnap a kid to make a point wasn't going to stop there. She would keep nipping at his heels until he honored his word.

A chill of foreboding slithered down my spine, but I was used to wearing a target on my back.

Sirens pierced the air with their wails, and Mom stepped into the circle of Dad's arms.

"We love you, baby." She let him lift her into a bridal carry. "Above all else, believe that."

Had we not grown so good at saying goodbye, I might have. As it stood, I believed they loved each other very much, and they loved the idea of the little girl they had known. But I was a grown woman now, and an agent. I was the deputy director. All of that must have convinced them it was okay to leave me to my own devices, that I would be okay without them, but they were wrong.

I needed my parents. I always had. But never in my childish fantasies had I pictured them not needing me too.

"Love you both," I forced out the words, aware every goodbye could be our last. "Safe travels."

"If you change your mind—" Asa slid his arm around my waist, "—you know how to find us."

After a curt nod, Dad flew away with Mom looking over his shoulder, tears in her eyes.

Wrung dry of emotion, I stood there, ready to face the gawkers when they arrived to find their vaunted deputy director wearing a moldy tarp instead of the signature black suit. I could only imagine how that would go.

"I'm...back," Clay panted, "with...clothes." He tossed a plastic bag to Asa. "All I could...find..." he braced his palms on his thighs, "...short notice."

"Come hold the edge of the tarp." Asa set the bag at my feet. "She can change behind it."

I ought to be thanking them, but I couldn't speak past the lump in my throat.

"Hurry...Dollface." Clay helped Asa create a screen. "The others will...be here in...less than five."

Nodding, I bent down and pulled out a pair of shorts with one purple leg and one gold leg. I slid them on, not bothering with the price tag. The gold tee was three sizes too big with *I love Mardi Gras* written in green and purple confetti. Last was a pair of green flip-flops with beads for straps.

"Not a lot to choose from," Clay apologized, still slightly winded. "There were no real stores nearby."

"You ran from the nearest souvenir shop?" That broke through my haze. "That must be miles away."

"There's a mall less than three miles away," Asa said wryly. "Exactly where did you come from, Clay?"

"You fail to take into account I was on the bus, not at the marina." Clay suddenly sounded much less breathless. "I hit a gas station on the way here, okay? But that was still a good half mile run in the heat."

Aside from the fact I could see the nearest gas station from here, and our warmest day only hit seventy-five degrees, I was still grateful for his efforts on my behalf.

"Thanks." I pushed down on the tarp to let them know I was done. "I appreciate it."

"You sure you're okay?" Clay took my hands and held my arms out from my sides, inspecting me for damage. "Ace told me what happened." He examined the skin on my hands. "Not a scratch on you."

"I have no idea." I dipped my chin. "I don't know what happened or how."

Sympathy swept across his features, softening them until it hurt to look at him.

Missing time. Acting against his own will. Waking to a scene he had no memory of creating.

No one more than Clay understood how I felt in this exact moment.

"We'll figure it out." He kissed my forehead. "Okay, Dollface?"

"Yeah." I pieced myself back together so that I could face the agents. "Okay."

"Almost forgot." He produced a shiny object from his pocket. "Colby got you set up with a new phone."

The rice experiment must have failed spectacularly if she gave up on reviving a piece of tech.

"That fast?" I knew you could walk into a store and walk out with a phone, but sheesh. "She's good."

"She's better than good." His chest expanded with pride. "She's the best."

Black SUVs pulled into the marina, blocking the road, and agents poured out to begin damage control.

A familiar face peeled away from the others and strode toward us with purpose.

"Fergal." *Ha.* I remembered his name this time. "I didn't know you were in the area."

"I wasn't." He cast Asa a curious look. "My presence was requested."

Only the faint amusement in Asa's eyes calmed me. He knew what was going on. Even if I had no clue.

"Where's your junior agent? Walters, right?" Clay scanned behind him. "How did he recover?"

The *y'nai* had relieved Walters of his hand for attempting to slice through one of Asa's braids.

For once, the *y'nai* and I had been on the same page about the punishment fitting the crime.

"He was transferred to accounting." Fergal's lips twitched. "He's better suited to a cubicle."

As if he had been waiting for this opening, Clay cut in. "How's Earl enjoying his coworker?"

"Earl?" Fergal snorted a laugh. "He was de*void* of all company, so Walters was a nice treat."

Snickering, Clay slapped him on the back. "Oh, I like you."

The vampire bared his fangs in a smile, but I was distracted as another agent I recognized ambled over.

"Jase Isiforos," I greeted him, recognizing the Miserae daemon from our last case. "Did you receive an engraved invitation as well?"

"I did." He bowed to me and then Asa. "You didn't know?"

"Our new deputy director requires trustworthy lieutenants to ensure her powerbase remains secure," Asa, who had been busy, answered for me. "She was impressed with your work and your candor."

The pretty speech reminded me of just who Asa was and how well he knew the importance of securing allies to remain alive. Granted, I didn't know Fergal or Isiforos well, but Asa was right. I had been impressed with them. They did their jobs, which was rare enough. But they also exhibited empathy toward victims, which was a remarkable find in our ranks.

"You each need to build your own team." I acted as if this had been my idea all along. "You'll both report directly to me. I'll help when I can, and divert resources when I can't, but you'll require your own backup that you can depend on. Choose people you can count on. Submit lists to me, and I'll make it happen." It hit me then, how else I could show my faith. "For that matter, if you can think of anyone else who would make a good lieutenant, someone you won't mind working shoulder to shoulder with, pass on those names too."

"Thank you." Fergal blinked, his pupils dilating from shock. "I... appreciate the opportunity."

"Dad will blow a gasket." Isiforos pounded a fist over his heart. "To serve the high prince's mate is an honor."

Asa bumped his shoulder into mine, and his grin peeked out where only I could see.

"Fergal," a woman dressed in a hazmat suit called to him. "Are you AIC?"

"Yes." He looked to me, and I nodded, happy to promote him, then he answered her, "I am."

The cleaners descended en masse, and with my permission, he went to direct them.

"What happened here?" Isiforos studied the aftermath of the spell. "Or is that above my paygrade?"

"Just know that if you abuse Rue's trust," Clay said cheerfully, "you could be next."

"I would expect nothing less." His smile spread wider. "Nice outfit, by the way. I didn't know we were doing casual Fridays." He thought about it. "Or that it was Friday."

Pride clear in his posture, he jogged off to corral the humans emerging from their boats and RVs.

"I do so enjoy striking fear into the hearts of my subordinates." I plucked at my shirt. "Can we go now?"

"You're the boss." Clay tugged on the ends of my hair. "*Can* you go now?"

"Yes," I breathed, throat scratchy and sore.

Finally, I had found a perk of the job. I could make a huge mess and leave others to clean up after me. Maybe this gig wasn't so bad after all. Or maybe that was the first mistake anyone in power made. Assuming what made their life easier was best.

"Thank you." I touched Asa's elbow. "For doing this."

For knowing me well enough to choose the people I would have selected for myself.

"I'll call a Swyft." Asa brushed his lips over mine. "We'll need a ride to the RV."

We had too many valuable targets on board to risk the Mayhews circling back for us. The RV wasn't what I would call inconspicuous. Unless you were driving the strip in Vegas.

A lime-green SUV arrived to pick us up, its driver distracted by a murder podcast. He drove us to the RV, which was parked next to a bakery. Wonder whose idea that was? Dollars to donuts, that was why Clay arrived huffing and puffing. Stuffed with pastries, the run probably gave him a tummy ache.

He wasn't breathless so much as seconds from hurling, but he manfully chose to fake the former over the latter.

>>*Have you dispatched the creature?*

First text on my new phone, and it was the director. As if I needed confirmation he had eyes and ears everywhere. Just not *my* eyes and ears. Updating him on our progress was one of the balls I dropped on this case. Thrown, really. As far as my arm allowed. I was surprised he let me get away with radio silence for this long.

Maybe he afforded the deputy director more leeway than I anticipated. Or maybe he had already fit me for a noose and was waiting for me to run out of rope and hang myself.

>*Yes.*

He didn't have to know it was a catch and release.

>>*Did you identify those responsible for its summons?*

>*The Toussaints are at it again.*

>>*What purpose did they have for the beast?*

>*A ritual ingredient. The usual.*

>>*No one else was involved?*

A hollow carved its way through my stomach, the certainty he was about to quit playing games and admit he sent me hunting for Dad.

>*Another local coven. The Garniers.*

>>*No one else?*

Tempting as it was to throw Luca under the bus, she might drag Dad beneath the wheels with her.

>*Looking for someone in particular?*

>>*I expect a full debriefing upon your return.*

I bet he did. Jerk. I wish he would man up and confess what he knew.

It would be so much easier to lie to him if he told me the truth.

"Try the fried pies," the Swyft driver said when we opened our doors. "Cherry's the best."

"Thanks for the tip." Clay rubbed his midsection. "I'll be sure to test your theory before we leave."

On the sidewalk, I glanced at the sign above the bakery then back to Clay. "Well?"

"Well what?" He strove for innocence. "Why are you looking at me like that?"

"Is he right?" I waited. "The cherry was best?"

"Poor guy is delusional." He tsked. "The apple kicked its ass into the next county."

Surprised to find I could smile, I made my way to the bus's door, and it opened before me.

"Hey." Marita pointed at her head gameshow-hostess style. "What do you think of my new 'do?"

A teeny Colby had climbed into her hair, which she wore in a fluffy bun.

"Spilling all our secrets, I see." I clucked my tongue. "I thought hairbow mode was our thing."

"I thought it was our thing." Clay climbed in behind me. "I'm hurt, Shorty."

"I was just explaining the rules," she said primly. "I told Marita I can only go out like this."

"A damn shame too." She lifted Colby gently onto her palms. "You're a little badass, you know that?"

Antennae aquiver, Colby turned her wide eyes on me, waiting for me to chastise Marita, but I was out of juice. I accepted Colby from Marita and flopped down on the bench, stroking her soft back.

"You don't look so good." She cuddled against my neck, hugging me tight. "Things didn't go well?"

"They did not." I let my head fall back against the window. "I'll fill you in later, okay?"

"Hey." Derry strode from the back. "I was just checking on the girls."

Jerking upright, I was seconds from rising. "Camber and Arden?"

"Eliza and Tibby," he clarified. "They're watching TV and cuddling."

"Mind going to your bunk?" I stroked down her back. "I need to talk to them."

"I have to put the finishing touches on my virus anyway," she said cheerfully.

The Ferret wouldn't know what hit her when Colby was done with her.

Rocking back on his heels, Derry hooked a thumb over his shoulder. "Want me to get them?"

"Yeah." I raked a hand through my hair. "I want this settled."

With a nod, he strode off to bring the young witches to me. Meanwhile, Marita sat beside me.

"Want to talk about it, when this is done?" She rested her shoulder against mine in solidarity. "You can talk to me, you know?"

"Thanks." I took her hand and squeezed it. "I appreciate the offer."

"But you won't take me up on it," she said without reproach.

"I don't know what happened, but I might need a sounding board once I figure it out."

"The door is always open." She winked twice. "Unless Derry and I are…you know."

"I do know." I spluttered a laugh, one of the last I expected for a while. "We'll talk soon, okay?"

Once Derry returned with the girls, he and Marita exited the bus and entered the bakery.

With only Black Hats present, I was ready to begin. The girls sat across from me, their arms linked.

"Tibby, you're in a bad situation. Your clan wants to—"

"I'll join." She gazed into Eliza's eyes. "As long as she can come too."

"Um." I rubbed the base of my neck. "That took less convincing than anticipated."

"I have an uncle in Black Hat," Eliza explained. "When your friend tackled me, I realized why you were here and what you would want from her." Her fingers laced with Tibby's. "I understand what it means to be Black Hat, and I'm okay with it." She wet her lips. "Tibby needs it. To be safe. I believe you can do that for her."

Had she an inkling there were two girls almost their age under a sleeping spell in the bottom bunk, she might not feel so confident.

"Eliza, are you sure you want this?" I gave her a moment. "It's for life."

"You'll be stuck with them," Tibby said quietly, "even if you get tired of me."

"What does that mean?" Eliza flushed red with hurt. "Are you... breaking up with me?"

"You don't have to give up your entire life for me."

"I don't have a life without you."

"Tell me Asa and I weren't this bad," I whispered to Clay out of the corner of my mouth.

"You were worse," he whispered back. "So much worse."

On my other side, Asa chuckled softly, overhearing our conversation with ease.

"We've decided," the girls said in unison. "We're joining."

"You're welcome to take the night to consider your options."

Tibby had none, but Eliza could decide to stay in New Orleans with her...

Awkward.

I had vaporized her father and several of her coven members. She could return home, but he wouldn't be there waiting for her. I ought to break the news, but Clay squeezed my knee in a silent warning.

Armed with the facts, Eliza might let grief cloud her judgment when she needed it most.

"We're sure," Tibby assured me. "Beyond certain."

"We don't even need to pack." Eliza nodded. "We're ready."

"Call Isiforos," I instructed Clay, a weight settling on my heart. "Tell him to come pick up our new recruits."

"Will do." Clay rose. "Let's go get you two some necessities." He waved them out. "It will take a few days for all the paperwork to process, and a week for you to receive your first paycheck as a trainee."

Another first? One for the Black Hat history books?

Recruiting two young women who wanted the job without having done anything to earn it.

Both girls were headed straight to Fergal for training. I trusted him—*gulp*—to guide and protect them.

"Put it on the company card." I flicked my wrist. "Whatever they need."

"Mind if I borrow Ace?" Clay slanted a mock glare at the girls. "These two look sneaky."

I saw the opening for what it was, and I gave a nod that weighed so much, I was shocked my head didn't pop right off my shoulders.

With a soft kiss, Asa left me to my fate.

There was, after all, another set of girls that needed to be dealt with.

Trudging to the back, I allowed myself a momentary reprieve to peek in on Colby. "Listen out, okay?"

Worst-case scenario, I might need help controlling Camber and Arden if this went south.

"Okay." She flew at my face and hugged me. "You got this."

"Let's hope so." I eased her back into her gamer den. "It won't take but a second to wake them."

Her marching orders in place, Colby perched behind the curtain, ready if I needed her.

Sliding the fabric open on Camber and Arden's bunk, seeing how they clung to one another, even in their sleep, brought a sour taste to my mouth as bitter memories surfaced from their last brush with magic.

Camber and Arden huddled together, their fingers laced, and their heads bowed until their hair tangled.

A touch of my hand to their foreheads woke them, and they sucked in ragged breaths, their eyes bright with panic.

"Rue," Camber gasped. "Where are…?"

"Get back." Arden recovered first. "I don't trust you this close to us."

Had she held a knife and driven it through my heart—and twisted it—I couldn't have been more hurt.

"That's fair." I lifted my hands and backed away. "We need to talk."

"You kidnapped us," Camber recalled, her voice shrill. "The only person I want to talk to is a lawyer."

"A restraining order isn't going to make this go away." I wished I could hold their hands or stroke their hair, but I no longer had that right. "You've seen the truth. You know what I am, what the others are, and that means you have a choice to make."

"We choose to go home," Arden growled. "We choose to never see you—any of you—ever again."

The trials they endured had dulled Camber's edge, but they honed Arden's to razor sharpness.

"We won't tell anyone," Camber whispered, "if you let us go."

This was the exact conversation I expected to have with Eliza and Tibby, who didn't know me from a hole in the ground. Instead, girls I had watched grow up begged me to forget I ever knew them.

Black witches ate hearts for a reason. For power, yes, but also for that black magic high that let you forget how people looked at you like you were a monster from a fairy tale the instant they learned who and what you were, what you could do.

"Those are both options," I allowed, "with the right precautions in place."

"Precautions?" Arden set her jaw. "What?" She scoffed. "Will you wipe our memories?"

"Yes." I watched horror spread across their faces. "If that's what you want."

"What if we don't?" Camber's bottom lip trembled. "Does that mean living with what we know?"

"Yes." I linked my fingers. "If that's what you decide."

"I don't want to know." Camber shook her head hard. "I still have nightmares about..."

What the Silver Stag copycat did to them both.

"All right." Coward that it made me, I relaxed a fraction. "I can arrange that for you."

"Will it hurt?"

"No, sweetie." Another fracture spread across my heart. "You won't feel a thing."

With the resources at my disposal, I could request the best for her, and I would. The witch could untangle the spell that had opened Camber's eyes to our world too, so she could close them again.

"I don't want to forget, and I don't want the spell broken." Arden stuck her fingers in that fracture and ripped it wider. "I don't want to be blindsided again." Her cheek twitched as she turned to her friend. "This way, I can watch out for both of us." She kept her eyes on me, her stare hard and cold. "Tell me one thing."

The word got stuck in my throat. "Ask."

"Have you ever tampered with our memories?"

"Yes." I wouldn't lie to her again. "I helped you both forget the worst of the kidnapping."

"It was your fault." She spoke with absolute certainty. "That's why you screwed with our heads."

A rustle of fabric behind me warned the hole I had dug was about to get deeper.

"She was trying to help you," Colby shrilled, "not hurt you."

"That moth spoke to us." Camber's breathing turned choppy. *"How did that moth speak to us?"*

The thing in Camber that broke that night, the fragile core of her that I had nurtured and done my best to heal, splintered. She melted onto the mattress, curled on her side, and pulled the covers up to her shoulders. Rocking back and forth, she sobbed into her pillow with quiet cries that left my eyes stinging.

"I can help you sleep, if you want." I expected her to rebuff me, if she replied at all. "When you wake up, you won't remember anything. You'll be back at the townhouse, ready to pack and go home. It will be as if none of this happened."

"Do it," Arden agreed on her behalf. "She can't handle much more."

Unflinching, Arden sat with her friend while I reached around her, touching Camber on the hand.

"Tell me about the man who kidnapped us," she demanded when Camber relaxed into slumber.

"A black witch attacked you." Colby puffed up with indignation. "Rue saved you both."

"How did a black witch end up in Samford, Alabama?" Her gaze drilled into mine. "Why did he pick us?"

"He followed me," I confessed. "He chose you two, because he knew how much I love you."

"You don't keep secrets from people you love." Arden didn't want to hear me. "Not like this."

"She had no choice." Colby bristled so hard she bumped up to cat size. "She had to—"

"Who are you?" Arden got to her feet. "*What* are you?"

To protect Colby, I told her what I could afford her to know, and I leaned hard into known witch lore to make it easy for Arden to grasp the depth of the bond between her and me.

"She's my familiar." I ruffled Colby's antennae. "She's not responsible for any of my actions."

As a matter of fact, not that it would help my case, but Colby was a victim of them herself.

"Where are the others?" She scanned the RV. "Clay and Asa and…Aedan."

"They're giving us privacy."

"That's what changed, isn't it?" Fresh hurt carved her features. "Things were fine until they showed up."

"The less you know about the details, the safer you'll be."

"We both know that's not true."

"The more you know, the harder it will be to keep the truth from Camber."

"If I have trouble, I'll ask myself—" More tears fell. "What would Rue do?"

"I deserve that." I sank my fingers in Colby's fluff to keep her from launching at Arden. "I'm sorry."

"Sorry you got caught."

"Sorry people like me don't get to live in small towns and have small lives and enjoy small happinesses."

A flicker of *something* passed over her features. "You're not coming back?"

Though I knew better than to ask, I must not be done flagellating myself yet. "Do you want me to?"

Her lips parted, but she didn't give an immediate response. I don't think she had an answer.

"Nothing has to change. You two can co-manage the shop. I'll increase your pay to make up for the extra workload. If you need help, you're welcome to hire a part-time employee. You don't need me to make Hollis Apothecary profitable. It's as much your business as it is mine."

"The two of us?" A slight tremble shook her jawline. "Aedan isn't coming back either, is he?"

"He has business in Samford, so he'll be staying on my property for the time being." I measured her reaction before adding, "He won't return to the store, and he won't contact you again."

"Is that his choice or yours?"

"You called him a monster," I reminded her. "That tends to stick with people like us."

"Monsters?"

"People who grew up believing the worst of themselves only to have someone they love confirm it."

"I don't know what to do." She shrank into herself. "About you. About him. About any of this."

"You don't have to figure out everything today. One life-altering choice is plenty."

"Yeah." She reclined onto the bunk. "Okay."

"Let me make some calls, and I'll get someone out here for Camber."

A fragile thread of what I wanted to call hope strung between us. "Can't you do it?"

"I want the best for her, and that's not me."

Fingers touching the curtain, she stifled a yawn I didn't believe for a hot minute. "I'm going to nap."

The fabric slid closed, both of us knowing she wouldn't be sleeping anytime soon.

"That could have gone worse." Colby leaned against my throat. "At least it's over."

"You're right." I leaned right back. "It is over."

My simple life, my simple job, my simple friendships.

All of it.

Everything.

Over.

17

Sometime before dawn, Arden elected to witness Camber having her memories altered. I wasn't surprised she didn't trust me to oversee the process, but it still hurt. Everything hurt. And yet, I discovered it could still get worse when she chose Clay over me to escort Camber back to Townhouse A.

Without saying goodbye, or anything else, she left, and then I was alone with Isiforos.

"Need anything else?" He stood at my elbow. "I'm about to leave with Ms. Toussaint and Ms. Garnier." He studied my profile. "Are the other girls coming too? Camber and Arden, right?"

Chills broke down my arms to hear a Black Hat mention them so casually.

"No." I shook my head. "They're not recruits."

"In that case, I'm off." He winked at me. "I have a hot date with a local cambion."

After he left, Fergal arrived at the RV, which was currently functioning as the world's most embarrassing mobile office, with reports for me to read and sign.

Now that both sets of girls had gone their separate ways, I didn't mind my lieutenants joining me.

Fergal updated me on the lake massacre, but most of it went in one ear and out the other. Selfish of me, I know, but I was too busy nursing my own broken heart to envision how the victims' loved ones would take the news.

None of them had been good people. Black witches, as a rule, weren't. But I should have felt something.

Something other than the boundless nothing within me.

Distantly, I wished I hadn't sent Derry and Marita home, but I thought then I wanted to grieve in private.

Not for the first time tonight, I was wrong.

"Ready to go?" Asa stuck his head into the RV. "Clay's waiting."

The SUV idled in front of the bakery, our bags and Colby already inside, but I saw no sign of him.

That could only mean he was buying snacks for the trip home.

Grateful for an excuse to leave, I followed him down the stairs. "Aedan?"

"He left." Asa dipped his chin. "He didn't want to be here while Camber was…in session."

"That makes two of us." I walked into his arms. "This case was a nightmare."

"I've contacted Moran." He kissed the top of my head. "She knows to expect us at the farm."

Another fissure spiderwebbed across what remained of my battered heart. "I hadn't thought that far ahead."

Living so close to Camber and Arden was how we became friends. The kind thing to do was to remove myself from the equation, so they didn't have to see me at work, or at home. I owed them that much for turning their worlds upside down.

"Aedan will take care of it." He stroked my jaw. "You haven't asked where we'll be staying."

"The bunkhouse?" I leaned into his touch. "Or tents?"

Those were the only two viable options in such a remote location with no time to prep for guests.

"We will be living our tiny house dreams." Clay, who had sneaked up behind me while I was moping over this latest turn of events, passed me a chicken and waffle donut. "We can discuss logistics on the way." He stuffed one in Asa's mouth when he opened it to speak. "Or we could, if you would get a move on."

On the way.

Not *on the way home.*

I appreciated the distinction as much as I loathed its necessity.

"There's one benefit to moving you haven't considered." Clay urged me into the SUV with gentle hands. "Stavros can't find you at the farm."

"I hadn't thought of that." I toyed with my seat belt. "No more surprise gifts or visits."

It did nothing to ease the bone-deep ache of losing my home, but it was a good point.

"And," Colby squealed, swooping onto my shoulder, "I get my own house."

"You what now?" That shocked me into feeling—panicked. "Your own house?"

"If we had more time, I could have commissioned our new *field office* to our specifications, but alas." Clay climbed in behind me. "I had to get what I could find. That means you and Ace have a one bedroom, I have a one bedroom, and Little Miss Gamer Pants will also get a one bedroom."

"I don't know how I feel about her living on her own."

"I'll be maybe four yards away." She scoffed. "Plus, I'll need the extra room for my rig and all my stuff."

All the custom equipment would have to come out of her room for her to be comfy elsewhere.

"I should also mention I've ordered some acrylic tunnels meant to let cats explore the great outdoors from behind clear plastic. We can mount them on the roofs, so she can walk over for a visit instead of flying. That will keep her safer and give her a way to enjoy the sunshine and fresh air without us."

"The centuria will protect her," Asa added, climbing behind the wheel. "She'll be safe."

"Come on, Rue." She rubbed against my cheek. "It's temporary."

For the sake of her bright spot of hope, that life could one day go back to how it had been, I relented. "Okay."

"Yes." She zoomed through the SUV. "This is going to be *awesome*."

I was glad one of us thought so.

The centuria had done their best to make the tiny house community that had sprung up in their backyard comfortable for us. With their preternatural strength, they had arranged the three homes into a loose U shape, with Colby's house in the middle.

In the center of that U, they had dug a firepit ringed with stones and placed bright metal chairs around it. Solar lights ran to the houses' roofs from a large tree across from the small yard, creating an umbrella effect that made the scene welcoming. From the same tree, on a thick limb, blew a Jolly Roger.

The skull and crossbones design of the pirate flag was oddly comforting and reminded me of Blay.

Though, if given a choice, he might have picked a basket of oranges for the banner instead.

It wasn't home, but it was homey, and my family was here.

That was what mattered the most.

As we pulled in, the headlights flashed over Aedan, who carried crushed boxes from the solar lights.

Once Asa parked, I got out and trailed after my cousin, glad to see he was safe and sound.

"How are you doing?" I bit my lip. "Dumb question."

"The centuria have plenty of work to keep me occupied." He

wiped sweat from his brow. "I'll miss the quiet of the shop, but it was never meant to be a permanent solution."

As tempted as I was to tell him Arden asked after him, cared about him even when she was furious, I kept my mouth shut. I didn't want to give him hope where there might be none. If she wanted to talk, she knew where to find him. If she didn't, she knew how to avoid him. That was the best I could do.

"I'm sorry you're hurting."

Done stuffing the boxes into a metal barrel to burn later, he turned. "You've lost more than I did."

"I've had time to make peace with it." Yet, it hadn't been nearly long enough. "All that mental prep didn't do me a whole lot of good when the bill came due, but at least I've had years to stew over it."

"She was never going to love me back."

This was not a conversation he should be having with me. I was too awkward with my own feelings to help someone else navigate theirs. But we were family, so I tried my best. "I think...she might have."

"I don't mean the shop boy." He struck a match and tossed it in. "I mean *me*."

"She's descended from witches. Whether she knows it or not, there's magic in her veins. She might be more open to the idea than we give her credit for. She did choose to keep her memories."

"She didn't want to forget what I am." He bowed his head. "She didn't want to want...me."

And she had ensured she couldn't forget what he was or what I had done to her and Camber.

"She'll come around, or she won't." I hooked an arm around his waist. "All we can do is wait and see."

That went for both of us.

"If you guys had a creek," Aedan said, forcing his hurt aside, "I would move in. These houses are *nice*."

"Clay bought them on the company dime, so I'm sure they're the best you can purchase prefabricated." I glanced over my shoulder at the beckoning glow of the lights. "I haven't gone exploring yet."

The truth was, it would become real when I stepped inside Asa's and my new residence.

Residence, not home.

Only one place would ever be that for me.

The house and town in which Rue Hollis was born.

The house and town that might as well have been a million light-years away.

In tune with me as always, Asa sensed my black mood, and he came to investigate.

"I have a surprise for you." About to follow him, he jerked his head at Aedan. "I meant him."

"Awkward." I shoved Aedan at him to cover my embarrassment. "Bring him back in one piece."

Once they walked off, Clay strolled over and stuck a slice of loaded baked potato pizza in my hand.

"Where did you get this?" I took a bite, not caring that it burned the roof of my mouth. "I didn't see a delivery driver."

This far out, I doubted they would come. The flavor profile wasn't typical Samford fare either.

"The great thing about winged daemons? They don't mind popping a few towns over for grub."

The centuria did need to acclimate so they could manage human interactions, so I let it slide. For now.

"Any idea what that's about?" I pointed my slice toward Aedan. "Asa looks pleased with himself."

Guiding me a little ways ahead, Clay pulled me to the side to watch the great unveiling from a distance.

"What is that?" I hadn't noticed it under the tarp Asa whipped off for his reveal. "A watering trough?"

The galvanized oval looked to be about three feet wide, eight or so feet long, and maybe two feet high.

"Technically, yes." He laughed, stuffing his face. "It's a stock tank pool."

"What does it do?"

"It holds water."

"Cute."

"I know I am, but I never get tired of hearing it."

"What is the purpose of this pool?"

"That spell really wiped you out, huh?" He softened his tone. "It's a spare bedroom for Aedan."

A fist squeezed my heart until I worried it might burst at the thoughtful gesture.

"Aedan has had a rough few days. You both have." Clay stole my slice before it went cold and ate it. "Asa thought it might be a good idea for him to split his time between your place and the farm, so we can keep an eye on him."

As I watched, Asa shook Aedan's hand, his rigid posture conveying his uncertainty.

Aedan, eyes glimmering, pulled him in for an awkward one-arm hug.

"I really do love him."

"Aedan?" Clay licked the grease off his fingers. "He's a good kid."

"Him too, but I meant Asa."

"Yeah, yeah." He made gagging noises. "You two are still disgusting. You don't have to rub my face in it."

Slanting him a look, I decided to play dirty. "I noticed you giving Moran a tour of your new house."

A cough lodged in his throat, and he pounded a fist on his chest, dislodging a wad of pizza on the dirt.

"She asked to borrow a cup of sugar," he wheezed. "I was being neighborly."

"Mmm-hmm."

While I didn't doubt we had groceries—Clay believed in a well-stocked pantry—I doubted Moran had sugar on her mind when she followed him inside his new space.

Well, at least not the granulated kind.

"Can I change my mind about the sea monkeys?"

Seeing as how I had already forgotten I owed him new pets, I said, "Absolutely."

"Oh good." His grin was pure evil. "I want a jellyfish instead."

"One day, I'll learn not to agree before I hear your sales pitch."

"God, I hope not."

"Wait a minute." I grabbed his arm. "There were jellyfish in Pontchartrain."

"Really?" He placed a splayed hand on his chest. "You don't say?"

"Tell me you didn't catch one."

"One might have swum into a noodle hammock, and I might have named him Mr. Squiggles."

"And you, what, accidentally had a saltwater aquarium set up in your new house?"

"Accidents happen."

"Did you see the pool?" Colby, who must have sneaked off with Asa, pinwheeled overhead. "Asa said he even bought a kit to make it a hot tub when it gets cold."

Central Alabama didn't really do cold. Mostly, fall and winter were lukewarm. Sometimes even cool.

Halloween costumes were skimpy on some years for good reason, and more than once, I had worn shorts on Christmas.

But it was still a nice gesture, one I was sure Aedan would appreciate.

"We should get some of those noodle hammocks Marita had," Clay decided. "Those were nice."

"Would you even fit in that pool?" I eyed his muscular build. "Without breaking it?"

"I'm not talking about *that* one." He whipped out his phone with a flourish and showed me a behemoth that would have been at home in any amusement park. "I'm talking about *this* one."

For such a short trip, maybe six hours total, Clay had been a very busy golem.

"You realize our residency is temporary?" I had to make myself believe it. "That's a big investment for a few weeks or months."

Please don't let our exile stretch longer than that.

"The centuria don't know much about fun." Clay put away his grand plans. "I figure a lazy river and a few water slides are a good start. There's an adjacent hot tub, so it should appeal to everyone."

"Especially in this heat," I joked, touched by his vision but concerned too. "This is temporary, right?"

A pretty lie would have been welcome right about now, but I knew he would tell me the ugly truth.

"You know how I said one day I might want to buy my own land and build my own house? One close to you, but not in your face?" He spread his arms. "I like it here. I like how there's always someone awake. How there's always something to do and someone to do it with. Out here, I won't have to lay in bed for eight hours and breathe quietly until everyone wakes up unless I feel like it."

"Oh, Clay." I touched his arm. "I didn't know it bothered you so much."

"I didn't either." He rubbed his bald head, a sure sign he was home and off the clock. "Until I started hanging out at the farm."

"It doesn't hurt that Moran lives here, huh?"

"I do enjoy the scenery, it's true, but this isn't the time for starting relationships."

"You're probably right." I stared up at the moon. "Things are complicated for everyone right now."

"Moran deserves to live a little before she settles down." He rolled a shoulder. "With anyone."

"Building a waterpark is a good start," I teased. "She's going to love it."

Already, I could picture the parties he would host. He could live his best twenty-four-hour life out here.

"Especially when she finds out I've ordered water cannons to shoot fliers out of the sky."

"Umm." I shared a glance with Colby, who was giggling. "That sounds...fun?"

For the landlocked daemons.

"The platform will have digital locks installed so the cannons can't be activated without the passkey."

Colby landed on my head, leaning over my forehead to look me in the eyes. "So I don't get caught in the crossfire."

A mild panic attack gripped me as I pictured her blasted out of the sky, her fragile wings torn to shreds.

Palming his forehead, he sighed at his partner in crime. "I wasn't planning on spelling that out."

Now that she had, I could look forward to nightmares about her free-falling to a watery doom.

"Hey, Rue." Aedan jogged over to us. "Mind if I stay tonight?"

"You don't have to ask." I squeezed his hand. "You're always welcome here."

Color suffused his cheeks, and he took a long breath that eased the pinch of his shoulders. "Okay."

"Let's get a fire going." Clay waved us toward the pristine pit. "We have s'mores fixings."

I let them go on ahead while I waited on Asa, who had been a few strides behind Aedan.

"That was very kind of you." I closed the remaining distance to him. "I think he was worried that leaving him behind at the house was tantamount to leaving him behind period."

"He's family." Asa rubbed my back. "This is what we do for family, right?"

Why everyone asked me, when I had the least experience with loving familial relationships, stumped me every time. It made me wonder if Aedan repeated my advice to the others, leading them to believe I had any clue what I was doing. How could anyone who knew me think I was an expert on feelings? Or on right and wrong? Seriously?

"Right," I agreed, because I wanted it to be true. "That's what we do for family."

With a mischievous smile, he guided me into the trees to a clearing where an old rope swing hung from an ancient pecan tree that might have once been part of an orchard but was now a lone sentinel. The wooden seat was weathered and cracked, but the rope had been replaced recently, if the bright red nylon was any indication.

"Hop on." Asa held it steady for me. "You'll enjoy this."

"If this cracks, and I bust my butt, and you tell Clay, I will never let you in my pants again." Laughter sparkled in his bright eyes, and I stared at him, utterly captivated. "I love you."

"I know." He helped me on. "I'm not convinced you want to, but you do, and that's what counts."

"Does anyone *want* to love someone?" I gripped the rope and climbed on. "It's like baring your chest and asking someone to crack open your rib cage, stick a fork in your heart, and rip it out by the arteries."

"That very Rue sentiment only makes me appreciate your faith in me all the more." He shoved against my lower back to get me moving. "Now." He waited until I was a blur. "You and I need to talk."

"Did you trap me here to lecture me?" I leaned back, catching his eye before he pushed again. "That's dirty." I kicked off my shoes. "Cruel, even."

"What happened in New Orleans..." He kept a steady pace, his mouth tight while he debated his words. "It frightens me that you possess so much power, so much knowledge, but had no awareness of it consuming you."

The tiny nudges in my head worried me as much or more.

Had that been the old me piping up? The new me chiming in? The new me fighting with the old me?

Or had it been the grimoire whispering sweet words of conflict?

But I voiced none of those worries. No. I had bigger fears living inside me. "I could have killed you."

"That's beside the point." His hands pressed against my spine. "You could have died."

"Me killing you while in a fugue state is not *beside the point*."

"There's someone who might be able to help, but I don't know how you feel about meeting her."

Summoning my wings, I lifted off the seat and glided out of range of the swing. "Who?"

"High Priestess Naeema."

Hand rising to my throat, I touched the choker bound to the pendant. "Your *grandmother*?"

Given his fond remembrances of her, and the magnitude of her gift, I hadn't expected him to be jittery at the idea of us meeting. More than likely, his mother would be there. Maybe that made him antsy?

"Your time is precious right now, I know, but your predicament is urgent. A day should suffice. Maybe two." He smiled at my surprise. "The time difference works in our favor."

An entire day spent in the pocket realm where challenges were held cost us a handful of minutes here. A couple of days there might stretch into weeks if we weren't careful with our realm-to-realm conversions.

"Okay." I worried the bracelet of woven hair on my wrist. "Let's do it."

The choker was her creation, so she might have insight into how it transmuted and what to do about it.

Plus, it gave me an extension to decide how much to tell the director about this case when I reported in.

"I'm tolerated in her court, but I will always be viewed as a symbol of my mother's suffering." He shuttered his expression too late. "You're an extension of me, in that regard. They may openly shun you, for that and your past."

Ah.

That explained his turmoil.

He worried fascination would push me into a wholesale slaughter of snooty fae.

Honestly?

He was right to be afraid of what I would do to protect him.

"You don't think I can survive the fae court?" I banished my wings. "You think I'm that fragile?"

"No." A proud smile stretched his cheeks. "I'm more worried they won't survive you."

"You're so sweet." I kissed him. "As long as they behave, they have nothing to fear."

"Yes." He kissed me back. "That's what I'm afraid of."

ABOUT THE AUTHOR

USA Today best-selling author Hailey Edwards writes about questionable applications of otherwise perfectly good magic, the transformative power of love, the family you choose for yourself, and blowing stuff up. Not necessarily all at once. That could get messy.

www.HaileyEdwards.net

ALSO BY HAILEY EDWARDS

Black Hat Bureau

Black Hat, White Witch #1

Black Arts, White Craft #2

Black Truth, White Lies #3

Black Soul, White Heart #3.5

Black Wings, Gray Skies #4

Gray Witch #5

Gray Tidings #6

The Foundling

Bayou Born #1

Bone Driven #2

Death Knell #3

Rise Against #4

End Game #5

The Beginner's Guide to Necromancy

How to Save an Undead Life #1

How to Claim an Undead Soul #2

How to Break an Undead Heart #3

How to Dance an Undead Waltz #4

How to Live an Undead Lie #5

How to Wake an Undead City #6

How to Kiss an Undead Bride #7

How to Survive an Undead Honeymoon #8

How to Rattle an Undead Couple #9

The Potentate of Atlanta

Shadow of Doubt #1

Pack of Lies #2

Change of Heart #3

Proof of Life #4

Moment of Truth #5

Badge of Honor #6

Black Dog Series

Dog with a Bone #1

Dog Days of Summer #1.5

Heir of the Dog #2

Lie Down with Dogs #3

Old Dog, New Tricks #4

Black Dog Series Novellas

Stone-Cold Fox

Gemini Series

Dead in the Water #1

Head Above Water #2

Hell or High Water #3

Gemini Series Novellas

Fish Out of Water

Lorimar Pack Series

Promise the Moon #1

Wolf at the Door #2

Over the Moon #3

Araneae Nation

A Heart of Ice #.5

A Hint of Frost #1

A Feast of Souls #2

A Cast of Shadows #2.5

A Time of Dying #3

A Kiss of Venom #3.5

A Breath of Winter #4

A Veil of Secrets #5

Daughters of Askara

Everlong #1

Evermine #2

Eversworn #3

Wicked Kin

Soul Weaver #1

Printed in Great Britain
by Amazon